THE DARKNESS was barely more than a name. Already the stars were an icy sheet flung across the sky. To the east, at the open end of the valley, a glass moon was beginning to float clear of the horizon, and in the silence a horseman waited. Neither animal nor rider stirred as the clear light slowly fingered the stunted hawthorns around them into silhouette.

He sat erect, every sense alert, his taut, dusky features almost invisible in the shadows. His lean figure and broad shoulders were swathed in a long black cloak, its fullness draped behind him over the horse's rump, hanging almost to the ground in graceful folds. Strong supple fingers held the rein on the horse's warm neck. He moved imperceptibly in the saddle and touched the rifle strapped to the pommel before him. But he did not loosen it. Time for that later.

In front of him the turnpike stretched deserted, the toll-house a few hundred yards away in total darkness. The gate was closed and chained, the moon throwing the shadow of the bars, elongated and menacing, across the road surface. He watched as a solitary hunting-owl drifted on soundless wings across it and heard its sharp call echoing in the silence. In the distance it was answered by the long quavering hoot of its mate. The moon was drifting higher now and the whole broad valley of the Wye and the mountains of Wales beyond were bathed in light.

It was time.

He raised his hand, and out of the shadows a group of silent women appeared, rising from the bracken. They were armed with cudgels and stones, and three of them carried axes. Like his, their faces had been darkened. He looked at them for a moment grimly, his eye passing critically from figure to figure as he loosened the gun before him on the saddle. Then he gave a quick, hard smile.

'Do it now, daughters,' he said.

CHAPTER
ONE

FROM THE hillside they could see it all. The flames had taken hold quickly, licking up the frail walls of the toll-house, hungrily consuming the roof, sending showers of sparks high into the night air.

Stella Vaughan steadied her snorting mare Cariad with difficulty as she watched the scene in the distance in shocked disbelief. A crowd of figures was milling around the building, making no effort, she realised in horror, to extinguish the fire; on the contrary, as the roof fell in, the circle of spectators let out an exultant roar. The savagery of it sent a shiver down her spine.

'What is it? What's happening?' she cried.

Her brother George's horse, rearing as it smelled the acrid smoke, had carried him a little way from her across the dark field. 'Rioters!' he shouted back excitedly. 'Destroying the toll-gate by the looks of it, and the toll-house with it!' Abruptly he remembered his duty to his sister. 'Come on, Stella, there's nothing we can do. It's dangerous to stay here. I must get you home before they see us.'

Above the shouting they could hear a woman's screams now, and the frantic barking of a dog—lonely miserable sounds, echoing above the angry bellowing of the men.

Beyond the smashed toll the road led away into the distance, a pale blur in the moonlight. As George and Stella hesitated, about to turn away to ride up the field, a troop of horsemen had appeared out of the darkness, moving fast, the moonlight reflecting on their drawn swords.

'It's the dragoons,' George yelled, reining back the cob. 'Someone must have fetched them from Brecon!'

There were lookouts posted on the distant road, for, almost at the same moment, a shout was raised among the rioters around the remains of the toll-gate, and within seconds they had begun to disperse. A shot was fired and then another, and once again the woman began to scream.

'Come on!' Reluctantly, George tore his eyes from the scene. He managed to manoeuvre his frightened horse next to his sister's and leaned down to catch her rein. 'Some of those devils may try and escape this way, and there's no knowing how dangerous they might be.' It was obvious to Stella from his tone that he would have liked to ride down the hill and join in the fighting.

She was breathless with the effort of controlling her plunging mare, and for a moment she allowed George to retain his hold on her horse. Her heart-shaped face was white beneath her feathered hat, her dark hair escaping in little tendrils which stung her eyes and caught at the corner of her mouth as they galloped side by side up the field. She clutched the saddle tightly, trying to calm the nervous pumping of her heart as she steadied Cariad, and managed to slow her at last in time to turn into the narrow lane which led up towards their home.

George caught her up. 'You know what I think we've just seen, Stella?' He glanced at her, his face keen with excitement. 'I think that was a Rebecca Riot, right here, not half a mile from Bryn Glas.'

Stella stared at him, sick with shock still at what she had seen. 'It can't have been,' she said desperately. She pushed the stray curls of dark hair off her face impatiently. 'They wouldn't do . . . that.'

George glanced at her. He had forgotten for a moment his sister's passionate support of the riots in west Wales, which had so shocked the rest of the family.

He hesitated, his sense of justice fighting with a sudden desire to see his spirited sister embarrassed by one of her passionately defended fads. 'Well,' he said, 'you are always reading about them in Papa's newspapers. Isn't the destroying of toll-gates one of their trademarks? It was too far to see if they had disguised themselves as women. Don't they always do that as well?' he sneered. 'Well, do you still think them romantic heroes, sister, now you've seen them in action.'

'You're being unfair!' Stung by his tone, her cheeks coloured sharply. Her imagination had been caught, it was true, by the tales of adventure and heroism among the

Rebecca leaders, and her soft heart had been touched by the tales of poverty and famine which had sparked the riots off. 'I support them because they are fighting against injustice, George. The tolls are terribly unfair and you know it. That is why they pull down the gates.'

'And what they have done to the Joneses down there was fair, I suppose?' George said gently, leaning forward to slap his cob's neck.

Biting her lip, Stella looked away from him as she thought of the terrible screams rending the night air. Mrs Jones, kind little Mrs Jones, who sometimes took the tolls for her husband, had so loved her neat little house with the roses festooned over the porch and the huge lavender bushes where she would drape her newly-washed linen to dry. 'I don't believe those were Rebeccas,' she said defiantly after a slight pause.

George relented a little. 'Perhaps not. There certainly haven't been any here in Brecon and Radnor up to now. Well, whoever they were, I hope the dragoons catch them. Then Father and the other magistrates can deal with them. Transportation is too good for them. They should all be hanged!'

He allowed Stella to ride ahead of him as the lane narrowed again and they had to duck beneath the fruit-laden hazels. She steadied her side-stepping mare, picturing again the fire, and the milling, shouting figures in the darkness and suddenly, in spite of herself, a quick shiver of excitement ran up her spine as she guided Cariad through the oppressively still woods towards the stables at the back of the house. She straightened her shoulders and glanced back at George. 'If it was they,' she cried defiantly, 'they were doing only what they have to. It is the only way to make people take notice. They are brave men, driven to desperation.'

Luckily she did not hear her brother's snort of derision.

The yard was lit by several lanterns, and two boys came running out at the first sound of the horses' hooves on the cobbles.

'Mr George, Miss Stella, are you all right? Did you hear they fired the toll-house?' One of the boys ran to Cariad's head and held her as Stella slid to the ground. 'The townspeople from Hay came here to find your father', he rushed on, the words falling over each other in his haste to get them out. 'To sign the order to call out the dragoons. As he wasn't here they had to ride to find the other magistrate, Mr Williams. They were afraid it would be too late.'

'We saw it all.' George dismounted and ran the stirrups up the leathers before handing his horse's rein to the boy. 'Attend to them well, Ianto, they're both sweating,' he said. 'And wait up for my father,' he added, seeing the boy's distraction. 'He should be back soon.' He took Stella's arm. 'Mother must be alone. She'll be terrified with no one but Eliza there. Come on!'

The lovely old stone-built house was quiet and in darkness save for the front room. There lamps burned and a fire had been lit against the sudden cold of the autumnal evening. Margaret Vaughan was sitting near it, her face pale, the embroidery frame at her side untouched. Her elder daughter Eliza was reading to her, seated by the table, but, as George and Stella hurried in, both women looked up. The book slid from Eliza's lap and fell to the floor with a thud.

George strode over to his mother and dropped a kiss on the top of her lace cap. 'Are you all right, Mama?'

She reached up and patted his hand. 'Better, now you're both back safely. I only wish your father were here too.' Turning, she surveyed her younger daughter as Stella ran across the room towards the fire, her eyes bright, and her hair beginning to come unpinned as she took off her feathered hat and threw it down. Margaret sighed, more worried now by the sight of her daughter's expression than by the news of the riot. The girl was so pretty, she found herself thinking for the thousandth time, but that vivid wildness had to be tamed for the child's own sake. Even as she watched, Stella whirled round, the skirt of her crimson habit brushing the fringes of the rugs on the sofa.

'Oh, Mama! We saw everything! The dreadful fire! Papa will help the Joneses, will he not, to get a different position and a new home?' Stella begged. She ran to her mother and took Margaret's cold hands in her own. 'George thinks it may have been the Rebeccas. If it was, they only meant to burn the gate.' She hugged her mother and turned back to the fire. 'Whoever it was, it'll be a sharp lesson for the detestable man the Joneses worked for, with his toll-farming and his extortion. The poor people cannot pay so much for tolls on top of all their other troubles. You must see,' she cried impulsively, 'it had to be done.'

There was a moment's shocked silence. Then Eliza stood up, primly smoothing her own immaculate hair into place.

'Don't let Papa hear you talk like that, Stella. He sends people to prison for less,' she said scathingly.

George sat down and stretched his legs out to the fire with a happy groan, his urge to take part in the fighting forgotten. 'Take no notice of her, Eliza. You know Stella, she loves to try and shock, as always. When she's married to Owen she'll change her tune.'

Margaret was studying her children closely. George was right, of course. Marriage to a strong husband was what the girl needed, and Owen Morgan was the perfect choice—wealthy, good-looking, ten years older than Stella, and heir to a baronetcy. She sighed, shrugging away the treacherous wish that it had been Eliza he had offered for; Eliza, who was in so many ways much better fitted to the role of his wife.

Stella was laughing as she raised her hands to try and salvage some of her hairpins. 'I'd like to see him try!' She stood on tiptoe to see in the mirror over the fireplace, and her skirt swung uncomfortably close to the smouldering logs. 'That's if I marry him! Do you think he'd beat me, George? I shall have to ask him if I see him tomorrow. Perhaps he'd feed me on bread and water and make me go barefoot until I change my ways! I think I shall take some of my Chartist tracts with me to show him. Then he won't want to marry me at all, and I shall be safe!'

George groaned. 'It'll serve you right if he did beat you.' He shook his head. 'And if he doesn't, Father will if he sees you reading that stuff.'

'She doesn't know what she's talking about, George,' Eliza commented acidly.

'Oh, yes, I do.' Stella turned on her sister. 'I'm talking about the terrible poverty and misery of those people—people like those rioters out there—' she waved her arm towards the window. 'Men and women whom we should be helping instead of grinding into the dirt.'

'Eliza's right, you are talking nonsense, Stella. You know nothing about it,' George retorted. 'They have to be controlled for their own good. There is perfectly adequate poor relief for those who genuinely need it, but many of those men are lazy good-for-nothings—'

'That's not true!' Stella flared. 'They work hard when they can find work. And it's people like Papa and Owen's father who should be helping them!'

'Stella, dear.' Margaret saw the colour deepen in her son's face and recognised the warning signs that his temper was mounting. 'Let us not have a political discussion now. I suggest that you both go and change before your Papa returns. Megan will be serving supper as soon as he comes, and you, George, are putting horse-hairs all over that chair.' She tightened her lips as Stella and George glared at each other. 'Did either of you remember to bring me the packet I asked you to collect?' she went on wearily.

George frowned. 'I'm sorry, Mama. Of course. That was why we were so late back. We waited for the mail coach.' He reached into his pocket and produced a small parcel, grinning suddenly. 'I'm prepared to wager this is a birthday gift for Papa. Am I right?'

His mother took it from him. 'That is none of your concern, George,' she began with a smile. 'As you well know—' She broke off in mid-sentence and let out a little cry of alarm as a furious shouting erupted from somewhere in the depths of the house.

George's grin vanished abruptly as he strode to the door and, pulling it open, looked out into the dark passage.

'What's going on out there?' he bellowed. 'Perry? Meredith? What's happening?'

Behind him the women looked at one another, and nervously Eliza went to stand close to her mother as three figures appeared in the doorway. The butler and their father's valet appeared to be supporting a third man, while behind them the boy Ianto hovered in the passage, a pitchfork in his hand. The man hanging between Perry and Meredith was dressed in torn rags, his blackened face streaming with blood.

Margaret gave a small scream. 'Dear God! What's this? Meredith, who is it?'

'It's one of the rioters, ma'am.' The butler grasped the man's arm more tightly. 'We found him in the shrubbery. He was trying to hide there.' He nodded towards the valet, who stepped forward with a bundle of dirty clothing which he unrolled in the lamplight to reveal a huge shabby skirt and a torn shawl. There was a moment's shocked silence. 'Women's clothes, by God! So they were Rebeccas,' George breathed. He stepped towards the man who cringed backwards. 'That's right, isn't it, you filthy cowards. You form yourselves into groups, disguise yourselves as women, call your leader your "Mother" and then you burn and riot and murder. Who is it, Meredith? Do you recognise him'

The butler shook his head. 'No one from round here, Mr George, as far as I know. But we'll soon find out—'

'Stop! Oh stop!' Stella had been standing speechless with horror, watching the prisoner, who hung helplessly between his two stalwart captors. The blood was streaming from a jagged wound in his forehead, trickling down his face, soaking into the dirty cloth which was knotted around his neck. As Meredith raised his hand threateningly to the man, she threw herself forward, forgetting everything but her anguish at the sight. 'Let him go instantly or the poor man will bleed to death before our eyes! How dare you treat him like this!' She glared at Meredith who, after a moment, somewhat helplessly stood back.

'Stella!' George turned on her. 'This is none of your business. Don't interfere!'

'It is my business when a man is brought into my father's house and allowed to bleed to death,' she retorted, almost in tears. She turned back to Perry. 'Let him go and send Ianto to fetch a cloth or something to staunch his bleeding.'

'Stella!' Margaret, supported by her elder daughter, had retreated to the fireplace. 'George is right, dear. This is a matter for the men. And I think—oh, dear God!' Her voice rose to a scream as the prisoner, seeing every eye turned away from him, seized his chance. From somewhere in his baggy trousers he produced a long knife. Wiping the blood from his eyes with his arm, he brandished the blade threateningly in front of him.

'Stand back, all of you,' he growled. 'Don't touch me or I will kill someone!'

Meredith and Perry retreated several steps, looking from the man to George and back, as the prisoner stood poised in the lamplight, the knife glinting in his swinging fist. It was Stella who reacted first. She was staring at him, her clear grey eyes steady; it had not crossed her mind to be afraid. 'Please, don't be silly,' she said quietly. 'It'll only make things worse for you.' She approached him, holding out her small hand for the knife. Too astonished to move, the man surrendered it without a word; by the time he had realised what he had done it was too late, the servants had jumped on him once more and within seconds they had bound his arms behind him.

Stella stood where she was, the knife still clutched in her fingers, its handle sticky from the man's blood, as George, recovering, took command of the situation. 'Take him to the empty cellar and lock him in,' he ordered. 'My father will deal with him in the morning. And here,' he touched the discarded clothing with his foot. 'Take this and keep it safely. It is the evidence which will send him to Van Diemen's Land.'

They watched in silence as the prisoner was hustled out of sight, then George closed the door and leant against it. His eye fell on Stella, who was still holding the weapon, her face white.

'You little fool!' he exploded. 'Do you know how near you came to being killed? These men are no better than common murderers!' He took the knife from her and laid it on the mantelpiece, rubbing the palms of his hands distastefully on his trousers. 'Don't you ever do anything like that again, Stella. Ever. Do you understand?'

She bit her lip. 'He didn't hurt me,' she said defensively. 'He gave me the knife!'

'Stella, be silent!' Her mother interrupted suddenly, her voice shaking. 'I think I have heard enough from you this evening. Please go to your room now. I do not wish to see you again tonight.'

'But, Mama . . .' Indignantly Stella turned to face Margaret and Eliza by the fireplace. 'You must agree with me. It is unjust to—'

'Stella!' George's voice was peremptory. 'Mother is right. You have said enough.'

She glared at him for a moment. Then without a word she went to the door and let herself out into the dark corridor.

The house was silent once more as she made her way to the hallway, where a candle glowed softly on the table at the foot of the stairs, the family's bedroom lights clustered unlit around it. Taking one, she held the wick to the lighted flame. As she waited for it to catch and burn clear she was listening intently, but no sound reached her from the far-away cellars; she could hear nothing but the faint bubbling of the wax as the candle flickered in her shaking hand.

She was still trembling when, having made her way unseen up to her own room, she set the candlestick down on the dressing-table and stood waiting for a moment until the flame steadied. Her windows were fastened, the curtains tightly closed and, feeling suffocated, she ran to pull them back and throw open the casement so that she could stare down the valley. Moonlight bathed the distant hillsides in clear cool light; far away beyond the silver streak of the River Wye she could see the Black Mountains, dark in front of the star-sown sky, and she could feel their mysterious pull reaching out to her, beckoning her as they always did with their strange remote beauty. She shivered. Somewhere out there desperate men, like the one incarcerated in their cellar, were hiding in the shadows, creeping down lanes and over fields back to their homes as the dragoons quartered the country looking for them, and with them, perhaps, went their leader, 'Mother Rebecca' himself. She shivered again. The cold air still carried the acrid smell of smoke.

She heard her father's horse long before she saw it, the even thud of the cantering hooves in the lane growing louder as he rode nearer, passing the house and going straight round to the stables. Then from somewhere she saw the glow of lantern-light swinging crazily on the gravel as Ianto ran forward to meet him, and she could hear the excited lilt of the boy's voice as he took the horse's bridle.

Abruptly she turned away from the window. She could not bear to think of the man in the cellar who must face her

father's wrath; Henry Vaughan was a just man and a
first-class magistrate, unlike so many of his colleagues, but
he was also very hard. He would see it as his duty to punish
the rioters. It would not occur to him to look further to try
to discover the misery and pain which had driven them to
their actions: the social conditions of the early 1840s that
had so stirred her soft heart when she read about them in
the moving articles by Thomas Campbell Foster in her
father's *Times*. She glanced at the leather letter-folder on
her little writing-desk, where the ones she had been able to
rescue and cut from the paper lay hidden beneath some
sampler patterns. If men like Foster could understand, why
couldn't her father? She sighed, her eyes fixed unseeing on
her own reflection in the little Chippendale mirror on her
table. Somehow she herself had to help the cause. Surely
there was something she could do?

The idea came to her suddenly out of the blue, and she sat
down abruptly on the chair before her dressing-table,
shocked by the audacity of it. Absently she began to
remove her hairpins one by one, a small uncertain smile
hovering round her mouth as, her heart beating swiftly with
fear, she worked out her plan. When the last coil of dark
hair was unfastened, she shook out her long tresses and,
reaching automatically for her brush, began to tease them
into order. It was all so simple. All she needed was courage.

She woke twice in the night with a start, thinking she had
overslept, groping in the darkness for the little repeater
button on the clock by her bed. The first time it struck two,
then four. A few minutes later she rose and felt around on
the end of her quilt for her peignoir. The house was fast
asleep. In an hour or so the servants would wake, but she
would, she hoped, be back in her bed long before that.

With her hands outstretched to feel her way, she crept
down the passage which led past her parents' room, holding
her breath lest one of her father's dogs hear her from their
customary place in the dressing-room and begin barking.
Then on down the broad sweep of the stairs, past the
grandfather clock with its measured tick, her bare feet
making no sound on the thick carpet.

Once inside the side door into the servants' wing she

stopped and listened, but there was no sound yet of anyone stirring. The stone floor was cold beneath her feet now, and she caught her breath as she let herself into the kitchen. The range glowed gently and she stopped for a moment, glad of its warmth. Then she reached for a spill and, thrusting it into the coals, waited for it to ignite. Several lanterns stood on the shelf near the back door and she lit one, and then made her way towards the cellar steps.

Her heart was beating uncomfortably as she ran down and held the light close to the door of the empty cellar which had been pressed into service as a cell. No sound came from behind it. The flickering shadows played over the heavy oak, revealing two bolts, both oiled and clean, shut fast. The key was standing in the lock.

Her hand was shaking a little as she set the lantern down on the floor, but it was without any hesitation that she stood on tiptoe and reached up for the top bolt.

The door opened with a heavy dragging sound which must, she was sure, be heard all round the house. She waited a moment, holding her breath, then, when nothing happened, she stepped into the cellar.

The man lay on the bare floor, in the corner, his hands still bound behind him, his eyes closed. With a little cry of horror Stella ran to him and fell on her knees at his side. 'How could they!' She moved her fingers gently over his forehead, where the blood had dried into a blackened crust. The man's eyes opened and for a moment he stared at her, dazed. Then he began to struggle to sit up.

'Wait, I'll help you.' Stella set the lantern beside him so that the light fell on his bonds. 'How my brother could do this! I'm ashamed of him!' She was pulling vainly at the knots.

'What did you do with my knife, girl?' The man spoke at last. 'These knots are pulled so tight I doubt if they'll ever open again.' He gave a sharp crack of laughter.

Stella bit her lip. 'Could you stand? There are knives in the kitchen. I can cut them there.'

'I'll stand. Give me a hand, then.' The man swayed to his feet and Stella grasped his arm.

'Quietly, we mustn't be heard.' Picking up her lantern she guided him out of the cellar, then carefully she relocked the door behind them.

In the kitchen she found a huge carving-knife and, gritting her teeth with the effort, began to cut through the rope while the man waited unmoving, wincing a little as the pain of her movements shot through his deadened arms. His harsh breath rasped in the silence.

'Why are you doing this, girl?' he asked, after a moment, over his shoulder.

Stella frowned, using every ounce of her strength to saw through the thick cord.

'I'm doing it because I agree with what Mother Rebecca believes; that's what they're called, your leaders, are they not?' She glanced up at him with a quick shy smile. 'You tell your Mother Rebecca I should like to meet her—him, I mean. If I could explain to my father what you are trying to do, what you believe . . . There—' The rope finally snapped and with a groan the man brought his arms round in front of him, rubbing his wrists.

'You want to meet Mother Rebecca!' he repeated mockingly. 'So you can tell your papa who she is and hang her from the gibbet, that's more like to be the truth.'

'No. I mean it. I want to help you all.' Hurt, Stella took a step back at his cutting sarcasm.

'Well, you've done me a good turn getting me out of this, but I'll not repay it by betraying my leader,' he said with a sneer. 'Now, out of my way. I must go.' And pushing her aside, he moved towards the door.

'Wait,' Stella cried. 'Let me bathe your head—'

'No time. Someone will come.' He was fighting with the lock on the back door. 'You get back to your bed, girl, and leave Rebecca and her daughters to fight their own battles.' Dragging the door open at last, he looked out. It was still dark. He took a deep breath of the fresh free air, then without a word he vanished into the night. Stella stared after him. He had not even said thank you.

Outside, a cockerel crowed tentatively and she started in alarm. Quickly she closed the door and relocked it, then replaced the carving-knife in the drawer. Tidying the rope-ends, she pushed them into the stove, blew out the lantern and put it back on the shelf, then, as quietly as she could, crept back down the passage towards the front of the house.

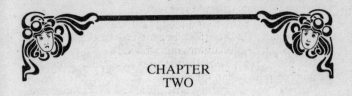

CHAPTER
TWO

STELLA WAS awakened by her father. He was towering over her bed, his handsome ruddy face contorted with anger.

'Well, miss, was it you?'

He glared furiously down at his younger daughter.

She lay, her long hair loose on the shoulders of her white nightgown, her grey eyes huge and startled as she looked up at him. 'Papa? What? What is wrong?' she murmured, genuinely bewildered for a moment.

'The prisoner has escaped; released by someone in this house!' he stormed at her. 'It was you, wasn't it? George tells me that you still have this romantic notion that you believe in what they're doing!'

'Papa?' She struggled to sit up, still dazed by her dream of angry soldiers galloping in the darkness, their horses' eyes glowing red as they passed.

She had fallen asleep almost at once on returning to bed, and her confusion was real as she glanced around the bright sun-filled room, the terror of the nightmare falling away as she realised that her curtains had been opened and the fire made up while she still slept. Her eyes sought out her father's face. He was shaking his head, exasperated, taking her perplexity for denial. 'One of the servants must have done it, I suppose, although they all swear they know nothing of it. God damn it! I shall be a laughing-stock!'

'The prisoner got away?' As the memory of her excursion through the cold dark house to the cellar flooded suddenly back, banishing her dream, Stella reached for her shawl and pulled it nervously around her shoulders.

'Some time in the night. No one heard anything. The dogs didn't bark. Those fools downstairs didn't think to leave anyone on guard.' He turned away from the bed, vehemently hitting his fist on the palm of his hand. 'Glynn Williams was called out to the riot last night and now he's going to hear about this, and we're due there this evening for dinner.'

Stella slipped out of bed and ran barefoot to her father's side. She hoped he would not notice that she was trembling. 'Papa, he won't blame you. You weren't here when it happened. If it was anyone's fault, it was George's. He took charge.' She cheerfully hoped her brother would forgive her for this little piece of disloyalty.

Henry Vaughan snorted. 'Well, the boy did his best, I suppose. He wasn't to know someone would let the fellow out. I shall just have to hope we can recapture him by this evening.' He looked down at his daughter fondly. 'Owen will be there, I hear,' he said, changing the subject abruptly.

She blushed. 'So I believe.'

'And you'll accept him if he offers for you tonight?'

For a moment she hesitated, looking out of the window across the broad river valley towards the mountains, shrouded in mist. Then she nodded. 'If you approve, Papa.'

He put his arm round her shoulder and pulled her hair gently. 'You know already that I have given him permission. I'm very pleased for you. And your mother is too, of course. One of her daughters to be a ladyship one day! Not bad, eh?'

She laughed. 'You'll have to bow and kiss my hand, Papa!'

'Baggage!' He slapped her gently on the behind. Then he pushed her away from him. 'Right, get you dressed and come down for breakfast. I'll have to arrange a search party. Not that this rogue will be within five miles of us by now. He will have vanished into the mountains long since, God damn it.'

Stella stared at the door as it closed behind him, then let out a long sigh of relief. The man had got away, and she had not had to tell a lie.

She went up a long time before she needed to, to dress for the evening. She had chosen her prettiest gown of lilac gauze, which was worn over a silk underskirt and several full petticoats, then she selected a warm pelisse to throw around her shoulders. Her dark hair was dressed low on her neck by Megan and decorated with Michaelmas daisies, and on her feet she wore pale kid slippers.

She was growing increasingly nervous about the evening to come, thinking about Owen Morgan and his imminent proposal of marriage. As he was staying with the Williamses only for another two days he would undoubtedly take this opportunity of asking her formally for her hand before returning to his father's estates in Radnor. She stared at the mirror, biting her lips to make them pink. She should be excited and thrilled by the prospect; everyone expected her to be. She knew it was the most excellent match, and her sister Eliza was positively green with envy, and yet . . . She sighed. She had so hoped to make a love match, to feel that strange something . . . She hesitated, groping in her mind for a word to cover a sensation she could not describe even to herself, but which she felt sure should be there. Turning from the mirror, she began to draw on her gloves. Perhaps, after all, as Mama had promised, it would come when she got to know Owen better.

She had been ready for over an hour when the Vaughan carriage was at last brought round to the door. Henry was to escort his wife and two daughters in the coach, while his son rode alongside on his chestnut cob.

The westering September sun was still warm as the horses trotted slowly away from the house, their matched bay coats glistening like silk. They wheeled out of the drive and on to the road which led steeply down the hillside, and then turned to follow the River Wye as it flowed in a gentle curve along the shallow valley. Beyond it, the steep wooded slopes of the foothills were turning to shades of russet and umber with the hint of autumn. In the distance the bare rocky shoulders of Pen y Beacon and Twmpa lay raw beneath the gold mackerel sky, beshrouded already by an amethyst haze.

Stella gazed towards them out of the lowered window, watching the shadows lengthen in the deep cwms where the sun had already gone, and the chill and damp of evening lay on the sheep-cropped turf. This time of day always saddened her. The days of early autumn still belonged to summer, but the evenings belonged already to winter. She could feel the gentle wind blowing from the mountain fanning her cheeks, and abruptly she leaned forward to pull up the window. The breeze carried whispers of bracken and bog myrtle, but it also held a hidden ominous chill. She cast off her melancholy with an effort. Warmth and candlelight and conversation would soon dispel her mood. And tonight was special, for almost certainly she was about to be engaged. She turned her back on the window and gave her attention to the others in the carriage.

They swept past a cluster of tiny stone cottages, and Henry Vaughan raised his hand in greeting as an old woman in a long black apron leaned on her spade, a pipe clenched between toothless gums, to watch them pass, while half a dozen hens flew squawking from beneath their wheels as Ianto whipped the eager horses into a canter.

The ladies had heaped cloaks and rugs into the carriage for the return journey, but now they sat relaxed as the heavy vehicle rattled westward down the road, enjoying the last warmth of the sunlight as they chattered eagerly about the evening ahead of them, and Margaret and Eliza did not draw breath until the horses began to slow. They had reached the site of the toll-house, and Ianto, who was acting as coachman, drew up slowly as they all stared out in sudden horrified silence. The wooden building had been burned to the ground. Nothing remained of the scene of the previous night's rioting but ashes and the trampled potato-plot which had served to feed the toll-keeper and his family. The smashed gate had already been replaced by a chain.

The keeper hobbled towards them to collect his nine-pence and give Ianto his chit. His face was ashen and there was a swollen bruise on his cheekbone. 'God save you, sir,' he murmured, touching his cap as he glimpsed the magistrate seated with his family.

Eliza drew in her breath sharply. 'Poor man. There, Stella! How can you side with the brutes who did that to him?'

Stella swallowed and looked down at her gloved hands. It was not the time to defend the rioters, and for the moment she was not sure that she could. She had been bitterly disappointed by the prisoner's reaction to her help. He had not seemed to her to be grateful at all for her dramatic rescue bid and had laughed when she said she wanted to meet his leader. She felt a small glow of shame as she thought again of what she had done. Abruptly, she put the thought away, and watched mutely as Henry Vaughan lowered himself from the carriage and went to speak to Jones, examining the scene of the fire. In spite of her pleas, Henry had refused to consider helping the family, but, as she watched, she saw the glint of silver as some coins changed hands and she felt a quick surge of warmth towards her father.

When the coach moved off, she turned and looked back out of the window and saw the keeper standing in the dusty road looking after them. Behind him, sprawled around an upturned box on which they were playing cards, were the toll's newly appointed guards, four uniformed dragoons.

Glynn Williams, one of Henry's colleagues on the bench, lived less than five miles from Bryn Glas. His house, a lovely stone mansion built a century earlier, stood in a park of old cedars and oaks in a gentle arm of the Wye. As their carriage swept up the raked gravel driveway to the entrance, Maria Williams herself ran out of the front door, her arms outstretched.

'Margaret! Girls! Oh, but it's good to see you! And dear Mr Vaughan. I was so afraid that you would decide not to make the journey, with all these dreadful people roaming the countryside. Now, you must all come inside. No! Not you, Stella dear.' She waggled her eyebrows in what she fondly imagined was coquettish girlishness. 'Someone is waiting for you, my dear, in the rose garden, and you have time, I think, for a stroll before dinner. If your parents think it proper, of course?' She paused expectantly.

Stella swallowed, but already her mother and father were exchanging glances and nodding. 'Run along, Stella,' her papa said with a fond grin, and without another glance at her he turned to follow his hostess up the broad steps to the front door, ushering his wife and elder daughter with him.

Drawing her pelisse around her nervously, Stella walked slowly on to the grass around the side of the house. Owen was waiting for her on the mossy veranda below the drawing-room windows. He smiled as he saw her, and stretched out his hands. 'Stella. I hoped you wouldn't think it improper to wish to speak to you like this, but there is so little chance for us to be alone.' He took her hand and raised it to his lips. He was a handsome man in his early thirties, tall and fair with a florid complexion.

'I'm glad you did.' Stella felt suddenly shy as she looked up at him. 'Very glad.'

They walked over the trimmed lawns towards the brilliant roses that were not yet blighted by the autumn winds. Beyond the trees, in the distance, the mountains were retreating into the mist. In their shadow it was beginning to grow dark.

'You know I have spoken to your father, Stella?' Owen guided her to the shadowy worn steps which led down between the flower-beds.

She nodded.

'He told me he would give us his blessing if you would consent—' He hesitated. 'Dash it, you know what I'm trying to say. Will you marry me?'

They had stopped walking, and now she turned and looked up at his face. Until that moment she had known that she would say yes, but unaccountably she hesitated. Behind them the red sun was enveloped in the bank of pearly whiteness and the garden lost its glow. Damp began to strike up from the ground and, feeling it, Stella shivered.

'Owen, I'm very fond of you and I know you like me . . .' She stopped, appalled at the dismay which appeared on his face. 'No, no, I don't mean to turn you down,' she said impulsively, hating him to be hurt. 'It's just that I must be sure that you know what sort of person I am. I'm not good and sweet and obedient like Eliza. I try to be, but I'm not. I'm bad-tempered sometimes, and rebellious, and I care about things I shouldn't.' Her voice had risen passionately.

Owen stared at her. Then he began to laugh. 'Sweet Stella. I know that. Besides, your father told me as much. He said I would have my work cut out trying to mould you into a dutiful wife.' He put his hands on her shoulders, and, drawing her close, kissed her gently on the forehead. 'But I'm willing to try. May I tell them we are engaged?'

She looked up at him, frowning. Then, quelling the treacherous little gnawing of doubt somewhere deep inside her, she nodded.

He folded her in his arms. 'Dearest Stella! When shall we be married? Let it be as soon as possible.' She could feel his heart beating beneath the cloth of his coat. The sensation disturbed her a little and she drew away.

'I think the nicest time would be the spring,' she murmured.

His face fell. 'But that's so long, sweetheart.'

'Not too long.' Now that he had released her, she felt happier. She gave him a radiant smile. 'I must get used to the idea of being such a great lady. Mrs Owen Morgan!' she teased.

'One day to be Lady Morgan,' he added, a little smugly. He snapped a pink rose from one of the bushes and put it in her hands. 'A rose for a rose, my love,' he said softly. He paused, savouring his phrase for a moment, then he gave her his arm. 'Come, it grows chilly. We must go back indoors,' and turning towards the house once more, he led her slowly across the lawn.

A roaring fire had been lit in the fireplace of the main drawing-room and on the mantelpiece two many-branched candelabra flared in the darkening room, each candle reflected a dozen times in the facets of the huge rococo mirror on the wall behind it. Besides the Williamses and the Vaughans, there were three strangers in the room when Owen led Stella inside.

All eyes were turned on the young couple and Stella found herself blushing painfully.

'At last. We were afraid you had got lost,' Maria Williams trilled, hurrying forward. 'My dears, but you look so cold! Come near the fire.' She pressed her own powdered cheek against Stella's as she pushed her towards the hearth.

Owen did not follow them. He glanced round the room from his position just inside the door. 'I am sure you will all be pleased to know,' he addressed the assembled company after clearing his throat, 'that Stella has consented to become my wife.'

There was an immediate buzz of excitement as the Vaughan family rushed forward with their congratulations. 'I'm so pleased, my child.' Her father took her hands and raised them to his lips. Then her mother hugged her, and Eliza and, finally, George.

Behind him, Maria had approached again. 'Stella, my dear! Oh, I am happy for you! But come. You must meet our other visitors. I am sure they will want to join in our good wishes. Here are Julia and Roger Campbell, who have lately moved into the district.' She presented a thin, elegantly dressed man with greying hair, and his wife, a small mousy woman with enormous eyes. 'And this,' she went on, leading forward the third stranger, 'is John Vivian, the solicitor who has recently joined Mr Griffiths in his practice in Hay.' She eyed her guest with evident pride.

Too enmeshed by her own entangled emotions about Owen to do more than glance round the room when she first came in, Stella had barely noticed the tall figure, dressed in sober legal black, waiting in the background. Now, when he stepped forward, she looked for the first time at his face as she held out her hand.

He was the most attractive man she had ever seen. As he stooped over her fingers she glimpsed piercing blue eyes set deep in a tanned face, dark winged eyebrows, a square chin and a determined mouth. He straightened at once and, meeting her gaze directly, held it, her hand still imprisoned in his own.

She felt herself reel slightly from shock at the impact of his scrutiny. She could feel her breath coming in light quick gasps in her throat as the colour mounted treacherously to her cheeks.

Aware suddenly of Maria's puzzled eyes on them, she looked down quickly, trying to draw her hand away, but he held it fast.

'So, Miss Vaughan, at last we meet. I have heard a great deal about you.' His voice was low-pitched and attractive, but for a moment she detected something almost like hostility in it.

Thinking she must have misheard, she risked another quick glance at his face. She was trembling slightly. 'I cannot imagine what you could have heard about me, sir,' she stammered.

'Can you not indeed?' There was no doubt now. His tone was deliberately taunting. 'But, Miss Vaughan, you are a celebrity in legal circles.' To her relief he released her hand. 'My new partner, Toby Griffiths, tells me that, single-handed, you carry a banner for every foolish cause, for every down-and-out villain, for every criminal, for miles around.'

She stared at him, shocked. 'That's not true!' she burst out, stung into self-defence. 'I'm sure he never said any such thing. I care about people, Mr Vivian, that is all. I hope that is not a crime!' Her eyes flashed dangerously. Why, the man was an ill-mannered and self-opinionated boor!

'Stella, dear! Mr Vivian!' Maria's shocked voice broke in reproachfully. 'Come, we are here to celebrate Stella's engagement!' She laughed lightly, and Stella saw John Vivian turn and eye her coldly for a moment. Then he gave a slight bow. 'I stand reprimanded, Mrs Williams. You are quite right. Forgive me, Miss Stella; how remiss of me not to add my good wishes for your future happiness. Mr Morgan is indeed a fortunate man to be marrying such a dedicated lady.'

The irony in the last two words was contradicted by the look of bland innocence on his face as he smiled at her for the first time. She felt her pulse quicken inexplicably, and crossly she looked away. Attractive John Vivian might be, she conceded to herself reluctantly, but his nature was obviously harsh and unpleasant and she had no wish ever to speak with him again.

She noticed suddenly that Owen was making his way towards them at last, and she clutched his arm as he joined her, fighting for composure as she smiled up at his reassuringly calm face.

John Vivian stood a head taller than Owen, and the former's slim figure made that of Stella's betrothed look positively stocky as she watched the two men eye one another. Vivian smiled. 'Congratulations, Morgan. It appears that you have appropriated for yourself the flower of the whole county.' There was no trace of sarcasm in his tone now, as he bowed in Stella's direction.

Brusquely Owen returned the bow. 'Thank you, sir. I do indeed consider myself fortunate beyond words.'

The two men exchanged a few more pleasantries and

then, to her relief, Owen led Stella away. As she crossed the room she was intensely aware of the fact that John Vivian's quizzical blue eyes were once more fixed upon her.

She did not look back.

In the corner Margaret Vaughan frowned slightly. She had seen the whole exchange and was puzzled by it. Why should this handsome stranger look at her daughter so intently, and why had Stella reacted with such unmistakable annoyance? The girl's high colour could be seen clear across the room.

Margaret sighed deeply. The engagement to Owen had not come a moment too soon.

She continued to watch John Vivian covertly, and was intrigued and not a little alarmed to see that even now he was standing alone, his thoughtful gaze was still fixed on Stella.

She started guiltily as Maria Williams materialised at her elbow.

'Good-looking, is he not?' her hostess whispered.

Margaret coloured. 'So I was thinking.'

'And, my dear, he is such a mystery man!' Her voice barely raised above a whisper, Maria drew her friend into a corner out of earshot. 'He is heir to Lord Ambleston, you know.'

Margaret's eyes widened in astonishment. 'Indeed?'

'Exactly!' Maria pounced triumphantly. 'So, why is he working as a country solicitor? A conundrum, is it not?'

Both women turned to stare at John Vivian. 'Maria.' Margaret laid her hand on her friend's arm. 'Would it not be expedient if he were to be seated next to Eliza at dinner?'

Maria laughed softly. 'It is already arranged,' she said smugly. 'I have everything planned.'

The long table was lit by three silver candelabra. Seated between her host and Owen, Stella watched, almost in a daze, as the company began dinner. The flickering lights played on the glasses and the silver, and on the jewellery of the women, and glowed ruby red in the wine. Directly opposite, her mother, resplendent in grey silk with the white lace on her cap, looked up and caught her eye, and Stella felt a quick glow of pleasure. The announcement of the engagement seemed to have brought to Margaret Vaughan's eyes a sparkle of happiness which Stella had not seen there for a long time, and she was glad.

On her mother's right sat John Vivian and, beyond him, Eliza. Stella saw her sister engaging the solicitor in vivacious conversation, the girl's pale skin tinted rose in the candlelight as Vivian turned to her, listening, and she frowned slightly. Obviously, she thought with a sharp pang of something not unlike jealousy, he was treating her sister more graciously than he had her.

Unable to resist taking the opportunity of surveying him while he was preoccupied, she stared at him surreptitiously. He had pleasant even features, certainly, and that, she decided critically, gave him a superficial attractiveness, but he seldom smiled and, when he did, the warmth did not reach his eyes. She could not imagine why she had initially thought him handsome.

She refused to allow herself to dwell on the strange disturbing emotions which had flooded through her at the touch of his hand. They were humiliating and more than eclipsed by her anger. She only wished that his presence in the room did not make her feel so uncomfortable.

She looked away, trying to concentrate her attention on her father at the other end of the table, but she could not help being still horribly aware of Eliza and John Vivian talking together in undertones on the far side of the epergne, and found herself wishing that Eliza did not look quite so happy in the solicitor's company.

She rebuked herself furiously. She should be glad he was being nice to her sister. After all, she herself had now found her own love. She was engaged, and other men were of no importance to her. She glanced down at the table where the rose Owen had given her lay beside her plate on the damask cloth, and saw with a tremor of sadness that the petals were already turning brown.

At the sound of her sister's laughter she raised her eyes almost unwillingly. But John Vivian's attention had left Eliza at last and he was looking now straight at Stella.

He studied her unashamedly for a long moment and she found herself unable to look away, mesmerised, the colour mounting in her cheeks as she was subjected to his cold appraisal.

'Stella?'

She jumped guiltily as Owen spoke to her. 'What are you staring at, my dear?' He sounded faintly reproving, following her gaze across the table as he sipped his julienne.

She glanced round uncomfortably, wondering if anyone else had noticed Vivian's strange preoccupation with her, but they were all listening now to Maria Williams recounting a story at the far end of the table. No one had, it seemed. Relieved, she turned back to Owen. 'I was thinking how wonderful it would be if Eliza could find the happiness I've found,' she whispered.

Owen grimaced. 'Well, if you're thinking in terms of that gentleman, I should think again,' he replied in an undertone, with a gesture towards John Vivian who was now talking to Margaret Vaughan. 'I gather he's a cold fish, and wedded to his profession.' He smiled at Stella. 'Don't worry, my dear. Eliza will find someone soon.'

As the footmen removed the soup bowls, and the fish course was brought in, the conversation became general once again.

'Well, Henry, what is this I hear about you letting one of Rebecca's children slip out of your hands?' Glynn Williams bellowed jovially down the table. 'By Gad, old boy, that's pretty bad going. You should have strung him up while you had him!'

Henry Vaughan's complexion darkened visibly. Stella saw his knuckles tighten on the knife he held in his hand. Her father managed a small smile as he looked around the table. 'I would have too, damn it, but he must have had an accomplice in the house.'

Stella stared hard at the embroidered napkin on her knees, praying that her face did not betray the emotion which flooded through her, as Glynn roared: 'One of your wretched servants, Henry? You'd better be careful or you'll find yourselves murdered in your beds. We've all heard the stories about the atrocities these people have been committing in the west of Wales where most of these riots go on.'

Raising her eyes, Stella found that John Vivian was

watching her intently once more, his face inscrutable in the flickering candlelight, and she caught her breath. He knew! Panic-stricken, she tried to still the sudden thudding of her pulse. How could he know? It was impossible. He might suspect, but that was all. How could anyone know what she had done? She forced herself to look away from him, frightened that he might read her thoughts, and concentrated hard on her brother, who had begun to speak. 'Why should they suddenly have appeared round here?' he asked with his mouth full. 'Do you think we're going to have more trouble with them? After all, they haven't shown their faces in Brecon and Radnor before, as far as I know.'

'They've got more sense,' Glynn said emphatically. 'And if they haven't, we'll soon deal with them with a detachment or two of dragoons. We'll brook no nonsense in our parish, eh, Henry? Where's that wine?' He turned and signalled to his butler. 'What is your view, my boy?' Squinting across the table through the candlelight he waved his knife at Owen.

'I'm not sure.' Owen put down his napkin and leaned back in his chair. 'They must be stopped, of course, that goes without saying, but have you been reading those articles in *The Times*? Pretty interesting. They really seem to feel these people have a genuine grievance.'

Stella looked at her fiancé quickly. 'You agree with me, then!' she said in delight, forgetting her preoccupation with John Vivian. 'You think these people are right in bringing attention to their plight. They need our sympathy and help for their families and children.

'It was not right to burn the Joneses' house,' she went on recklessly, 'but I'm sure the Rebeccas didn't intend to go so far. It was the man the Joneses work for whom they should have attacked. He is the real criminal, and the Rebeccas' leader was at fault in not controlling them better.'

'Stella!' Henry Vaughan roared at her down the table. 'No more of this nonsense, please.'

John Vivian was still watching her, and she saw a flash of amusement cross his face. 'I'm sure Mother Rebecca would have welcomed your advice, Miss Stella. Obviously you would be an asset to his side.' His tone was dry and, seeing the expression which crossed her father's face in the mo-

ment of silence which followed Vivian's shocking state-
ment, Stella felt a tremor of dismay clutch at her throat.

Owen reached across and touched her hand gently. 'Mr
Vivian is making fun of you, my dear,' he said calmly. 'No
one doubts the sincerity of your feelings.'

'Indeed not,' Vivian put in fervently. 'Forgive me, Miss
Stella. Your sincerity is obvious. However misguided.' His
eyes gleamed maliciously as he watched her through the
candlelight, and she looked away abruptly as she saw Eliza
lean across and, just for a second, touch his arm to claim his
attention back.

Owen frowned at Stella, his expression forbidding.
'Stella, this is not a suitable subject for ladies. It is much
too serious. I suggest we discuss something else. That
mare your Father was going to give you, for instance.'

Snubbed, Stella blushed with anger. 'Cariad,' she said
sulkily. 'She's lovely.'

'Lovely, but in need of schooling,' put in George, heap-
ing succulent flakes of river trout on to his fork. 'She's a bit
wild.'

'Like her mistress.' Owen smiled at Stella.

Stella bit back the furious retort which sprang to her lips,
and looked down at her plate.

'You enjoy riding, Miss Stella?' It was the cool voice of
John Vivian which cut through the general good-natured
laughter.

She looked up suspiciously, clenching her fists in her lap.
'Very much, sir.'

'And she's good,' George put in, his tone conciliatory as
he recognised the dangerous sparkle in his sister's eyes. 'We
were out on the hillside last night when they fired the
toll-house. The horses were terrified and she sat Cariad like
a trooper.'

'How commendable.' Vivian reached for his glass and
raised it to Stella, the candlelight winking on the heavy gold
signet-ring on his finger. 'I so admire a lady who knows how
to sit a horse.'

Again that hidden mockery, meant for her alone. Stella
returned his look defiantly, conscious of Owen beside her,
listening to the exchange. If only her fiancé would go on
standing up to him. Put him down with some sharp, well-

chosen retort. But Owen merely smiled amiably across the table. 'Eliza, too, is a fine horsewoman,' he said mildly. 'And you, Mrs Campbell,' he inclined his head towards the woman who sat on John Vivian's far side. 'Do you ride since you came to Wales?'

Stella saw the woman respond to Owen's questioning, fluttering beneath his charm. 'Mr Campbell wouldn't let me, sir,' she said with a quick glance at her husband. 'He was afraid of these terrible rioters even before we came here. We read about them in the papers when we were still in Cheltenham. And now, after last night . . .' She raised her hands explicitly, as words failed her.

John Vivian smiled at her. 'I feel sure you have nothing to fear, ma'am. It is very much a local matter. Only those who openly involve themselves would run the slightest risk of any unpleasant encounters.'

Stella held her breath. He had not looked at her and yet she had a strange feeling that his words had been directed at her. Was it a warning? Or a threat? She found she was trembling slightly as she wondered for the second time if he had guessed who had released the rioter from Henry Vaughan's cellar.

Cautiously she raised her eyes and found the intense blue gaze fixed unwaveringly on her face once more. Once more he raised his glass in her direction and she realised uncomfortably that somehow, across the table, John Vivian had issued a wordless challenge to her. And it was one which somehow, sometime, she would be forced to meet.

When Maria Williams led the ladies to the drawing-room, leaving the gentlemen to their port and cigars, Eliza drew Stella into a corner.

'What do you think of him?' she whispered eagerly. Her face was flushed and her eyes bright with excitement.

Stella smiled faintly. 'I suppose you mean Mr Vivian?'

Eliza nodded. 'Isn't he handsome?'

'Indeed he is.' Stella turned towards the window where the open curtains showed the lawns bathed in cold moonlight. 'If you like men so dark of colouring. He is sunburned like a labourer after the harvest.'

Eliza gave a gurgle of delight. 'That is because he has to

ride out on cases the whole time and in all weathers. And he is a superb rider. Mrs Williams told me. Anyway, you are no judge of men. You think Owen is handsome, with his pink face and straw-coloured hair!' With a shrug, she flounced away to sit beside Mrs Campbell on the sofa, and soon the two young women were giggling quietly behind their fans while Stella watched them for a moment, struggling with the strange anger which had come over her once more at the thought of the man her sister admired.

'My dear, now at last I have the chance to wish you well properly.' Maria Williams interrupted her thoughts, suddenly appearing at her elbow. 'I am so pleased you're to marry Owen.' She too was watching Eliza on the sofa.

'Thank you, I'm very happy,' Stella replied. She hesitated. 'My sister seems much struck by Mr Vivian,' she went on, touching almost unwillingly on a subject which some strange instinct told her she should leave well alone.

Maria frowned. 'My dear, I am so sorry about John's outspoken comments earlier. I feel sure he did not intend them to sound so severe.' She smiled coyly. 'I think he comes from a background where he expects ladies to take no interest in matters which are better left to the gentlemen.'

'Indeed?' Stella bit back the retort which instantly rose to her lips. Instead, she asked, demurely, 'What is his background? Where does he come from, do you know?'

Maria beamed. 'Indeed I do,' she murmured confidentially. 'My dear, he is the son of the Earl of Ambleston's late brother; the seat is in Pembrokeshire, you know. And there is an enormous fortune. Such a catch he would be, for Eliza!'

Stella bit her lip. 'How strange, then, that he should practise the law if he is so favourably endowed,' she said, more tartly than she intended.

'Just what your mother and I were saying earlier,' Maria said eagerly. 'And I trust that Mr Williams will have asked him something of himself over the port, although I am quite certain that he is most eligible. Your mama need have no fear on that score. I am sure that he was looking with interest at Eliza during dinner.'

Stella gave a wry smile. 'Indeed he was,' she agreed, with

a silent prayer that he would confine his attention to her sister for the rest of the evening.

But she need not have worried.

When the tea urn was brought in and the gentlemen appeared from the dining-room, John Vivian was not with them.

'He begged to be excused, my dear,' Glynn said to his wife. 'He has to work this evening; a case he is involved in, apparently. He seems a very conscientious gentleman, I must say, though I can see his presence will be missed.' Stella could not fail to see the knowing smile he directed at Eliza, nor her sister's blush, but she herself felt nothing but relief that she need not see him again that evening, and turned to slip her arm through Owen's with a lighter heart.

It was late when Henry Vaughan at last sent for his carriage and ushered his family out into the hall. Owen, like the Campbells, was to remain as an overnight guest, so theirs was the only vehicle on the cold moonlit drive, the horses' breath steamy in the night air as they trotted round, silver-shadowed, from the stables with a sleepy Ianto on the box. The weather promised fair for the next day, but beneath the glittering stars the dew lay heavy with a sheen which would soon be frost. Stella caught her breath as Owen pressed her hand to his lips in farewell, and found she was shivering violently.

It was warm in the carriage, however, where there were rugs and foot-warmers to keep the passengers comfortable, and as they wheeled out of the drive and on to the dusty road, in minutes Margaret and her younger daughter were asleep. Henry stretched in his seat and reached out his hand to Stella's beneath the fur rug.

'Happy, daughter?'

'Of course, Papa.'

'Are you sure, Stella?' He turned a sharp eye on her face as a shaft of moonlight pierced the window. 'He'll make a good husband, of that I'm certain. It's an excellent match.' He broke off as the coach lurched into a pothole. 'God dammit! They take these tolls from us, so you'd expect the roads to be better than this!'

Stella smiled. 'That sounded positively rebellious, Papa. The trouble is that Ianto is driving too fast.'

She leaned forward to lower the window and peered out. The dark shape of George's horse moved alongside. 'All right?' he shouted cheerfully.

'Tell Ianto to slow down. Papa is getting quite peppery,' she called back.

George laughed, but already the horses were slowing.

Moments later there was an alarmed cry of warning from the box. 'Mr George, Mr Vaughan—' and Ianto was pulling the plunging horses to a complete halt as George's animal reared up beside the carriage.

'What the devil—' Before George could protest further the road was full of shadowy figures; two were at the coach horses' heads, while two more pulled Ianto, yelling loudly, from his box. Then George, too, was dragged to the ground.

Before Stella or Henry Vaughan could move, the carriage door was pulled open and a blackened face peered in. The hand that reached inside was holding a pistol.

'Out!' a gruff voice ordered. 'Out, in the name of Rebecca!'

CHAPTER
THREE

MARGARET VAUGHAN'S terrified scream brought no answer
in the night. There was nothing for it but to climb from
the coach and stand huddled in the road as they were
instructed.

Stella's heart was beating fast with fear. There was
nothing gallant or romantic about the dozen or so men who
surrounded them. They all wore the disguise of shawls and
skirts, but there their likeness to women ended. Their faces
were blackened and all were armed with pitchforks or
staves. Two men carried guns. One of these approached
Henry Vaughan and gestured him forward away from the
huddled group.

'I have a message for you, Magistrate Vaughan. A warning, see,' he said slowly. Deliberately he cocked the gun in
his hand. 'You have sworn to deal with Rebecca's daughters if they come before your court. Our Mother doesn't
like to hear that kind of talk. She takes it personally, see.
She's fair, though; she believes in warnings. She warned
Jones at the toll, but he took no notice so his house was
burned to the ground. I hope you'll take notice, Magistrate
Vaughan.' The man reached into the pocket of his vol-
uminous skirt and produced a letter. 'This is for you,
Mr Vaughan. I advise you to read it carefully.' He thrust it
into Stella's father's hand.

No one moved. Next to Stella, George and Ianto stood
motionless. Only her mother's stifled sobs rent the silence.

Then one of the skirted figures stepped forward. He
whispered to the man with the gun, who nodded, then
motioned Henry towards the carriage. 'You may get back
inside your grand coach now, Mr Vaughan, and read your
letter at your leisure.' He turned to the men who held
George and Ianto. 'The boy can go back on the box, and the
other gentleman must ride inside. We need his horse.'

Spluttering with rage, George found himself being
pushed into the carriage after his father. Margaret climbed
in next, shaking so much she could barely stand, and then
Eliza. But when Stella tried to follow, she found herself
being held back. Terrified, she began to struggle, but it was
in vain. Strong arms held her easily, and as the coach horses
were whipped into a gallop she was forced to watch the
Vaughan carriage swaying up the road with her family
inside, and Ianto hauling desperately on the reins as he
tried to gain control of the horses.

Within seconds she was being lifted up on to George's
cob. Someone took the bridle and she was led swiftly and
silently off the road down into the woods which bordered
the water-meadows along the river. 'Please, oh please,
where are you taking me?' she called, but the men ran on
without looking at her, and, half paralysed with terror and
breathless from the jolting of the slippery saddle, she did
not ask again.

They moved soundlessly and with considerable speed,
seemingly unhampered by their ludicrous garb, picking
their way unhesitatingly towards the silver river while Stella
perched perilously on the stocky horse. It trod stumbling
into the water and she felt hands reach up to steady her, but
the Wye ran shallow there over its shingly bed and they
crossed without mishap in spite of the men's skirts trailing
in the cold ripples.

Only when they were out of the silent dew-silvered
meadows where the red and white cows grazed beneath the
moon, and once more in the darkness of the woods, did
they slow to a walking pace. One of the men detached
himself from the group and came to walk beside her. She
caught the glint of his eyes in his blackened face as he
looked up at her.

'Mother Rebecca wants to see you,' he said. He reached
up to slap her horse on the rump. It threw up its head, and
he laughed as she clutched desperately at its mane.

There was something about the angle of his head, the
twist of his mouth, which she recognised as she stared
uncertainly down at him. 'You're the man they caught,' she
said at last. 'The man I helped. It is you, isn't it?'

He gave a crooked smile, his teeth gleaming suddenly

white. 'Maybe, maybe not,' he said. And with that she had to be content.

Her fear had lessened now. The men did not seem disposed to hurt her; on the contrary, they had provided her with a horse. She looked from one to another carefully, but their disguises were thorough and she could distinguish no features even in the moonlight.

The first dead leaves lay in crisp swathes on the ground, and the horses' hooves rustled steadily as they began to climb steeply up the wooded hillside. Near by, below them, she could hear the gurgling chatter of a stream and all round the light patter of leaves as a breathy wind stirred the trees.

They had been going for some time, up ever-steepening country, when the man leading her horse called the group to a halt in the thickest shadows. He glanced round at them and then addressed the man at Stella's side. 'Best go no further with the horse, Dai,' he said softly. 'We'll go quieter across the mountain without it.'

Dai nodded. He looked up at Stella. 'You'll have to walk from here, girl,' he said. He reached up and, before she could protest, his hands were on her waist and he had lifted her from the saddle. The horse was led away and she saw it tethered in the trees.

Nodding at the two men nearest her, Dai reached into his pocket. At his signal they closed on Stella, taking her arms. She gave a small cry of fright but Dai shook his head. 'There's no need to be scared, girl. They're not going to hurt you. I'm going to tie something over your eyes, that's all. Mother Rebecca doesn't want you seeing where her house is, now, does she?' In his hands he was holding a black scarf. As the two men gripped her elbows, he tied it tightly around her eyes, blotting out the moonlight.

Stumbling, she found herself being guided on up through the steep woods, her skirts trailing in the crisp leaves, and then the ground changed. They were walking over close-cropped turf and she guessed they had come out some-where on the open mountainside. The wind was cold on her face. She could feel it teasing her hair where Dai's hands, knotting the blindfold, had half dislodged her heavy chignon. The hands on her wrists were calloused and strong and there was no way she could raise her arm to push away the scarf, but they were also careful, guiding her over the rough ground. The men continued to walk in silence; the only sound, save the gentle moan of the wind, was her own laboured breathing as they began to climb again.

She could not guess how long they had been walking when at last they stopped. She slumped against one of her captors, gasping at the stitch which tore at her side, and an arm went round her shoulders, steadying her. Then Dai's voice spoke in her ear. 'Nearly there, girl.'

Somehow she negotiated a rough wall, half-lifted, half-scrambling over the loose stones, then in the silence she heard the broody mumbling of a hen.

She was guided into some kind of building and brought up short by the hands which held her. After the biting cold outside it was hot and airless, and she felt herself gasping for breath.

'We've brought the girl, Mother,' Dai announced.

There was a moment's silence. Then a voice spoke. It was a deep whispering voice, heavy with the lilt of the mountains, vibrant and attractive. Stella shivered violently at the sound of it.

'Let her sit down, Dai bach, then you can remove the blindfold. I want to see her face while I talk.'

She blinked, dazzled, as the black scarf was removed from her eyes. She was seated before a scrubbed table in a stone-walled room. In front of her a fire blazed up the chimney and at her elbow a candle shone directly into her eyes. Throwing the scarf on the table, Dai shuffled out, shutting the door behind him with a clatter of the falling latch.

For a moment Stella thought he had left her alone, then she realised that there was someone else in the room. A figure sat in the high-backed chair beside the fire, the face in shadow, the flames throwing the outline of broad shoulders into silhouette. The rest of the room was dark.

'So, Stella Vaughan,' the figure whispered again. 'You expressed a desire to meet Mother Rebecca.'

Stella swallowed nervously, leaning away from the candle, trying to see him, but the light was in her eyes and his face was dark.

'Yes, I did,' she faltered at last.

'And now you have met her, no doubt, being a woman, you have something to say?' The deep voice prompted.

Stella tried to collect her whirling thoughts. There was so much she had wanted to say to him when she was rehearsing her views safely at home, but now she was here, in his presence, her courage failed her. All she could think of was that she was alone with a dangerous man. She had expected someone quite different to lead the people in their struggle: a farmer, perhaps, like the fatherly men she knew as neighbours, but not this strong, muscular figure who even in the anonymity of the darkening shadows radiated tightly leashed power. She gripped her hands together nervously on her lap and, straightening her shoulders, looked at him across the dazzle of candlelight. 'I wanted to help,' she said as firmly as she could. Every nerve in her body was tensed. She wanted to stand up and run, but the powerful stillness of the man who sat opposite her in the shadows held her a frozen captive.

'And how can you help?' A log slipped, sending a shower of sparks out on to the flagstones. He did not move. 'By releasing one poor prisoner from the threat of transportation?'

She blushed uncomfortably. 'That's a start, surely?' she said with a touch of defiance. 'You're wrong, though, to burn people's homes—even toll-houses—you must see that. Violence only makes things worse for your people—'

She broke off as the man gave a short bitter laugh. 'Don't lecture me, Stella Vaughan. A society that lets parsons and squires grow fat and allows the children to die of starvation in the fields is a society whose rules I do not listen to.'

Shocked, she stared at him. 'But there are ways of helping the poor—'

'Helping? By transporting them, by hanging their men-folk and throwing their children into the workhouse?'

He rose to his feet abruptly, and stood, his back to the fire. He was dressed in trousers and a shirt of some dark material. The firelight behind him reflected in the polished leather of his boots. But his face, like those of his men, was blackened, and she tried in vain to see his features. 'The only way to reach the powers that rule this land is to hit them where it hurts them most. By striking at their property. By burning their houses and firing their ricks!'

Stella stared at him, silenced by the vehemence with which he spoke. This was no labourer or hill shepherd. This man was educated and very dangerous. She licked her lips nervously, shifting in her chair as she tried vainly to see him more clearly, helplessly aware of the strange magnetism which must hold his followers loyal, reaching out to her in spite of her fear.

'What can I do, then?' she asked at last.

He smiled grimly. 'Haven't I put you off, then, Miss Vaughan? Can you still want to help after all I've said?'

'Not if that means burning houses,' she repeated with stubborn courage. 'But there must be something else I can do.' The candle beside her was dripping hot wax on the table and she stared down at it, no longer looking at him.

'There is,' he said softly. 'You can go back to your father and ask him if he has read the letter he was given this evening. As I expect you have heard, Mother Rebecca writes a great many letters, Miss Vaughan, and your father's is short and to the point. He is to stop sentencing poor starving men to transportation, he is to help our daughters in the struggle for lower rents and tolls, he is to prevail upon his neighbours on the bench, Mr Williams and Sir Robert Morgan, to do the same. I hear you have some influence, now, with the Morgan family. I suggest you use it.'

Stella gasped. 'How did you know about that?' she said, hot colour reddening her cheeks.

'I have my spies,' he said with a grave flash of amusement. 'Even on the mountain we know of this evening's engagement of Owen Morgan and the beautiful, spirited, Miss Vaughan.' He studied her face for a moment as she tried to regain her composure, his arms folded across his chest, and his tone was once more forbidding when he spoke again. 'Our tempers are short and our longing to use the flame is very strong. I should hate to burn your house over your head, Stella Vaughan, but if that is what it takes to win our cause, then burn it I will. So far, this part of Wales has escaped the full brunt of Rebecca's anger. Whether or not it continues to do so is perhaps up to you alone.'

She gave a little cry of protest as the violence of his words rang in her ears. 'But my father will never go against the law,' she cried desperately. 'Don't you see, the law must be changed! Then he can help you. Please understand. Burning houses will only turn them all against you! You can't win like that, you can't!'

'We can, and we will.' His voice was grim. He took a step towards her. 'And you will help us by being my spokeswoman. Now it is time for you to go home to your no doubt distraught family. You will forgive me if I replace your blindfold. In the moonlight the countryside is as bright as day, and I cannot rule out the chance that your father might persuade you to show him where our humble headquarters is hidden.' He laughed softly as he reached for the scarf.

Stella leaped to her feet, sending the chair crashing backwards on the flagstones. The table was still between them, and the halo of smoky light from the candle blinded her as she backed away. 'There is no need. I won't tell him, I promise,' she cried, her breath catching painfully in her throat. She could feel the panic fluttering beneath her breastbone as slowly and deliberately he folded the scarf and began to move round the table towards her.

But there was nowhere to run: she was trapped in the small room, and at last there was nothing for it but to turn away from him to face the wall and wait, afraid to look up into his darkened face, not wanting to see his eyes as he approached her with the blindfold. In spite of herself she began to tremble violently as he tightened the knot.

He rested his hands lightly on her shoulders. 'Why are you trembling?' he murmured. 'Are you afraid at last?'

She stiffened. 'No. I'm not afraid,' she lied stoutly. 'I just don't like not being able to see.'

He laughed. 'How like a woman. Quite the heroine, aren't you, Stella Vaughan?'

She realised that his fingers had strayed to the nape of her neck, and one by one he began to remove her surviving hairpins. With an exclamation, she raised her hands to stop him, but he caught her wrists and pulled them away.

'The heroines of romance, my dear, wear their hair long and flowing,' he said sternly, 'and you have hair as soft and as black as a blackbird's wing. You should not be allowed to

tame it.' She could do nothing but stand helplessly, both her
wrists pinioned in one of his hands as he loosened her silky
tresses with the other and allowed them to tumble down her
back. 'That's better,' he said critically. Then he went on, his
voice mocking her darkness, 'I wonder. If you are the
heroine in this particular little romance, Miss Stella, how
have you cast me? The hero or the villain?' He chuckled.
'Of course Owen Morgan must be your hero, which leaves
me the villain's role. I would rather be the villain; it means I
can behave despicably with complete lack of conscience.'
She could feel the warmth of his breath on her cheek as he
released her wrists and ran his hands gently up her arms,
and then she gave a gasp as they slid round to cup her
breasts. He pulled her hard against him and she felt his
taut, muscular, body against her own. A quick flame of
desire such as she had never known shot through her and,
unable to struggle in his grasp, not even wanting to be free,
she felt herself being turned to face him, her lips raised to
his in the silken blackness of the blindfold which hid him
from her.

His kiss sent hot fire searing through her veins, quench-
ing her protests as her body reacted violently and of its own
volition to the masterful touch of the man who held her. She
wanted to cling to him, to hold him in her arms, but he had
her tightly pinioned and she could not do more than raise
her willing lips to his. For a long moment they remained like
that, her soft mouth beneath his hard one, then at last he
drew away and she heard a harsh quiet laugh.

'So. This prim, virginal exterior is just as much a disguise
as my black face. Underneath you are a woman of passion.'
He caught her hands and held them in a grip of steel. 'We
shall meet again, I think, and then, I promise, you and I
shall get better acquainted.'

His lips brushed hers again for a second and then, almost
before she realised what had happened, he had moved
away from her once more. He propelled her at arms' length
towards the door. 'Dai,' he called, 'you and William escort
this lady back to her house. See she gets to her father safely.
Goodnight, my dear,' he whispered in her ear. 'I'll keep
your hairpins as souvenirs.'

She heard the door open.

Then Dai was there, and another man, holding her arms, and she was stumbling back across the wall, her thoughts a tumult of fury and shame as they hurried her down the cold dew-wet hillside once more.

They walked swiftly on the downhill journey, not talking, half carrying her as she stumbled with exhaustion on the rough ground. The gurgle of water told her when they were once more near the wood, then she heard the rustle of leaves beneath their feet and knew they had left the bare mountainside. Still shaking, she raised her hand to move the scarf, but Dai stopped her. 'You keep that on for now, girl, I'll not have you seeing us in our proper clothes,' he said. 'Wait now, I'll ride this horse of your brother's and you can come up behind me.'

She was lifted on to the crupper of the saddle and found herself unwillingly clutching his belt, her eyes still bandaged, as the horse began to move. The occasional touch of a shoulder against her knee told her the other man was walking beside her. The journey seemed much longer on the return; she knew when they forded the Wye, and she knew that they were climbing the hill on the far side, but when at last they stopped it took her by surprise.

'Right.' Dai slipped from the horse and helped her forward into the saddle. 'I'll lead you the last bit home,' he said softly, 'then you can go in by yourself.'

She felt the horse move, felt the reins in her cold fingers on his neck. The wind whipped her long hair, fanning it over her shoulders, and she clutched the cob's mane as he lengthened his stride, cavorting sideways, and suddenly she knew she was alone. There was no longer anyone at the horse's head.

She raised a hand to pull at the scarf as the animal, sensing her sudden fear, began to snort in terror, but the knot was tight and it had caught in her hair and she could not free her eyes. In her panic she lost the reins and clutched desperately at the saddle.

'Help me! Oh, please help!' she called, hearing the terror in her own voice as she pulled hysterically at the material around her face, and then, miraculously, help was there.

'Stella! Stella, hold on, I'm coming!' She heard Owen's shout from the distance as, beneath her, the horse began to buck in earnest. Then Owen was there beside her, soothing the cob and she felt strong arms go round her, dragging her to safety.

'Wait, my darling. Let me get this off your eyes.' Owen's voice was stern, as behind him in the distance she heard an outburst of angry shouting. A shot rang out and another and there was a scrabble of hooves as the cob reared high above them. Owen let out a violent curse. 'Keep still. I've a penknife in my pocket. Don't move while I cut this damn thing off you! The knot has pulled so tight!'

She stood still, trembling on the verge of hysteria as he slid the cold blade down her cheek. Then at last she could see. Sobbing wildly, she threw herself into his arms as figures ran towards them, lanterns swinging, and she saw that she was in the paddock just below the stables at Bryn Glas.

'Is she hurt?' It was her father; a gun, the barrel still smoking, clutched in his hand.

'I don't think so. Only frightened.' Owen, having disengaged himself from her, was staring at her with concern on his face. Then he stooped and lifted her into his arms.

'I'll take her up to the house, Mr Vaughan. Did you see them?'

'I think I hit one of them.' Henry Vaughan smiled grimly, his ruddy face illuminated by the smoking lantern. 'And we'll get the other one too. And, make no mistake about it, these men are going to hang for this night's work!'

CHAPTER
FOUR

THE DRAWING-ROOM was lit by half a dozen lamps as Owen laid Stella on the sofa. Margaret threw herself on her knees beside her daughter, weeping violently.

'My darling child! My baby! Did they hurt you? What did they do to you?'

Owen touched her on the shoulder. 'Mrs Vaughan, if I might suggest, a little brandy—'

Margaret glanced up at him through her tears. 'Of course, you're right. I'll get it. If you're sure she's not hurt—'

'She's not hurt.' He smiled down gravely and reached to help Stella's mother to rise.

Stella was staring up at him as her mother left the room, still bewildered by the lamplight. 'I was so frightened, I couldn't free my eyes,' she said faintly. 'I thought the horse was going to bolt and I couldn't see. I—'

'Hush.' He knelt beside her in her mother's place. 'It's all over now, and you are quite, quite safe.' He reached out and rather timidly touched her forehead. 'This is the most terrible thing, Stella, quite terrible. I couldn't believe it when George rode back to fetch us. Glynn called out the dragoons. The whole countryside is being quartered and we will find every one of these men. They shall pay very dearly for laying hands on you.' He clasped her hand gently in his and carried it to his lips. 'They didn't hurt you, did they, my dearest? Do you feel well enough to tell me anything? Did you recognise anyone? Or hear any names?'

Behind him the firelight was flickering on the walls, the shadows running across the ceiling as the lamps smoked from the draught of the open door. Stella looked at her hand, imprisoned in Owen's. His fingers were long and white, elegantly manicured, quite unlike that other hand, the hand of Mother Rebecca which she had glimpsed so briefly. That hand had been lean and brown.

She opened her eyes and met Owen's gaze. 'I saw nothing. They kept me blindfolded the whole time.' She looked away from him unhappily, not quite knowing why she lied. 'It was terrible. But they didn't hurt me at all. They were very polite.'

'What did they want?' He stared at her intently.

'They told me I had to persuade Papa to agree to what they wanted in their letter.' Her voice was steady now, her courage returning as the horror of her ordeal receded.

With a sigh, Owen stood up. He went to stand with his back to the fire. 'He hasn't had time to tell me about the letter yet, but it will be full of threats and demands, of course. They always are.'

Behind them the door opened and Mrs Vaughan reappeared, carrying a tray with a decanter and some glasses. Owen stepped forward to relieve her of her burden, setting it down on a low table.

'Has Mr Vaughan returned?' he asked quietly as he removed the glass stopper and laid it on the tray.

She shook her head. 'He went chasing after those men. Ianto says one of them was shot. There was a lot of blood and he said my husband and the men would easily catch up with him.' She shuddered.

On the sofa, Stella pulled herself up against the cushions, instantly alert. 'What did you say, Mama? Did they catch one of them?'

Owen and Margaret exchanged glances. Then Owen brought her a glass with a little brandy. He knelt at her side once more. 'Don't be afraid, Stella. If they don't get them tonight, they will tomorrow. Whatever happens, you are safe.'

She sipped the brandy a little reluctantly and screwed up her face in distaste. 'They didn't hurt me, Owen. I'm not afraid.'

He smiled. 'Brave girl. All the same, you are shocked. I suggest that you allow your Mama to take you up to bed. I shall see you in the morning.' He bent and awkwardly placed a little kiss on her forehead.

Mrs Vaughan cleared her throat. 'Will you stay here tonight, Owen?'

'No, thank you.' He rose to his feet. 'I shall ride back to the Williamses' place and give them the news that Stella is safe. But I shall return tomorrow and enquire how things are, if I may?' And with one last worried look down at Stella's face, he headed for the door.

Mrs Vaughan saw him out to the hall. Then she returned, drawing her shawl tightly round her shoulders as she quietly closed the door and turned to face her daughter.

'Stella?' She hesitated. Then she strode purposefully to the sofa and sat down on the end of it, her eyes fixed on Stella's face. 'My dear, you look stronger now, so I must talk to you. Your father thinks you were taken by these men because it was you that released the prisoner from the cellars. It was you, wasn't it?'

Stella dropped her gaze to her hands, still clutching the glass. 'Mama—'

'Tell me the truth, Stella. I must know.' Margaret Vaughan's clear grey eyes, so like her daughter's, were quite steady as she surveyed the girl. Then she slumped back against the fringed cushions. 'No, you don't have to say anything. Your guilt is written all over your face. Oh, Stella! Why? How could you have been so disloyal?'

Stella closed her eyes wearily. 'It was not disloyal, Mama. I happen to believe very strongly that these men represent families who are in great need; they do wrong only because they are driven to it.'

'So, no doubt, every murderer justifies himself!' Margaret snapped back. 'You are being naive, Stella. That man could have hurt you; he could have robbed us, or even killed us all in our beds. And you see what it led to? You are abducted; you could have been murdered, ravished, anything!' She dabbed at her eyes with a wisp of handkerchief.

Stella's cheeks coloured sharply. 'All that happened, Mama, was that they took me to Mother Rebecca at his hideout in the mountains, and he talked to me.'

'What about?' Her mother's tone was scornful.

'About poverty and need and the things these people are fighting for—' Stella looked away from her mother's shrewd gaze, remembering the stinging scorn of his voice; the disbelief; her own mortification. She drew herself up unsteadily and put down her glass. 'Mama—if you will excuse me, I think I shall go to bed. I have a headache and I'm very tired. No, don't come. I'll ring for Megan if I need help.'

Her mother did not move. But as she watched Stella leave the room, she shook her head with infinite sadness.

In the dark passage Stella leaned against the door for a moment, breathing deeply to steady herself. Her wet shoes were in ribbons, her feet cold and blistered, and as she made her way slowly towards the stairs she limped painfully, supporting herself with her hand against the wall.

Now that her fear had quite gone she was remembering the full humiliation of her interview with Mother Rebecca. Unconsciously she raised her hand to her lips and stopped in her tracks, embarrassed by the glow of desire which flowed through her as she felt again the pressure of his mouth on hers and the strength of the hands which had released her hair and touched her breasts. She pressed her hands to her face, overcome with guilt and shame that her own body should have responded as it had to his touch. How could she! For a moment she was breathless. Then suddenly she was blazingly angry. What kind of woman did he think she was? She would show him that she was not to be trifled with! And somehow she had to make him see that her support was not to be ridiculed either. Straightening her shoulders, she walked with new resolution towards the stairs.

Eliza was lying in wait for her on the landing. 'Stella! What happened? Were you hurt?' Her sister was dressed in her nightgown, with a cashmere shawl round her shoulders.

Stella shook her head. 'I'm tired, Eliza. Do you mind? We'll talk in the morning.'

'Oh no, we'll talk now.' Eliza followed her into her room and closed the door firmly. 'Do you know what happened to us? Ianto managed to stop the horses only when we were nearly home; the coach nearly overturned! It was terrifying! Then there was a terrible row. George wanted to ride back for Owen and Glynn Williams at once, and Papa said No, we must get the constables from Hay, but George went anyway. Papa didn't want Owen to find out what you'd been up to. He thinks you let that awful man loose this morning, and that Owen would call off the engagement if he found out about it. Think of that!'

'I did let him out.' Stella threw herself down on her bed.

Eliza stared at her. 'You did? You admit it?'

'I had to. Mama guessed.'

'And what does Papa say?'

'I don't know. He's not back yet.'

'Stella! He'll probably have you whipped!' Eliza's eyes were enormous. 'How could you do it?'

'Very easily.'

'And what will Owen say?'

There was a pause. Stella frowned. 'I don't know. Perhaps they won't tell him.'

'He would never understand. Never!' Eliza whispered.

Pushing herself off the bed, Stella went to the bell and pulled it, then crossed to her mirror and stood staring at her reflection in the glass. Her face was flushed now, her grey eyes bright, her dark hair hanging loose and wild about her shoulders. The face was that of a beautiful gipsy. She stuck her tongue out at it, then she turned back to Eliza. 'If he loves me, he will understand,' she said defiantly. 'If he doesn't, then he is not the man for me.'

Stella did not feel so courageous, however, the next morning, when her father sent for her to his study. He was seated behind his broad desk, while beyond him the french windows were open to the garden. It was another warm misty day, with the rich scents of early autumn drifting in across the carpet.

Stella had dressed carefully in a morning gown of pale striped silk. It was unadorned, save for the small brooch at the collar. Her hair was neatly pinned. She stared at her father a little defiantly as she crossed the room towards him. 'Good morning, Papa.'

'Good morning, child. I trust you slept well?' He motioned her towards the chair by his desk, and she perched on it nervously. He did not wait for her to answer his question. 'Stella. There are several things we must discuss.' He frowned. 'The first, of course, is your conduct the night before last, when you freed this man from lawful custody.'

The formality of his tone frightened her, but she said

nothing, and her father went on. 'You deliberately misled me, Stella, when I questioned you about it. That was dishonest—'

'But Papa, you yourself—' Stella interrupted him, jumping up. But he went on speaking, without pause.

'Your mother has already pointed out to you what might have happened, and I am sure that you have seen the error of your ways. In the circumstances, I do not intend to pursue the matter beyond this warning: do not ever be tempted to meddle again with these Rebeccas.' He paused. 'You may be interested to know that the man you released was one of those who brought you back here last night, and that he has been recaptured.'

Stella gasped. 'You caught him?'

'He was wounded in the leg. He left a trail a blind man could have followed. Unfortunately, his accomplice got away—'

'Where is he?' Stella asked.

Her father gave a harsh laugh. 'Where you could not reach him, my dear, even if you were so inclined. He is in the lock-up at Hay. I have seen to it that they bind up his wound, too, in case your tender heart is worried about that. I have no intention of letting him die of lack of blood. He is to stand trial, among other things for your abduction.'

'But he brought me back!' she cried. 'Papa, you cannot forget that—'

Henry Vaughan narrowed his eyes. 'Oh yes, I can, Stella. I am not going to be prevented from doing what is right. The only reason these rioters returned you unharmed, the reason they took you in the first place, so I understand from your mother, was so that you could persuade me to act upon the letter they gave me last night.' He rose, placing his hands flat on the desk before him. 'In that letter your friend Mother Rebecca calls on me to pervert the course of justice. If I do not agree, he threatens to burn this house over our heads. The impudent wretch even gives me a date by which he expects me to act on his demands, or else. Yes, you may well look horrified! But have no fear. No one is going to terrorise me, or my family. And I shall have a whole regiment of soldiers here for our protection if necessary when that date comes.' He paused for a moment, watching her. 'Now you see why I intend to overlook what you did, Stella. I am convinced that you did not realise what you were doing. You thought it romantic to play the heroine, no doubt. You will know better in future.'

Stella stared at him. How could they think her so transparent and shallow, she thought rebelliously, as her father echoed unknowingly the very words that Mother Rebecca had used. She stood up, but although a spark of anger flashed in her eyes, she managed to speak calmly. 'I'm sorry, Papa,' she said, struggling to sound repentant.

Her father smiled. 'I knew you would see sense. Now, one more thing I have to ask you, child; then you must go out to your fiancé who is awaiting you in the garden. Try again to think about last night. Is there nothing, nothing at all, that you can remember which might give us an idea as to the identity of their leader?'

She hesitated. He was watching her intently. 'You know,' he said, 'we have one clue besides the letter which is obviously in a disguised hand. This.'

He held out the black scarf which had been used to bind her eyes. 'Owen brought it to me this morning. He put it in his pocket last night without thinking. Take it. Tell me what you think.'

Reluctantly, Stella held out her hand and took it. The tight knot had not been touched; the rent where Owen had cut it from her face had begun to fray into wisps. She looked at it, puzzled.

'I see no clue, Papa.'

'Feel it, girl. What sort of material is it?'

She crumpled it in her fingers. 'Why, it is silk.'

'Exactly.' He smiled triumphantly. 'Expensive, fine quality, silk. Not exactly what you would expect from the cottage of a starving labourer, is it?'

She thought of the expensive polished boots, but she shook her head. 'It could have been stolen, Papa.'

'No, no.' He brushed aside the suggestion. 'If it were stolen, they would have sold it for money, not used it to tie up some stupid interfering chit! No, whoever used this, Stella, had no care for its worth. I suspect our Rebecca is a gentleman.' He laughed. 'One or two of them have been, you know. The rioters are too ignorant to write these letters themselves. Read it. It is the work of a highly educated man.'

She looked at the letter he threw across the desk at her and shook her head. 'He spoke like a simple shepherd,' she said quietly. 'But I suppose he disguised his voice.'

'Of course he did.' Impatiently her father took back the letter and perused it once more. 'The man is an impudent scoundrel, but he'll pay for it. He'll pay with his neck!'

Stella shivered. Outside on the grass she could see Owen now, pacing slowly between the flower-beds, his hands clasped behind him, his head bent in thought. Her father, following her gaze, swivelled in his chair and stared at him silently. 'You are very lucky, Stella. Many men would have broken their engagement for less than this. To embroil yourself, however innocently, with the rioters could cause a fearful scandal. It reflects on my position as a Justice of the Peace, and on Sir Robert Morgan's as well.'

Stella coloured uncomfortably. 'You told Owen, then?'

'Of course. If he is to be your husband, Stella, he must realise the kinds of impetuous actions of which you are capable.'

She lowered her eyes. 'I'm sorry, Papa.'

'Just as long as you never do it again, child. Now run out to him.'

She did not wait to be told a second time. Darting through the french windows, she fled across the grass to where Owen awaited her.

His face lit with contentment as he saw her. 'Stella, my darling. How are you?' Catching her hands in his, he held her at arms' length and scrutinised her slowly. Then, tucking her hand beneath his arm, he resumed his patrolling of the flower-beds. 'Your papa has spoken to you?'

She nodded.

'Were you able to tell him anything about your captors?'

'Nothing, Owen. I recognised no one and I couldn't see where they took me.' She stopped, disengaging her hand, and looked up at him, her grey eyes serious. 'Owen, I would understand if you wished to break our engagement. It was wrong of me to help that man to escape, I do see it. But there must be other, legal, ways of representing the interests of these poor people, and you should know that I still intend to try to help them.'

He held her gaze for a moment, his face serious, then he smiled. 'Sweet Stella. Do you really think I would condemn you for caring about the poor and oppressed? Of course you must; I shall see to it that you have sufficient pin-money to do whatever you wish to help them once we are married.'

They were at the far end of the garden now, the thick yew hedge between them and the windows of the house. Ardently he put his hands on her shoulders and drew her to him, pressing his lips against hers.

With a gasp of distaste she drew back, feeling nothing; no desire, no excitement, only a dull resentment at the inexperienced fumbling of his touch. 'Owen! Please!' She was furiously angry with herself. How was it that she could respond so shamelessly to the arrogant caresses of an outlaw when the kiss of her own fiancé left her cold? 'Owen!' she repeated faintly. 'Please let me go.'

But he continued to hold her. 'Oh, Stella, when shall it be? Let us announce a date so that we can be married soon. Sweet Stella. I want you so much!' Once more his mouth was seeking hers and she stopped struggling, submitting reluctantly to his kisses, feeling the grasp of his fingers biting her arms through the thin sleeves of her gown.

'Why not at Christmas, Sweetheart?' he murmured at last. 'Let it be Christmas.'

She pulled away. 'I shall discuss it with Mama, Owen,' she said quietly, trying to keep the stiffness out of her voice. 'I shall ask what she feels would be proper. Now we must go back. Papa will be wondering where we are.' She forced herself to take his arm and smiled at him as if to make up for the coldness in her heart.

As they walked slowly back through the gardens towards the house, they met George, obviously on his way back from the stables. He was dressed in breeches and shirt-sleeves and seemed in high good humour.

'Morning, Owen. Morning, Sister,' he shouted as he saw them. 'You'll be glad to hear my horse is unscathed after last night. I've had him out for a bit of a trot around and he's as sound as a bell.'

Stella gave her brother a quick look under her eyelashes.

'Thank you for asking, George. I'm unscathed, too,' she
said with a touch of sarcasm.

He smiled sheepishly. 'I can see that. I shouldn't think
the rioters could send you home quickly enough if you
treated them to one of your lectures. You'll have to watch
her, Owen, or she'll turn into a shrew—' He ducked out of
reach with a shout of laughter as Stella lunged after him,
shaking her fist.

Owen's smile was indulgent. 'Your sister's spirit,
George, is quite delightful and I am sure it can be moulded
with the correct training,' he said pompously. He took her
arm again, guiding her possessively towards the house.
'What news is there in the county this morning, George?
The countryside must be in ferment.'

George nodded eagerly. 'It is. The story of what happened to Stella is everywhere. Papa wanted it kept quiet,
but Ianto must have spread the word. You are quite a
heroine, Stella! The men are furious, of course; Papa's nose
has been pulled properly. They are out for revenge. Word is
they know where the Rebecca hideout is. It is up in the
mountains beyond Llanigon. We are for going up there and
smoking the "ladies" out!' His eyes were shining with
excitement. 'Of course we can't take the law into our
hands—Papa and Glynn Williams would be furious—but if
Mother Rebecca happened to get one of her garters tied
around her neck in the skirmish, that would be just too bad.
Are you with us, Owen?'

Owen had dropped Stella's arm as he listened, and he
gave a low whistle. 'I certainly am! Where did you learn
about the hideout?'

'Some of the chaps who go cockfighting. I'd be surprised
if some of them didn't ride with Rebecca themselves last
night! We were buying them all beer at the Swan Inn and
one or two became a trifle indiscreet.' George gave a hard
laugh. 'I came back for Ianto and the boys. Not a word of
this to Papa, Stella, he's just ridden off to see Glynn, so the
field is clear!'

She stared from one to the other. 'You can't! It's dangerous! George, Owen, you can't do it. Those men had guns!'

George gave a sly smile. 'So have we. I didn't come back
only for the men. There's no point in hunting for sport

without the right weapons, eh, Owen? I'll lend you some-thing out of the gun-room. We'll pepper their petticoats!' Both men roared with laughter.

Owen patted Stella's arm. 'Go in, my dear. I'll see you this evening at dinner. Your papa has been kind enough to invite me.' Without a second glance, he followed George towards the back of the house.

Stella was left staring after them in dismay as George, his voice still ringing with confident amusement, clapped his arm round his companion's shoulder and led him out of sight through the stable arch.

'Take care,' she called after them desperately; but already they were out of earshot. They would not listen anyway. To them it was a game: hunting men instead of foxes. She shuddered. If they had heard the words of Mother Rebecca, recognised the bitter determination in his voice, they would not be setting off so blithely now.

She stood staring at the hedge where they had dis-appeared, her mind a jumble of thoughts. Her brother and her fiancé were armed; they had surprise on their side and numbers, perhaps. They wouldn't be harmed. And the Rebeccas? Did she still care about them? Would she mind if Mother Rebecca were caught? Her mouth was dry, her heart pounding uncomfortably as she forced herself to think of him again: his confidence, his arrogance, his bitter determination to bring down the established order and his insolent promise to see her again. Her cheeks flamed. No, she would not care. He deserved to be caught!

She was roused from her troubled thoughts by her mother's voice, as Margaret's face appeared at the study window.

'Stella! Hurry! I've ordered the trap so that Eliza may drive us into Hay. There are several things I want to buy, and you said you needed new ribbons for your bonnet.'

She gave her daughter no time to argue, sweeping her indoors where Eliza was already setting her hat on her curls before the hall mirror. Eliza turned as Stella appeared. 'We thought we'd call on Mr Griffiths,' she said lightly, tying the plum-coloured ribbons beneath her chin. 'Papa has asked us to give him his regards.'

Stella smiled in spite of herself, suddenly recalling the

dinner of the night before. 'And if Mr Vivian should be there it would be uncivil not to speak to him, of course,' she replied.

'Of course!' Eliza glared at her. 'Do you object?'

'No. Why should I?'

She had almost forgotten John Vivian and her antipathy towards him. Last night's dinner-party had receded so completely after the events which had followed it.

She remembered it now with a slight frown, and the frown deepened as she realised that her desire not to see that particular gentleman again was as strong as ever, even though it no longer mattered whether or not he had guessed she had released the prisoner. Puzzled, she stared for a moment over Eliza's shoulder into the mirror, seeing her own face, troubled and sad, next to her sister's pert and pretty one. With a sigh she turned away and made for the stairs, meaning to change into a walking-dress. If Eliza wanted to run after John Vivian, that was her sister's business. He meant nothing to her.

CHAPTER
FIVE

STELLA FOUND her thoughts returning to John Vivian as the trap bowled down the lane towards the bridge over the river. The mocking challenge in his blue eyes and the arrogance of his handsome face still troubled her, and she suspected ruefully that he would be enormously amused to hear of her misfortune of the night before. She only thanked heaven he could never know the true extent of her humiliation.

As she watched Eliza's gloved hands on the pony's reins, she resolved not to give him the chance to gloat over her abduction. As soon as their shopping was done, she would make some excuse to return to the trap and wait while her mother and Eliza made their call.

It was market-day in Hay, and the town was crowded, as Eliza guided the trap through the narrow cobbled streets. Margaret had grown pale suddenly as she sat between the girls, clutching her reticule nervously, and Stella saw her gazing apprehensively at the crowds, her happy mood quite gone.

Stella leant forward. 'Mama? What is it? What is wrong?'

Her mother gave a small laugh. 'It's silly, isn't it? But I can't help looking and wondering; among these men might be the ones who carried you off!'

'Oh, Mama, they caught him!' Eliza clicked her tongue soothingly at the pony.

'Only one of them,' Margaret insisted. 'There were a dozen men around our carriage last night. They are probably in town here today. Bragging of what they did!'

Stella kept quiet about George's report. She touched her mother reassuringly on the arm. 'Mama, they wouldn't. They would be terrified to show themselves in case we recognised them, and if they were here they couldn't harm us.'

'You're not afraid?' Margaret peered at her younger daughter with respect.

'No, I'm not. Angry, perhaps, but never afraid.'

They left the trap at the rear of one of the crowded inns and walked arm in arm through the crowded stalls and up the pavement towards the town centre and the old castle where the Reverend Humphrey Allen lived in the house that had been built in the ruins. Their path took them below the walls of the St John's lock-up, and Margaret glanced fearfully at the barred windows as they hurried by. Stella, too, looked up. But there was no face at the narrow aperture.

They stopped first at their mother's favourite milliner, and Margaret produced a list of silks and ribbons while her daughters looked idly at a display of bonnets. It was Eliza who spotted Maria Williams through the shop's shaded window. She ran to the door and called out. Maria, her face glowing from the sunlight, bustled in and stopped short at the sight of Stella.

'Sweet child, are you well enough to be out?' she exclaimed.

Stella smiled. 'Of course, Mrs Williams, why shouldn't I be?'

'But Owen told us such terrible things! How you were carried off, bound and helpless, into the mountains. My dear, I had made sure your mama would keep you within doors!'

Margaret, her attention diverted from the assistant behind the counter, bridled visibly. 'There is nothing wrong, Maria, I assure you. These men may be villains, but they behaved like perfect gentlemen the whole time. No one set so much as a finger on Stella.' She dropped her voice abruptly, conscious of the assistant's wide-eyed stare.

'And she wasn't gagged and bound?' Maria sounded quite disappointed.

'Certainly not!' Margaret retorted, horrified, as Eliza gave a snort of laughter.

'I'm surprised they didn't, the rubbish she talks,' she said with cheerful malice. 'They blindfolded her, though, with an expensive silk scarf. Papa says—'

'Be silent, Eliza!' her mother snapped. 'I want no more

tittle-tattle from you! Don't listen to her, Maria. The girl
has lost her wits.'

With a forbidding glare at both her daughters, Margaret
turned back to the counter.

Their shopping complete, they bade Maria farewell and
were walking slowly back down the street, pausing to
admire an array of wares on a pedlar's tray, when Margaret
let out a small cry of pleasure. 'Why, there is Mr Griffiths!'

Stella's heart sank, but it was too late for excuses. She
could hardly return to the trap now. There was nothing for
it but to follow her mother as, crossing the street, Margaret
accosted the tall, sober-faced, solicitor who was walking
slowly down the hill, leaning heavily on his silver-topped
cane.

'Why, Mrs Vaughan, ma'am,' he exclaimed. 'Miss
Vaughan, Miss Stella. How very nice to see you all. I trust
you are keeping well?'

Stella, as she gave him her hand, was touched at the firm
squeeze he gave her fingers. 'A little bird has told me, Miss
Stella, that you are affianced. May I wish you every happiness, my dear. I was so pleased to hear the news.' He said it
earnestly, keeping hold of her hand. 'Mrs Vaughan, we are
only a step from my office, so please may I offer you all a
small libation in honour of the engaged pair?' He reached
into his waistcoat pocket for a gold fob. 'Yes, I have an hour
before my next appointment. Please allow me to precede
you.'

Margaret and Eliza exchanged smiles as they followed
him down the street. Neither of them noticed that Stella
had gone a little pale.

Chattering amiably, Griffiths led them towards a tall,
narrow, grey stone buildng at the corner and let them
in. To Stella's relief, the hall was empty. The old man's
room was on the ground floor overlooking the street, a
pleasant book-lined office with an enormous partner's
desk, and several dusty chairs all completely swamped by
papers.

'There, my dears, sit ye down, sit ye down!' he ex-
claimed, sweeping three of them clear of books. 'Barnabas!
The sherry wine and some glasses, if you please. And see if
Mr Vivian is in,' he called out of the door. 'You met my new

young partner last night, of course.' He beamed round at them. 'A most able young man. Most able.' Nodding, he seated himself on the edge of his desk.

Stella forced herself to smile as Eliza glanced at her, her eyes shining, but their mother had already taken the cue. 'Has he been with you long, Mr Griffiths? I was surprised my husband had not met him.'

Griffiths looked cheerfully over his spectacles. 'Indeed not. Scarcely two months. But he is a great success; very popular with our clients. Ah, here is Barnabas with our refreshment.'

The clerk entered alone and set the tray on the table with a bow. 'Mr Vivian is out at present, sir, but I expect him back at any moment,' he said.

'Good, good, excellent. Have him join us when he comes in, there's a good fellow.' Griffiths was already pouring out the wine.

'Is he a relative, perhaps?' Mrs Vaughan persisted ingenuously as the door closed behind the clerk. 'He seemed quite the gentleman, but the name was not familiar . . .'

Stella, sitting on the very edge of her chair, found she was holding her breath as the old man raised his glass and twisted it experimentally in a dusty ray of sunlight which had strayed through the window. 'Aha!' Griffiths smiled and waved a coy finger at her. 'You have him discovered, my dear lady. He is indeed a gentleman. And an educated one. A graduate of Balliol. His people are extremely well off, I understand, and his father was titled, but,' he sighed, 'like so many young men these days, John is something of a rebel. He wants to make his own way in the world, I gather. And there is no doubt he will be a success. No doubt at all.' He paused. 'But we are forgetting the purpose of our little celebration. Stella, if I may call you so, to you, my dear. May I wish you every happiness in your future life!' He raised his glass and Stella found herself smiling, touched at the old man's gallantry.

Minutes later the door opened and John Vivian walked in.

'Barnabas tells me you want to see me, Toby—' He broke off sharply as he saw the visitors, and after a slight hesitation he bowed, removing his tall hat with a flourish.

'Forgive me, I had no notion that you were entertaining. I'll come back later—'

'No, John. Stay.' Toby Griffiths shuffled to his feet. 'I was hoping you would join us for a drink. We are celebrating Stella's engagement.'

John Vivian had approached Margaret and shaken her hand. Now he paused and turned to Stella.

'Good morning, Mr Vivian,' she said coolly. Ignoring the sudden inexplicable pounding of her heart, she raised her eyes to his face. 'How nice to see you again.'

His hand, still clad in its white glove, was cool and firm. 'Miss Stella. I trust you are well this morning?'

From the light irony in his voice she knew at once that he had already heard what had happened and, although she tried to remain calm, she felt herself growing uncomfortably pink. 'Well enough, sir, thank you.' She withdrew her hand quickly as Eliza stepped forward.

'Mr Vivian, did you hear of Stella's adventure?' she asked, simpering. 'We were all so frightened!'

'Were you indeed, Miss Eliza. I'm sorry to hear that,' John replied, accepting a glass from his partner.

'What's this?' Griffiths looked anxiously from one to another of them.

'We were held up by the rioters last night,' Margaret Vaughan explained reluctantly. 'They carried Stella off with them, but they returned her unharmed.'

The old man's face paled visibly. 'Dear heaven, what a terrible thing! Indeed, it's not safe to go anywhere these days.' He shook his head sadly. 'But the troopers have been called in, and they will get matters under control, of that I am certain. Why, two of the ringleaders of those people who were tried in Brecon are being sent for transportation this very week. Stella, my poor child, were you very much distressed?'

Stella shook her head. She had not looked at John again. 'No indeed, Mr Griffiths. I assure you, it was all quite exciting really.'

'Everyone has been trying to get her to tell about Mother Rebecca,' Eliza put in. 'But she says nothing. Do you, Stella?'

Stella glared at her. 'There is nothing to tell, Eliza, as I keep repeating.' She took a sip from her glass.

John Vivian was watching her intently. He had seated himself in the corner of the room, and setting his glass down on the table, put his hat and cane on a pile of books and laid his gloves down. 'You must be a very courageous young lady, Miss Stella,' he said quietly. 'Most women would have had the vapours, at least, after such an experience.'

'Well, I am not most women, sir,' she retorted, and she looked up and gazed straight at him.

His eyes held hers mockingly. 'Indeed you are not. You are quite exceptional.' He smiled suddenly and she caught her breath. Her first impression at the Williamses' house had been right, after all. He was attractive when he smiled, more attractive than any man she had ever known. She swallowed, and looked down at her glass hurriedly, twisting the delicate stem between her fingers, conscious that he was still watching her. 'And,' he went on relentlessly, 'you are about to tell me that you have never had the vapours in your life.' She could hear the laughter in his voice.

'You are right, sir.' She managed to look up.

'Which is just as well,' his blue eyes were dancing, 'if you are going to make a habit of putting yourself in a position to be singled out for such personal attention by all the rogues in the country.'

Beside her, Eliza and her mother were both talking excitedly to Toby Griffiths, describing the holding up of the carriage as, his face drawn and concerned, he refilled their glasses, her mother cheerfully oblivious that her daughters were indulging in a beverage of which she would normally have heartily disapproved.

Stella glared at him. 'I don't know what you mean by that, Mr Vivian,' she retorted, realising suddenly that Eliza had ceased to listen to her mother and Mr Griffiths and was now gazing at her. 'You seem to feel that I deserved to be taken by those men!'

'You yourself said that you sympathised with them,' he returned smoothly.

'Enough, John my boy, enough,' Toby Griffiths interrupted. 'Leave the child alone. We all know about her unfortunate support for these people. But all that is over now. She has found out for herself what sort of men they are.'

'And what sort of men are they?' John Vivian asked softly. 'Did they treat you the way you would have wished, Miss Stella?'

She could feel the colour flying to her face at his tone. Her mind flashed back to the night before: the strong hands on her hair, the intimate caresses, the kiss of Mother Rebecca. It was almost as if he had guessed. She stared at him desperately. This man seemed to be able to read her thoughts, just as he had at the dinner-party when he had known, she was sure, that it was she who had released Dai from the cellar.

She became conscious of Eliza's jealous gaze still fixed on her face and, swallowing her anger and embarrassment as best she could, she managed a very creditable smile.

'I was quite unharmed, thank you,' she said with as much dignity as she could. 'But they will in any case pay for their rashness. One of them is caught already, as you know. And others will be soon.'

'Indeed?' He raised an eyebrow. 'You have great faith in the power of the law.'

'I do not mean the law,' she said. 'I mean people who have already taken matters into their own hands.' She frowned unhappily in spite of her resolution to appear calm.

'And who have taken matters into their own hands?' he pressed quietly.

'My brother and Owen—' she broke off, realising suddenly that her mother was listening as intently as Eliza, her eyes widening with fear. 'Oh, Mama, I'm sorry,' she burst out impulsively. 'They made me swear not to say a word. They were doing it for me! I tried to persuade them not to go, but they wouldn't listen.' She stared down into her glass for a moment, then she forced herself to continue. 'They have gone up into the mountains to hunt for the rioters.' She hesitated, as the silence in the room grew oppressive. 'George says that one of the men in the Swan Inn this morning claimed to be a follower of Rebecca and he told them where the meeting-place in the mountain is. They have gone to try and capture the Rebecca leader and they have sworn to hang him, if they catch him, for what he did to me.' Raising her eyes once more, she glanced defiantly at the young solicitor.

He was watching her thoughtfully. 'So,' he murmured. 'Your honour is to be avenged. How gratifying that must be for you.'

She blushed angrily, but before she could retort, her mother's angry hysteria had overwhelmed her.

'Why didn't you tell your father? Dear Lord, Stella, those boys will be killed! Don't you care at all about your future husband and your brother? Are you completely cold and unfeeling? Dear, dear, Lord!'

Margaret rose in a cloud of grey silks and bombazine, divested herself of her glass and reclaimed her packages. 'Dear Mr Griffiths, we must go. As you can see, I must contact my husband. Eliza, Stella—come, girls, quickly! We must pick up the trap and see if we can't avert a disaster!'

She held out her hand to the older man first, then to John Vivian. 'I am sorry to leave so abruptly, Mr Vivian, but as you see I am sorely tried,' she murmured tearfully. 'Won't you call on us one day soon? We should so much like to see you at Bryn Glas.'

He thanked her gravely. 'I should be delighted, ma'am. And really, I doubt if you should upset yourself so much. Young men will be young men, you know. Their exuberance will have run out long before they get to the mountain. And the chances are that they are wrong. The worst that will happen is that they will spend a tiring day quartering the countryside to no avail.'

'You really think so?' she peered up at him, a little comforted.

'I really do, ma'am.'

He turned to Stella. Taking her hand, he raised it to his lips, as Margaret began to chivvy Eliza into hurrying. 'Your brother and Owen Morgan will be very angry, will they not, when they hear you have betrayed their confidences,' he said. Then he smiled mockingly. 'I'm surprised you didn't go with them. You would have enjoyed watching Mother Rebecca hang, surely? And you are obviously quite fearless in your pursuit of adventure.' He was still holding her hand.

She gasped, trying without success to snatch it away from him, 'You know that's not true! I don't want him caught. Or at least—oh, I don't know *what* I want!' Her last words came out almost as a wail.

'Poor Stella.' He released her slowly with a smile which made her heart contract sharply. She stared at him for a moment, conscious of the amused glance of the old lawyer behind her and of her mother and Eliza making their way to the door, as he went on, 'I shall look forward to calling upon you all at Bryn Glas to hear how the revenge was accomplished. I hope your brother forgives your betrayal once he has recovered from the tongue-lashing he is obviously going to receive from his mama!' She turned and ran to the door after her mother, and did not look back.

'What did he say to you?' Eliza pulled at her sleeve as soon as they were in the street.

Stella frowned. 'He was reprimanding me for betraying George!' she said furiously.

'Why should he do that?' Eliza stopped. Her eyes were accusing.

'I can't imagine!' Stella answered repressively. 'No doubt he was making fun of me again. I have never met anyone so rude and so . . . so impossible!' To her astonishment, she found she was near to tears.

Henry Vaughan had still not returned when they reached home. Agitated, Mrs Vaughan rang for one of the servants, but it was Megan who answered the bell; all the men were gone with George. Margaret stared in horror at Stella and Eliza. 'Do you realise what this means?' she shrieked. 'We are quite defenceless! If those rogues came up here now, there would be no one to save us. No one! Stella, this is all your fault! We are completely at their mercy.' She pressed her hands to her face to suppress a sob.

Eliza put her arm round her mother. 'Mama, hush. We are quite safe. After all, George has gone to find these men. He would not allow them to come here and harm us! Come, let me take you upstairs to lie down. Papa and George will both be back soon, then all will be well.' She ushered her upstairs, leaving Stella to walk slowly into the parlour and throw her gloves and reticule down on a chair. Her head was spinning.

John Vivian's mockery, her mother's reproaches, Eliza's glowering, all combined to overwhelm her and she flung herself down on the sofa, ashamed to find her eyes once more filling with tears. Angrily she blinked them back as Eliza returned, closing the door softly after her. She stood in front of Stella, her face icy, and launched into an attack at once.

'You were flirting with Mr Vivian, Stella. Mama noticed it, too. I think you are wicked and forward! Not content with being engaged to the most eligible man in the two counties, you flutter your eyelashes at every handsome newcomer who appears!'

Stung, Stella jumped up. 'That is not true—not at all. I find Mr Vivian cold and arrogant. I hate him! If you listened at all to what he was saying to me last night or just now, you would know that he was making a cruel jest of everything I believe in!' She turned away quickly, so that Eliza would not see how near to weeping she was.

Eliza stared after her for a moment. Then her scowl changed to an amused smile. 'You are silly, Stella. Of course he makes fun of your ideas. So does everyone who has any modicum of good sense.' She paused, before saying, 'You really don't like him, then?'

'I really don't like him,' Stella echoed vehemently.

'Good,' Eliza had gone on without pause. 'Because I do like him, quite a lot.'

Stella swung round and gave her sister a searching look. 'Eliza, dear—'

'What?' The suspicion and defiance in Eliza's face were obvious.

'Nothing, only—you will be careful.' Stella hesitated, a picture of his dark, handsome face floating before her eyes for a second. 'I have a feeling that Mr Vivian could be quite dangerous to know.'

Eliza gave her a beaming smile. 'I had reached that conclusion myself, sister,' she said.

She joined Stella at the window, obviously pleased with herself, and looked out. Then her expression changed to one of horror.

'Who are all those men?' she cried suddenly.

'Where?' Stella whirled round, her heart missing a beat. 'Not the rioters! Not in daylight!'

The two girls peered fearfully out, watching as a band of horsemen wheeled into view, cantering up the lower field from the lane.

'It's George,' Eliza said after a moment, with a sigh of relief. 'Look, he's riding that flea-bitten grey he picked up at the market. I didn't recognise it. And there's Ianto, and Owen behind them. They don't look as though they've been fighting,' she added, half disappointed, half thankful.

Stella closed her eyes in relief. 'If only they wouldn't try to take the law into their own hands. Papa will be so angry.'

George, when he appeared, was of a similar opinion. 'We had a meeting down at Llowes,' he said, when he and Owen joined them ten minutes later. 'There seemed little point in trying to find their hideout. They wouldn't be there in daylight and if they were we couldn't be sure of getting more than a handful of them. Better wait until tonight.'

'Tonight?' Stella stared at him.

George nodded. 'Word is out. They mean to go for the toll on the Brecon road tonight. And we'll be waiting there for them.'

'They'll get more than they bargained for, then, all right,' Owen added, rubbing his hands. 'And we'll first be sworn in as special constables by your father, Stella, so it will all be legal. My only regret is that this will mean cutting short our evening after dinner. We must explain to your mama. Where is she?'

'She's gone to bed,' Eliza put in hurriedly. 'She had a headache, made worse by the thought that you and George were in danger, and I certainly don't think knowing your new plan would improve her state of health.' She shuddered. 'Thank God I'm not a man!'

'Is Papa going with you?' Stella asked bleakly. Owen had seated himself next to her on the sofa by the window.

'Indeed he is,' he said enthusiastically. 'And Glynn Williams too.'

'And the dragoons?' Her hands were shaking slightly as she clasped them on her lap.

George shook his head. 'They'll be coming up to guard

the house on the night old Ma Rebecca's threatened to burn it,' he said, his eyes gleaming. 'Not before. The town can't afford it. And with luck they won't have to come then, either. By then we'll have 'Becca behind bars. The last one they caught is being shipped to the penal colonies for a twenty-year stretch.'

Stella stood up abruptly. Her face was white. 'You're enjoying this, aren't you. You really want to fight them tonight. You want him captured!'

There was a moment's astonished silence. George glanced at Owen and grimaced. 'You'll have your hands full when you marry my sister, Owen. As you see, she's an out-and-out unrepentant radical. You would have thought she'd have learned something after what happened to her last night, but no.'

Owen smiled at her fondly. 'I wouldn't have her any other way, George. Besides, she'll change. Once she's my wife I shall guide her thinking and she will see the errors in her present attitude.'

Stella opened her mouth to retort, but was interrupted by Eliza. 'I should love to see you do that, Owen,' she gurgled. 'May I perhaps attend your lessons?'

'Eliza!' George turned on her, shocked. 'How can you be so impolite. Apologise to Owen this minute.'

Owen laughed, however. 'They are as spirited as one another, George. Don't apologise for either of your sisters. I find them quite delightful.' He gave Eliza a wink. 'If a man were allowed two wives in this country, I should claim both of you instantly.'

George snorted. 'More fool you, sir.'

Eliza was blushing. She glanced at Stella, not quite sure how her sister would take Owen's attempt at gallantry, but Stella was smiling. 'I doubt if you could manage two of us, Owen,' she said demurely.

He grinned. 'You're right as always, my love. I doubt if I could. Nor would I really wish it, for I hear Eliza has set her cap elsewhere.' He bowed gallantly to Stella's sister, who gave him an impish smile.

'Perhaps I have, perhaps I haven't,' she said archly. 'But you would always be my first choice, were you free!'

'Then if Stella jilts me, you shall be my comfort,' he

murmured with a laugh. He took Stella's hand. 'Not that she would ever do so, would you, Stella?'

'Of course she won't,' George interrupted impatiently before she could reply. 'Now come on, Owen. We've things to discuss in the study, remember?' He winked. 'A brandy to help us lay plans, I think we said, did we not?'

Stella escaped as soon as she could to the privacy of her own bedroom. She was seething with frustration and anger. They did nothing but make fun of her. Her father, George, Owen and John Vivian. Even the odious Mother Rebecca. None of them took her seriously. None of them listened to her. If she had been a man, it would have been different!

She paced up and down the carpet, pausing every now and then to stare out at the mountains across the valley. A misty heat-haze hung over their brooding summits and she longed suddenly to be up there in the pure air, away from the house with its atmosphere of breathless waiting, and free of Eliza's suspicious jibes.

But why shouldn't she go for a ride up there? She thought suddenly of the beautiful black mare in the stables, probably as impatient and longing to gallop as she was. There could be no danger, surely, in broad daylight. She wouldn't go far. Not, as she would have liked, up to the bare ribs of the mountain where the curlew called and the lonely miles stretched in folded hills and valleys populated by nothing but straying sheep and ponies. No, she would just ride to the lower slopes where the horse could gallop on the short sheep-cropped turf and the unpleasant clinging cobwebs would be driven from her brain.

No sooner had the idea formed in her mind than she was putting it into effect. Pulling off her gown and throwing it on the bed, she groped in the ornate cupboard for a riding-habit. The one she chose was of heavy olive green material trimmed with black braid, and she put it on swiftly, buttoning the bodice, and reached for her veiled hat. She set it on her head before the mirror, and her movements slowed as she stared for a moment at her face. The grey eyes looking back at her were still full of anger and impatience.

Shaking her head, she opened her drawer, took out her leather gloves and pulled them on with a sigh. Then, well aware that no one would approve of her plan if it were discovered, she opened her bedroom door cautiously, and began to make her way downstairs. To her horror she found the stable yard was full of men and horses. At the gate she hesitated, half inclined to turn back, but already Ianto had spotted her. He pulled himself from his perch on the edge of the drinking-trough and approached her. 'Miss Stella?'

'I wanted to take Cariad out,' she said. 'Who are all these people?'

'Waiting to ride with Mr George and Mr Owen this evening, miss,' Ianto explained. He raised an eyebrow. 'Going hunting they are, as you might say.'

Stella felt a constriction in her throat. She swallowed and straightened her shoulders. 'Please saddle my mare, Ianto. I shall not require you to ride with me.' She remained where she was as he shuffled back through the noisy group, and disappeared into the far range of boxes.

Behind her, the house was still. She turned and glanced up at the windows, anxious to get away before George and Owen reappeared to join their uncouth companions, or Eliza went upstairs to find her and discovered that she was missing. She tapped her whip impatiently against the gate-post, ignoring the curious glances cast in her direction from the yard.

It was a full ten minutes before Ianto reappeared, leading the beautiful black mare. The horse was fresh and eager, dancing on her toes, and her ears pricked as she sidled through the crowd.

'She's lively, miss,' Ianto commented as he approached. 'You watch her. Are you sure you don't want me to come with you?' He crooked his hand for her foot and tossed her up into the side-saddle.

'No, thank you. I'm not going out for long.' She smiled down at him, feeling the mare's mouth with a gentle hand on the rein. 'You stay here with my brother.' She hesitated, her eye caught by a pile of pitchforks propped against the stable wall.

'Ianto, keep an eye on him tonight, won't you.'

He beamed. 'Don't you worry, miss. We'll give those boyos more than they bargained for.' He released her rein and stood back respectfully.

Turning the horse, Stella trotted her carefully out into

the lane. Only when she was sure she was out of sight of the house did she press the mare into a gallop, feeling the powerful strides lengthen beneath her as they cut across the fields and neared the river.

The thud of hooves on the meadow turf and the rush of the wind in her ears filled her with exhilaration, draining her mind of everything but the joy of speed. She leaned forward in the saddle, whispering encouragement into Cariad's ear, and the world was empty of everything but herself and her horse and the spicy air blowing down from the hills. She had to slow momentarily to ford the Wye below the bridge, but then she pushed on up the bank and once more they were galloping, clods of earth flying from the mare's hooves.

It was a route Stella often followed with George; one which circled Hay to the north-east and led eventually up towards the mountains where the horse's stride could lengthen again on the close-cropped grass of the hill's shoulder. The satin skin of the mare's neck was gleaming with sweat as she cantered through fields and meadows, and it was not until Stella had turned south into the woods which grew along the Dulas Brook that she reined in at last, relaxing a little in the saddle so that she could look about her. The heavy green of the leaves was dusty from the late summer's heat and touched here and there with crisp flecks of gold and russet, and the air smelt of smoke from a distant cottager's chimney. The woods were very silent.

Cariad's stride settled to an easy swinging walk, but the horse held her head high, her ears pricked, ready to dance at the slightest shadow on the stony track, and Stella found herself looking hard at the distant point ahead of them where the track wound out of sight, conscious for the first time of how quiet the day had become. Somewhere in the distance she heard the sad notes of a robin singing its wistful autumn song, then through the trees, as the horse trod softly on the leafmould which muffled the stones, she heard the gentle mutter of the water. For no reason she could think of she felt the tiny hairs on the back of her neck stirring. She gave herself a little shake. There was nothing to be afraid of here. The Rebeccas never showed themselves by day. Their leader was probably miles away in some great house amusing himself with the memory of their encounter. She pushed away the hot glow of shame which flooded through her at the very thought of him, feeling Cariad tensing in response to her own nervousness. The muscles in the silky neck quivered as a fly settled on her mane, and almost unconsciously Stella tightened her grip on the reins. She had, she acknowledged at last, been very foolish to come out alone.

Glancing despite herself over her shoulder, she nudged the mare into a trot, glad that the track, where it ran beside the brook, was dappled with sunlight. Once they were out on the mountain where she could see for miles in every direction, she would, she told herself, feel safe again.

The sound of the water pouring over the stones of the brook masked the sound of the other horse completely and the first Stella knew of its arrival was a piercing whinny from Cariad before the mare plunged, panic-stricken, off the track. Stella had a fraction of a second's glance at a figure on a tall chestnut as it cat-jumped across the brook towards her, fifty yards ahead, before she was carried in a crazy series of side-steps back into the copse. Branches tore at her, whipping her face, clawing her clothes, and she heard herself scream once with terror as she lost her grip and felt herself flying through the air.

CHAPTER
SIX

SHE LAY still for several seconds with the breath knocked out of her before she opened her eyes and cautiously began to try to move. There was no sign of Cariad; but the chestnut horse, she realised suddenly, was only a few feet from her. Its rider leapt from the saddle, and in a second was kneeling beside her.

'Of all the stupid idiotic females! To creep out of the woods like that! Are you hurt?'

It was John Vivian.

'Me idiotic?' she cried, near to tears. 'I was on the path. You had no business to cut in front of me like that! Any horse would have been scared. Where is she?' She raised herself on her elbow, staring round. 'If she has damaged herself . . .'

He glanced up, eyes narrowed in the twilight of the trees after the bright sun. 'She's hasn't. She's over there, grazing. Are you hurt?' He looked down at her critically. Then, unexpectedly, he grinned. 'You are lucky, Miss Stella. You appear to have fallen on a soft landing-place.'

She had indeed fallen into a thick tangle of nettles, and only her clothing and her gloves had saved her from being badly stung. She realised suddenly that the skirt of her habit was all awry, exposing an unseemly amount of lace-trimmed drawers and, blushing furiously, she reached down to pull it straight.

'Perhaps you would catch my horse for me, sir,' she said with as much dignity as she could muster, 'and see she isn't lame. I am perfectly all right.'

'You don't know till you stand up,' he said unfeelingly. 'Here, give me your hand.' He leant down without ceremony and caught her wrist to pull her to her feet, dragging her bodily out of the nettles. She gasped.

'I can manage perfectly well, thank you!' she snapped. 'If

you want to help, please catch my horse!' She was pulling her jacket straight. Reaching up to her hair she found her hat had gone, and a frond of curled bracken had lodged in one of her combs. She pulled it out angrily and threw it to the ground.

'My hat has gone!' she exclaimed.

'It is over there.' He inclined his head gravely towards a low bush where her green velvet hat hung by its ribbons, its veil snagged on the thorns. 'No doubt you wish me to recover that for you, too,' he went on. 'Which do you consider has priority, ma'am? Hat or horse?' There was a flicker of amusement in the steely blue eyes.

'Seeing that you have to stop to gather strength to do either, sir, I think it would be better if I did both myself,' she retorted with spirit, and she began to walk towards Cariad, furious to find her left ankle aching painfully as she put her weight on it. She was praying the mare would not humiliate her further by taking it into her head to gallop off. She raised her head warily as Stella approached, eyeing her mistress with suspicion, then, apparently content to be captured, she walked meekly forward and thrust her muzzle into Stella's hands.

'Bravo!' A faint cheer came from behind her. 'I wonder if the hat will be so compliant!'

Stella whirled. 'If you think my predicament is so amusing,' she said crossly, 'I am surprised you do not sit down on that log in order to enjoy it more!' Her eyes were blazing with anger and mortification.

'I can't do that,' he returned humorously. 'I dare say you'll need the log for a mounting-block. Unless of course you deign to set your little foot on my shoulder when you want to climb back in the saddle.' He laughed out loud suddenly at her expression and said repentantly, 'Oh, come on! Your eyes are murderous. Here, let me hold the mare for you. Then you can recapture your hat and put it on in comfort.' He took Cariad's rein from her and pulled the horse's ear gently as she nosed his pockets.

Retrieving the hat took several minutes, so snagged was the veil, and as she cautiously pulled it free Stella could not resist a furious glance at John Vivian while he was preoccupied with Cariad and would not notice her gaze. He was no longer dressed in the severe legal black of their meeting that morning but wore fawn breeches and a dark green riding-jacket. His horse, which stood obediently in the clearing, its reins trailing, was sweating profusely, its shoulders flecked with foam. He had obviously ridden far and hard. She stared past him, across the brook and up the bleak hillside which rose beyond the trees in the direction from which he must have come, and frowned. What in the world could this solicitor of Hay want up there among the sheep and the ravens?

Impatient with the veil, she gave it a hard tug, and the hat came free with a loud ripping sound. He immediately looked round.

'Patience, I take it, is not one of your virtues?' he said soberly, on a note of enquiry.

'Indeed it is not!' she retorted, jamming the hat back on her head, and pulling the veil into place. With luck the tear would not, she thought, be too obvious.

'Whereas your sister,' he mused, 'probably has it in abundance.'

'My sister is a paragon of the virtues, Mr Vivian,' Stella said firmly. 'She differs from me in every way. I suggest you snap her up before some other gentleman does so.'

She reached for Cariad's rein, but it was still looped over his arm.

'She would not,' he went on, ignoring her interruption, 'for instance, ride unattended on an unschooled horse in a district where dangerous armed criminals are known to abound.'

Stella flushed uncomfortably. 'I hardly think the hills are full of dangerous criminals,' she said. 'If it comes to that, you don't seem averse to riding there alone yourself, and I'm sure a man is in more danger than I would be.'

He gave a sceptical look. 'You being in a privileged position, you mean,' he said, 'known to be a friend to the Rebeccas?' He held up his hand. 'No, why deny it now, when you spent yesterday evening so strenuously promoting their cause. All well and good should you meet one of the "ladies", but there are other undesirable elements about. I meet them in my job all too frequently, alas. And I am armed accordingly.' He nodded soberly in the direction of his horse. Following his gaze, she noticed for the first time the stock of a rifle protruding from the saddle. He turned back to her. 'Surely you do not have to be reminded that a woman should not ride unescorted anywhere,' he went on quietly. 'Even if only by her maid.'

Stella glared at him. 'I need to be reminded of nothing by you,' she said defensively. 'I know perfectly well what is proper.'

'Then why do it?'

'Because I was angry and I needed to gallop.'

He raised an eyebrow. 'An honest answer, at least. May I ask why you were so angry?'

She hesitated. Then she shrugged. To refuse to answer would make her seem even more churlish and foolish in his eyes. But she was not going to tell him the truth, that it was his scorn and mockery, added to that of her brother and Owen, which had driven her into such a fury. 'If you must know,' she said, with a touch of defiance, 'my brother and my fiancé still feel they have to have their revenge on the Rebeccas for what happened to me last night. They are planning a raid on them.'

John was smoothing Cariad's mane, meticulously straightening each silky hair. 'So you mentioned this morning. I had understood the raid would be over by now.'

'No, not that one. They have another idea now.' She glanced up at him, her grey eyes troubled. 'One of the rioters was in the inn and betrayed their plans to George.'

'Betrayed?' he repeated sharply. 'How lucky for George. What did this man say?'

'That the Rebeccas are planning to burn the Brecon road toll-house tonight,' she explained reluctantly. 'George and Owen are insisting on taking the men to lie in wait for them there. Then they'll catch them in the act.'

'I see.' He thought for a moment. 'And this makes you angry?' He had not taken his eyes from her face.

'You well know, Mr Vivian, that my loyalties are divided,' she said, 'and you know my views, laughable as you find them. You must also know that I love my brother, and do not want him hurt or perhaps killed!' Her voice trembled for an instant.

'Do I gather from what you say,' he said solemnly, 'that

you do not care so much if Owen Morgan is hurt or killed?'

'Don't be stupid. Of course I do!' she flashed back. 'I care if anyone is killed.'

'And you still sympathise with Rebecca, even after your ordeal at her hands last night?' he went on, ignoring her protest. 'You are a brave young lady.'

She felt herself going scarlet and looked away quickly to hide her face. 'I thought you said I was idiotic,' she reminded him.

He grinned. 'It is possible to be both. Now, may I suggest that I help you to mount. Your impetuous gallop will help neither your brother, nor—' He stopped abruptly, his eyes narrowed suddenly, his expression forbidding. 'You were not intending to try and find the rioters' hideout yourself, I trust, and warn them of this change of plan?'

Stella took a step away from him. 'Of course not! I don't know where it is. Besides, I wouldn't . . .' Her voice trailed away helplessly as she felt her courage fail beneath his eyes.

'I think you would,' he said softly. 'I think it is just the sort of foolish thing you would do.' Was that admiration she glimpsed just for a second in his eyes? She felt her pulse quicken as she stared up at him, searching his face for some sign of feeling, but the hard anger had returned. 'Whatever the reason for your ride, you have gone far enough. You will return home now, do you understand? And I should like to think that, at least for the time being, you will not venture out alone again.'

Anger swept through her. 'You may like to think what you wish, Mr Vivian. It is hardly your affair what I do.'

She was acutely conscious of how close he was to her. Attired in evening clothes or sober black, he had exuded an air of restrained authority, his handsome features composed to fit the solemnity of the occasion. Now, in riding dress, his dark hair ruffled by the wind, she found herself sharply aware of the muscular shoulders beneath the dark green broadcloth and the strength of his tall lean body.

His eyes had not left her face. 'I have made it my affair,' he said, 'if only by being the cause of your fall, and if you will not go home alone I shall be forced to escort you.'

'There is no need, I assure you.' She summoned as much dignity as she could. 'As it happens, it is getting late. I should anyway have turned back now.' She put her hand on Cariad's rein, not liking to try and pull it from his hand. 'Please, don't let me detain you, Mr Vivian. You appeared to be in somewhat of a hurry when we met.' She wanted him to release the horse and move right away from it so that she could scramble into the saddle unaided.

Her gaze lingered on his hand for a moment as he caressed Cariad's neck, and she felt herself shiver convulsively. What was it about the man that made him so dangerously attractive? She stepped back abruptly, suddenly conscious that her heart was beating tumultuously. Retreating another step, she found herself pressed against Cariad's warm silky flank, unable to move any further from him. He had not moved. He ignored her attempts to reclaim the rein, and now he was straightening the stirrup for her. 'I hope I can trust you to go straight home,' he said. 'I find I have further business in this direction, so it would be a great inconvenience to have to escort you back to Bryn Glas.' He tested the leather with a snap, and smiled at her. 'But can I trust you?'

If only he would not smile at her like that. She preferred him angry—then she could hate him unreservedly. 'On this occasion you can.'

His smile deepened. 'Will you tell me when I can't, I wonder? Come, allow me to help you up.'

'There is no need.' She put her hand on the high withers. 'I can manage!' It was an easy jump, one she had managed gracefully a thousand times, but she had forgotten her injured ankle. With a little cry of pain, she fell against the horse, clutching the saddle.

'So I see,' he commented sardonically. 'How opportune that I am still here.'

She gasped as his hands closed on her waist, and she felt the strength of his arms, and the taut muscular body against hers. For a moment he held her, his eyes on her face, and she felt herself drowning in his gaze, her body pliant with longing.

With a violent sense of shock she realised she was clinging to him, and tried to pull away, but he held her easily, a slight smile flickering behind the steel-blue eyes as he reached to bring her chin up, forcing her to look at him again. His face was inches from hers and, with an anguished realisation, she knew suddenly that she wanted to feel that cruelly attractive mouth on hers. She closed her eyes and waited, trembling violently.

Did his lips brush hers, or was it just her imagination? Her eyes flew open as a low chuckle sounded in her ear. 'I told you these mountains can be dangerous to a lady riding alone,' he murmured. 'I think you had better go home before something happens to you we might both regret.' Before she knew what was happening, he had lifted her into the saddle, settling her as lightly as if she had weighed no more than a feather. He stood back with a look of amused triumph.

'Ride carefully, Stella Vaughan,' he said softly. 'And tell your mother and sister that I shall give myself the pleasure of calling upon them soon.'

With a slight bow, he turned and walked back to his own horse. In the saddle, he raised his hand once and set the huge animal at a gallop up the track away from her, heading back towards the mountains.

Speechless and trembling with rage and humiliation, Stella had to fight to keep control of Cariad, who plunged in circles, wanting to tear after him, and it was several minutes before she could calm the mare and turn in the direction of Hay and home.

Only then did she notice on the path, a hundred yards from her, a solitary horseman watching her intently. It was Owen.

CHAPTER
SEVEN

OWEN WAS standing immobile in her path as Stella walked
the mare sedately towards him. His grey cob was cropping
the grass on a loose rein, but he ignored it, keeping his eyes
fixed on her face. Self-consciously she raised her hand to
her hair, patting her hat and surreptitiously allowing her
veil to fall once more into place, wondering if the tu-
multuous thundering of her heart was as audible to him as it
was to her.

'Owen?' Striving to keep her voice steady, she called out
to him as soon as she was close enough. 'How did you know
which way I had come?'

'I guessed,' he said, shortly.

She glanced at him sideways, trying to read his stern
profile, but neither his voice nor his demeanour told her
how much he had seen. 'It was good of you to follow me.'
His angry face made her nervous.

'I trust you have got rid of your pique, Stella.' Turning to
her, he frowned perplexedly. 'We found it strange that you
left Bryn Glas so precipitously and without even a groom to
escort you. It seemed a little childish, and under the circumstances at the moment an act of unbelievable stupidity.'

Looking down at her hands, she felt herself blush miserably. 'I'm sorry, Owen, I realise that now. I was upset and
angry about the way you were all teasing me. Eliza has been
hateful—'

'Oh, come, Stella. That is hardly charitable. Your sister
is always charming.'

'In front of you, Owen, yes,' she retorted. She took a
deep breath. 'How did you really know which way I had
come?'

'George said you preferred this ride above all others.
And I needed to go into Hay anyway so I rode there first
and then came on. I wanted to visit the jeweller to collect a

gift for my bride-to-be.' He smiled at her at last. 'Don't you want to know what it is?'

She nodded. 'Of course I do.'

'First tell me something.'

'What?'

'Who was that man?'

Stella blushed crimson. 'I thought you could not have seen him,' she murmured uncomfortably.

'I could hardly avoid it, my dear. It seemed to me that he lifted you on your horse with undue familiarity.' His tone was chilly.

She stole a glance at him. 'He was kind enough to help me. Cariad was playing the fool and I could not mount her by myself, that is all,' she said stiffly. She tapped the mare's flank with her rein.

'Had she thrown you, then?' He looked at her with new concern.

'She did, but I wasn't hurt. She tripped, that's all, and I wasn't paying attention, so I flew into the nettles.'

Owen's face had paled. 'Stella, you could have been killed!'

'But I wasn't. I'm not even bruised. Please, Owen, forget it! Tell me instead what my present is.' She smiled at him coaxingly.

He sighed. 'Women are so inquisitive. Well, if you are sure you are all right, I shall show it to you on our way home. Once we are the other side of Hay.' He gathered up his reins. 'Who was it?' The question was repeated quite casually, but there was an undercurrent in his voice which made Stella stare at him in sudden fear.

'It was Mr Vivian.' She forced herself to give Owen a dazzling smile. 'It was his horse that startled Cariad, so he was really forced to stop and help me out of courtesy.'

'I see.' Owen was gazing straight ahead, concentrating on the glittering water of the brook, where a handful of yellow leaves whirled tumbling over the stones. 'You are lucky you weren't hurt. What was Vivian doing up here?' His eyes strayed, just as hers had done, to the bleak hillside already deep in shadow.

'He had business up there, he said,' she replied. 'I dare say Papa will know of the case if you ask him.'

'I dare say.' He stared once more up the hillside behind her, a worried frown on his face. Then he wrenched his horse's head from the weeds it was cropping and swung it to retrace their steps through the wood.

He did not take Stella straight back to Bryn Glas. Once through the town and over the bridge he led the way off the road into some water-meadows on the edge of the Wye and, opening a gate, he ushered her before him into a field, and then reined in. 'Let me help you dismount, sweetheart—it can offend no one, I'm sure, if we spend a few moments walking together beside the river.'

Her heart sank. She had no wish to dally with Owen at that moment and her ankle ached abominably, but she knew he would be deeply hurt if she refused. With a sigh, she slipped from the saddle into his arms and rested her foot cautiously on the grass.

Her gasp brought a look of concern to his face. 'I thought you said you weren't hurt,' he reproached her gently.

'I'm not. I turned my ankle over, that's all. Owen! Get up! There's no need!'

He had slipped to his knees and, raising the hem of her habit a couple of inches, rested his hands gently on her boot.

'You should take this off, sweetheart, in case the ankle swells.'

'Rubbish.' She put her weight on it grimly and stepped away from him. 'Come on, let's see the river. If we're late home, Mama will worry, and I don't want to cause her any distress—'

She watched him tether the two horses to the gate, and then, taking her arm firmly through his, he led her down towards the broad strip of white shingle which bordered the curve of the river. A kingfisher flashed across the path before them and Stella gave an involuntary gasp of delight. 'Owen, look, how pretty!'

'As pretty as you, my sweet girl,' he said as he stopped and gently pulled her to face him. 'May I kiss you, Stella?'

'Oh no!' Stella took a step backwards. 'No, Owen, it's not right.'

He laughed. 'Of course it is right. We are betrothed. Come here!' It was a command, though his hands on her shoulders were gentle. She glanced at his face. His eyes were closed; he had sandy lashes, she noticed, and a large velvety mole at the corner of his mouth.

'Owen—' she said faintly.

'Please, Stella.' His lips were warm and soft against hers. The kiss lasted only a moment, then he released her and smiled. 'You're trembling, sweetheart. There's no need. I'll not harm you, you know that. Here, let me show you your present.'

He was fumbling in his waistcoat and produced a small box. 'See, I went to Davies in Hay to buy this for you. Open it!' He pressed it into her hand.

Stella, her fingers shaking, fumbled with the lid and at last managed to lift it off. Inside, on a bed of lambswool, lay a delicate filigree brooch. She stared at it speechlessly, letting it lie winking in the sunlight in its soft nest.

'Here, let me.' Unable to watch another moment, he took it from her, and standing close, frowning with concentration, he pinned it into the collar of her habit.

Hesitatingly she lifted her eyes to his. 'It's beautiful, Owen. Quite beautiful,' she said in a whisper. 'But I can't accept it.'

His mouth dropped open. 'Stella, what are you saying?'

'I can't marry you, Owen,' she said sadly. 'I am sorry, I should never have said Yes. It was the most terrible mistake.' Fumbling awkwardly with the pin, she unfastened the brooch and held it out to him. 'You must release me from my promise and forgive me. I didn't want to hurt you, but I can't go through with it. I can't.'

Owen was staring at her and for a moment he seemed deflated by her words. 'Stella!' He took her hand blindly in both of his and held it against his chest. 'Stella, please. You cannot know what you are saying.'

She pulled away from him and went to stand on the river bank, stirring the shingle gently with the toe of her boot. 'I do know, Owen, and I bitterly regret hurting you. It was unforgivable of me to promise myself when . . .' She hesitated, staring at the glittering water with eyes that were blinded with tears.

'When? When what?' He stepped after her and there was anger in his voice. 'Do you love someone else, is that it?'

'No!'

'Then what is it? I demand to know.'

'I just cannot be certain of giving you the love you deserve.' She faced him resolutely. 'I care for you so much, Owen, but not as a future wife should love the man she is to marry.'

A deep frown appeared between his eyes. 'If I may say so, Stella, such a love comes with time; it is unseemly to expect or even think about it when we have been betrothed for only a day.'

'But it isn't unseemly,' she cried. 'I know it isn't. We should feel something . . . something special; we should be overwhelmed by it!'

'Stella?' He smiled awkwardly. 'My dear, forgive me, but I think you have perhaps been reading too many novels. Such emotion as you describe does not happen in real life. In real life men and women achieve, if they are lucky, calm contentment and mutual respect. To seek for more would be foolish and irrational.'

She looked into his eyes, troubled. 'Do you really believe that?' she whispered.

He nodded, catching her hands again in his own. 'I do believe it, but I was forgetting, sweet Stella, how young you are and how innocent. I should not reprimand you for your girlish dreams when you do not really know what you are talking about. Trust me, my dear, that is all I ask, and, believe me, our marriage will be a happy one. I will not be a stern or an unforgiving husband.' He gripped her hands tightly and she let out a little cry of pain. His brooch was still clutched in her hand and his sudden movement had driven the open pin into her palm.

Concerned, he opened her fingers and drew off her blood-spotted glove, dabbing the small wound with his handkerchief. Then, disapprovingly, he took back the brooch. 'Now, I shall refasten this for you and I wish to hear no more nonsense about ending our betrothal. It is settled, sweetheart, between your father and myself and there is no going back. I shall require you to wear this brooch as a symbol of our union until I can collect the family ring for you. I shall be very angry if you do not do so, Stella. Do you understand?' He looked at her sternly for a moment, and she found herself standing docilely, like a trapped animal, as he repinned the brooch to her collar.

The dining-room at Bryn Glas was long and low ceilinged, facing west, and from the windows the green valley stretched out towards a sky which was mottled and flecked with gold. Seated between Owen and her brother, Stella kept her eyes fixed on the sunset as Meredith and Perry served dinner.

'So, my boy, you are joining us this evening,' Henry Vaughan addressed Owen jovially as he shook out his napkin and bent over the bowl of soup before him. 'I confess I am looking forward to putting a stop to this nonsense before it really starts. These Rebeccas and their followers may be allowed to terrorise west Wales, but I'll be dashed if I will allow them to terrorise me! Threatening to burn my house, indeed! And giving me a date, if you please, as if the scoundrel were making an appointment to meet me at my club! But I'll trim his sails for him once I set hands on him tonight!' And gleefully he rubbed his hands together.

Stella said nothing, glancing surreptitiously from one to the other of the three men, and then looked sadly down at her plate. Nothing would dissuade them; nothing could defer the battle and there was no knowing how many men were going to be hurt, even killed. But at least John would not be there.

She pulled herself up short. She had allowed herself only a few seconds' thought about John Vivian since her meeting with Owen, and she did not intend to allow any at all in the future if she could help it. The emotions John roused in her had been too violent and too powerful for her to face. She opened her fan with a snap and fluttered it before her burning cheeks. He had humiliated and scolded her and she disliked him intensely, so why was it that she could not rid herself of the image of his face and this secret terrible suspicion that this was what love was like. Such a thing was not possible! She refused to contemplate it. The whole thing was quite ridiculous! All she could do was to make sure that she never saw him alone again, and to put him out of her thoughts for good. He was arrogant and dangerous, and he despised her, as he had clearly shown on several occasions. There was no more to think about. And she didn't care one bit if he were there tonight or not.

Luckily her preoccupied silence went unnoticed, as dinner was not on this occasion a prolonged affair. The men soon retired to the magistrate's study so that George and Owen and certain of those waiting in the yard could be sworn in as special constables and the plans for the evening laid.

Margaret Vaughan, tired and pale too at the thought of the coming battle, retired with her daughters to the parlour and, taking a seat near the window, picked up her embroidery. Eliza automatically reached for the book from which she was reading out loud and opened it, but she was watching her sister.

'Where did you get that pretty clip for your dress, Stella?' she asked.

Stella put her hand self-consciously to the shoulder of her pale blue gown. She had debated for a long time before her mirror whether to wear the brooch. Independence and defiance prompted her to put it into the curved drawer of her mirror and not to wear it again, but finally sense and a certain instinctive diplomacy persuaded her to pin it to the soft pale silk which swathed her breast. She was glad she had done so, for Owen's eyes, as she entered the drawing-room before dinner, had gone straight to the jewel and she had seen the tight frown which had adorned his brow since their return from the ride ease a little, to be replaced by a small smile. She faced her mother. 'Owen gave it to me this afternoon, Mama.'

'I thought he must have,' Margaret said with a quick smile. 'You rode with him earlier, didn't you, and I thought you looked a little tired. Your colour seemed very high at dinner.'

Stella blushed. 'Cariad was not behaving very well, Mama. She nearly pulled my arms out of their sockets. Owen rescued me just in time or I might have galloped all the way to Brecon.'

'Do you know, he's looking forward to tonight,' Eliza put in. 'They all are. Are men not extraordinary? There are bound to be broken heads and yet they are as excited about it as little boys. Even Papa!' She wrinkled her nose in disgust.

Margaret gave a small cry of distress. 'Oh, don't say that. What if your father should get hurt! Or any of them.'

'I shouldn't worry about them,' Eliza said with a sniff. 'They will no doubt look after themselves. But what about us? Once again we are to be left unprotected without a second thought! Suppose these rioters were to realise that every man on the place was with Papa. What on earth would prevent some of them from coming here and carrying out their threat to burn the house? Who would stop them?' She had lowered her voice dramatically. Then she laughed. 'Oh Lord, Stella, now even you have gone white! I was joking, silly. They won't come until the night they have promised. They could not possibly have found out that we are undefended, and by the time they find out the strength of Papa's forces at the toll it will be too late for any of them to change their minds and come here.'

Stella's mouth had gone dry, and for a moment she felt a surge of panic as she thought of Rebecca's threats to her home. Did no one else realise how dangerous that threat was? That she believed in their cause did not stop her from being terrified for her beloved home.

She glanced up at her mother, her fists clenched in the folds of her skirt to hide their sudden trembling.

'Mama,' she said faintly. 'Perhaps we should ask Papa to leave some men here with us.'

Her mother was looking worried, but she shook her head. 'My dear, I have already begged him to, but he feels it is quite unnecessary. He needs every hand at the toll-gate, he says, then he can be certain of rounding up all these men. He seems to think he is certain of catching them, so there will be no danger to us at all—'

'I'll speak to him!' Stella was already speeding towards the door. 'He can't leave us alone like this, he can't!'

Leaving her astonished mother and sister, she ran down the corridor towards her father's study. The fire still burned brightly and a decanter and empty glasses standing on the desk showed where the men had toasted their enterprise, but the room was deserted. She sped back up the passage towards the kitchen and out through the wash-house to the stable yard where the men were mounting their horses.

'Papa!'

Henry Vaughan was already astride his big bay cob as she threaded her way through the staring men towards him, careless of her gown in the muddy yard, and caught hold of his stirrup.

'Papa, you must leave enough men here to guard the house. You cannot leave us alone!' she cried.

'Hush, child,' he said sternly. 'Stand out of the way now. This is no place for a woman!'

'But, Papa!'

'Enough, Stella. There is no need for a guard. The fellow has warned us when he intends to come here; he will not strike sooner. And tonight he has other plans, anyway, and I trust that by midnight we'll have him and all his skirted followers behind bars! Go back into the house and reassure your mother. She's near hysterical with this business as it is, and I want no female fluttering to distract us. Go on. Go inside!'

With a shout to his followers, he kicked the horse past her and began to lead the way out of the gate, followed by the rest, some dozen farmers and townsmen on horses and a score more others on foot armed with pitchforks and cudgels. Many of them, Stella saw as they trotted past, had guns.

With a sinking heart she watched them leave, then she turned and looked up at the house. The westering sun was reflecting crimson in the window-panes and they looked already as though they were on fire.

With tears in her eyes she ran to the gate and peered after the men as they turned out of the lane and began streaming across the darkening field towards the river. There was nothing more she could do.

As soon as the sun had gone, the evening chill began to fill the room. Stella pulled a shawl round her shoulders and watched miserably as Megan put several logs on the fire. Bobbing a curtsy, the maid turned to Mrs Vaughan.

'Will I bring in the tea, madam?' she said. The girl looked nervously towards the window where Stella seated herself in the bay, gazing out into the darkness.

'Please do, Megan,' Margaret replied, setting down her

sewing and leaning forward to adjust the oil lamp on the table. 'And please will you ask cook and Peggy to help you check every door and window in the house and make sure they are securely bolted. And let the dogs out, if you please.' She smiled at the girl, whose eyes had widened in terror. 'I am sure there is no need for alarm, but we shall all feel safer if we've done all we can ourselves,' she reassured her, as Megan hurried from the room.

As soon as the door had closed behind the maid, Eliza let her book fall into her lap and looked at her sister. 'Look at Stella! She is waiting to be carried off once more by her friends to Mother Rebecca,' she said softly. 'Can't you tell, Mama! What makes you think, Stella, that they would bother to rescue you before they fired the house?'

Stella, her face white, turned on her. 'They have never deliberately hurt anyone; they only want to draw attention to their cause,' she cried defiantly.

Eliza gave a little sneer. 'Well, a lot of people seem to have got quite badly hurt by mistake, then. What about old Sarah Williams who was murdered at Hendy only a couple of weeks ago. And that was in your precious newspapers, I read it myself. A defenceless old lady, shot in cold blood!'

Stella bit her lip and turned back to the window. 'I had forgotten,' she said quietly.

Behind them on the mantelpiece the pretty ormulu clock chimed eight.

'Only a few hours,' Margaret whispered at last, 'and it will all be over.'

The knock on the door made them all jump as it reverberated in the silent room.

Eliza stared at her mother in horror. 'Who is it?' she whispered.

'It's Megan with the tea, child.' Margaret forced herself to smile as Stella went to the door. Sure enough, the maid stood outside.

'No sign of anyone anywhere, madam,' she said as she slid the heavy tray on to the table. 'Cook has all the doors treble bolted, and she's sent Peggy up to the attics to keep a watch for lights, but there is nothing to be seen at all.'

Deftly the girl arranged the cups and set the kettle down on the hearth. 'Cook says it is all rubbish and there is to be no raid at all,' she went on more cheerfully. 'Better things to do, they have, she says, than play at riots, with the apple-picking still to finish and the pony sale coming so soon.'

Margaret smiled, in spite of herself. 'Tell cook I sincerely hope she's right, Megan,' she said.

Megan bobbed a curtsy and was turning to leave, when they all heard the distant sound of a dog barking. She froze, her mouth open with terror, as Stella, shading her eyes against the reflections in the glass, peered out into the dark.

'Stella, come away from the window and draw the curtains,' her mother ordered, her voice sharp with tension. 'Go on, Megan. Get back to cook. There is no need to worry. The dog is probably chasing a rabbit.' Her back as stiff as a ramrod, Margaret leaned forward and began to pour the tea. With a gulp, Megan nodded, and tiptoed from the room.

Without looking up from her task, Margaret continued softly, 'Eliza, dear. There is, I believe, a pistol in the desk in your father's study. Perhaps you would be good enough to fetch it.'

Eliza gasped, but without argument she stood up and carefully marking her place in the book with the embroidered marker, put it on the table, picked up a candlestick and made her way out of the room.

Full of anxiety, Stella went to the fireplace and, sinking on her knees in a cloud of pale silk flounces, began to stir the logs with the poker. 'The dogs are quiet again,' she said after a moment. 'There can't have been anyone there, after all.'

'I'm sure there wasn't,' Margaret replied. She was still looking thoughtfully at her younger daughter when Eliza slipped back into the room, gingerly carrying the gun at arm's length.

'Do you know how to fire it, Mama?' she asked, setting it nervously on the table.

Margaret shook her head. 'All I know, dears, is how to point it, and that I shall do if anyone threatens my home.'

Stella took a deep breath and, turning from the fire, rose to her feet. 'I know,' she said.

The two other women stared at her.

'I have watched George,' Stella went on steadily. 'He has shown me how to load a gun and allowed me to fire it on several occasions. You mustn't tell Papa.'

Margaret cleared her throat uncertainly. 'My dear, Papa would be proud of you.'

Stella gave a quick smile. 'I'll fetch the bullets. I know where they are kept.' She took the candlestick which Eliza had put down on the card-table near the door and made her way out into the dark corridor. As the door shut behind her, she held her breath and listened. The house was silent and, save for the pool of light thrown by her own candle as she walked, completely dark. She imagined cook and the girls huddled together in the kitchen where the warm range threw a red glow across the old tiles, and she shivered violently.

Her father's study was empty and cold now, the fire a heap of white ash, the curtains open, the glasses cleared away. Nervously she stood in the doorway gazing round, staring at the blind windows which reflected so starkly the single cold white light of her candle, then resolutely she walked across to her father's desk. In the bottom drawer lay a ring of meticulously labelled keys. It took her only a few moments to find the correct one, insert it in the lock and withdraw the necessary ammunition from the box. Then, with a quick glance over her shoulder at the long windows, she fled back towards the warmth of the parlour.

Margaret and Eliza watched, half admiring, half afraid, as she primed and loaded the pistol. 'Are you a good shot, Stella?' Eliza asked at last. For once her voice held only respect.

'Fairly.' Stella squinted down the barrel.

'And you would shoot a man?' her sister said slowly.

'If he threatened to burn this house, I would.' Stella pictured for a moment the tall dark figure of Mother Rebecca and wondered if he would still mock her if she were holding a pistol to his head. And with a spurt of indignation she knew that he probably would.

Eliza picked up the book again as the clock chimed nine, but none of them could concentrate on the story; after a few pages she put it aside and started to pace restlessly up and down the floor.

Margaret was leaning back against the cushions, dozing, when clearly in the distance they all heard the sound of a shot. Her eyes flew open as Stella jumped up, and all three women stared numbly at the drawn curtains. Stella's heart was thumping painfully as a burst of distant furious barking from the dogs made Margaret, too, rise to her feet. Her face was white with fear as, seconds later, they heard the sounds that had alerted the dogs, the clatter of hooves from the lane at the side of the gardens.

Stella looked first at her mother, then at her sister; then she moved slowly to the table. The gun was cold and heavy in her hands as she lifted it from the embroidered table-cloth.

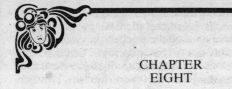

CHAPTER
EIGHT

THEY HAD waited for several more minutes before the sound of banging on the front door reverberated through the silent house, followed by an indignant shout.

Stella's fingers tightened on the gun as Eliza crept on tiptoe to the parlour door and opened it, peering out into the hall. Moments later, her face broke into smiles. 'It's Papa! I recognise his voice. It's all right, it's Papa! They're back! Megan, open the door!'

From the hall she could hear the sound of voices raised in anger as the bolts on the front door were at last drawn, and then Megan's cry of alarm as boots echoed on the polished boards. Almost at once Henry Vaughan was standing in the doorway. His face was filthy, and his coat badly torn and bloody. He surveyed the room with one glance.

'Margaret, Stella, Eliza, are you all right?' His gaze fell on the pistol which Stella was still clutching to her, and his face registered a brief astonishment. 'I hope that is not loaded,' he added in a threatening tone. Not waiting for a reply to his question, he turned on his heel and disappeared back along the passage as George strode past him into the room in his stockinged feet. His clothes were torn, and there was a long jagged scratch on his forehead. He appeared to be in a high temper. Flinging himself down on a chair, he tore off his cravat and opened his shirt collar. 'They were waiting for us!' he said. 'We never stood a chance. They made complete fools of us.'

Stella could feel the colour draining from her face. Abruptly she sat down, her legs no longer able to support her, her eyes fixed on the blood on her brother's temple.

It was Margaret who managed to stammer, 'Was anyone badly hurt?'

George shook his head. 'Only bruises. They overwhelmed us. They were out to make us a laughing-stock.

They never even touched the toll. They took Papa and
Owen and tied their hands and set them backwards on their
horses. They put labels round their necks!' He was spluttering with anger. 'Papa nearly had apoplexy! I've never seen
him so furious. I tell you that Rebecca will regret the day he
did this; he has signed his own death-warrant this time.'

'He was there?' Stella hadn't realised she had spoken out
loud till George swung round on her.

'Oh, yes, your precious friend was there, in his skirts and
his wig with his face as black as a coalminer's, ordering his
men about. "Gently with them, daughters, for they are
kind folk and not used to rough women like us",' George
mimicked in disgust. 'My God, but I'd like to find out who
told them we were coming!'

Stretching his legs out before him on the carpet, he
caught sight of Stella's stricken face. 'It was you!' he
exclaimed. 'You warned them, didn't you? Just as you
released that man last time.' He leapt to his feet and stood
towering over her.

Stella jumped up. 'I didn't! How could I?' she cried.

'You are being ridiculous, George,' Margaret added
sharply. 'Your sister could not possibly have done such a
thing. More likely it was your own bragging in the Swan
which alerted someone to what you planned!'

But George was still staring at Stella, his face full of
accusation. Ignoring his mother, he took a step towards
her. 'That is where you went this afternoon, isn't it. When
you rushed out of here, you went to find one of them to
warn them. Don't deny it, Stella, you might be able to fool
Mama with your protests of innocence, but there is guilt
written all over your face.' He grabbed her wrist. 'Do you
know what would happen to you if Papa found out? Do you
know the penalties for helping the rioters?'

'Let go of me!' She broke free of him and put the
tea-table between herself and her brother. She was trembling violently.

'Children, please,' Margaret protested weakly. 'Stop it.
You are making my head ache so. George, haven't we had
enough troubles without this? Apologise to your sister.'

'Certainly, Mama, when she has convinced me of her
innocence.' He advanced on her again.

'I am not going to stand here and listen to you accusing me!' Stella cried, near to tears. 'I didn't warn anyone. I didn't!' She had backed away from him until she was beside the long windows, and seeing George between her and the door, on sudden impulse she threw back the curtains with a rattle of rings and flung the french window open.

Behind her, George stopped in amazement. 'Don't be a fool, Stella. Don't go out. You don't know who might be out there!' He lunged at her, grabbing at her hand, but she eluded him, darting out between the curtains to the deserted moonlit terrace. 'Dash it all, Stella, I've no boots on!' His wail reached her as she looked about her, suddenly afraid of the silence outside and the blackness of the shadows. She had intended to do no more than run round to the windows of her father's study, which also opened on to the terrace, but a glance told her they were shut fast. She had no alternative but to descend the steps to the dew-soaked grass and make her way towards the corner of the house where the dining-room windows threw a long rectangle of light across the flower-beds. She could still feel herself shaking with indignation at George's accusation. The more angry because John Vivian had suggested the same thing.

The moonlight painted the wet lawns white, but as she cut through the alley of high beech hedges which angled across the lawn towards the house, the grass was pitch black and barred with shadows and she had no chance of seeing the dark figure who waited there until it was too late.

Her gasp of terror was smothered against his shoulder as he seized her and dragged her back into the deep shadow.

'So, Stella Vaughan,' a husky voice murmured in her ear. 'Are you so eager then for another kiss from Mother Rebecca?'

'You?' She tried to tear herself from his grasp, but he held her easily, spinning her sharply so that her back was towards him and she could not glimpse his face. Above her head he glanced cautiously towards the house, where the light from the open french windows still spilled out across the lawn. George had disappeared. The house was in silence. He smiled grimly, then propelled her swiftly out of sight of the windows through a break in the hedge. She struggled furiously against him, feeling the dew-wet leaves catching at her hair and her dress as she tried to free herself, and desperately she raked his forearms with her nails.

He swore quietly and changed his grip, catching her wrists and holding them crossed across her breast so that she was pinned against him. Then he laughed, as a shaft of moonlight lit the delicate wild creature in his arms and he saw the soft coil of her hair slipping loose over her shoulders.

'What are you doing here?' she cried softly. She gave up struggling at last and stood quietly, trembling in his grasp. She was shivering with cold; her shawl had fallen from her shoulders and hung uselessly over her elbows. 'Have you come to burn our house, just to set the seal on your triumph, is that it?' The words tumbled out bitterly.

'No, I haven't come to burn your house.' His mouth was close to her ear. She felt his warm breath fan her cheek. 'Not this time. Perhaps I came to see you; to find out why you failed to make your father see reason.'

'My father will never help you,' she retorted. She twisted round, trying to see his face, but he held her easily. His grip tightened, and with a sharp thrill of fear she felt his mouth on her hair as he pulled her hard against his chest.

'Stand still, you little fool,' he hissed. 'You don't want to see who I am, believe me.'

She froze, her heart pounding wildly beneath his imprisoning arms. 'Would I know you, then?' she whispered.

There was a moment's silence. Then unexpectedly he chuckled. 'Oh yes, Stella Vaughan. You would know me.'

Her brain was in a turmoil. She knew him! She knew the identity of the man who held her so intimately in his arms. A dozen faces flashed before her eyes, but none fitted the mocking insolence of the husky Welsh voice. She tried to think, but her mind refused to concentrate on anything but the iron grip which held her so effortlessly.

She forced herself to breathe slowly. 'Tell me how you knew my father would be waiting for you at the toll,' she said at last.

'One of our informers,' he replied after a thoughtful pause.

'My brother thinks I warned you about it.'

'Does he, now.' The quiet amusement in his tone infuriated her. 'And would you have done it, if you had known where to find me?'

'No!' she cried. 'No, I wouldn't. You are despicable! You deserve to be caught!' With a desperate lunge she almost broke away from him and, half turning, kicked out at him with all her strength.

But he caught her arms again with ease.

'Let me go or I shall scream!' she sobbed. 'Then you will be caught and hanged.'

To her chagrin, she heard a soft laugh. 'You won't scream, Stella Vaughan. That would be cowardly and you are no coward. Besides, you don't really want to see me hang.'

They were standing in the deep shadow of the hedge, a stream of silver moonlight illuminating the scythed path at their feet. A slow black shadow crept across the garden as a swathe of cloud drifted over the moon, and suddenly they were in total darkness. The hands which had been holding her so harshly propelled her round to face him.

Terrified, Stella at last looked up at him, but it was too dark to see anything at all of his features. She saw the pale gleam of his eyes for an instant, then his lips came down on hers, hot and demanding, his grip so hard that, forced back against his braced arm, she found herself held fast. Helpless against his strength, she ceased to struggle as she felt herself beginning to melt towards him. What kind of woman was she, she wondered miserably for a moment, that she could respond so wantonly to a man like this—then all the conscious thought was driven from a head dizzy with desire, her bones dissolving until she could barely stand and she had no thought of resistance left.

It was several minutes before he released her. He gave a quiet chuckle.

'Do you kiss Owen Morgan like that?' he enquired mildly.

'Certainly not!' Blushing furiously, she pulled away from him. 'That was unforgivable of you.'

'Very probably.' He pulled her against him again. 'But then I am the villain, am I not? I do unforgivable things all the time.' His laugh was husky. 'Tell me, why don't you kiss

Mr Morgan like that? Has he never tried to take you in his arms?'

'It is none of your business,' she returned furiously, struggling again with renewed determination.

'He's a bigger fool than I thought him, then,' he went on as if she hadn't spoken. He continued to hold her as easily as he would a child. 'I must confess I had him singled out this evening for your sake. Such a cowardly fop! He's not good enough for you.'

'How dare you say that,' she cried. 'He might have been killed. They all might.'

'Of course they wouldn't,' he retorted. 'They came to no harm at all, other than to their dignity. But next time they may not be so lucky, and it could be up to you alone to see there isn't a next time. Must I persuade you all over again that it is your duty to argue our case with your father?' His voice dropped, and she felt his arms tighten round her once more. Even as she framed the words of her furious response, his lips had found hers and she felt her mouth open shamelessly beneath his, her body his to command as she became aware of the hard masculine pressure of his thighs against hers. Desperately clinging to the shreds of her self-control, she pulled back from him.

'If I help you,' she said as repressively as she could, 'it will be because I still support your cause, not *ever* because of your methods of persuasion!' Her voice was shaken and breathless.

He laughed quietly. 'Just so long as you succeed, my dear. That is all that matters.'

As she stared up at him, she became dimly aware that out of the corner of her eye she could see the brilliant moonlight returning, sweeping gently across the garden in a broad silver path towards them as the clouds drifted southwards. Near by, an owl hooted softly. She held her breath. In a few seconds she would see his face . . .

A pandemonium of barking broke out suddenly from behind the house. With an oath he drew back into the hedge's shadow, dragging her with him.

'It is time I was on my way,' he murmured, 'and you must return to the house before your brother finds those boots he was lamenting and comes out looking for you. They'll wonder what you've been doing out here in the moonlight alone.' He laughed again. Then he kissed her almost tenderly on the forehead. 'Run back, and don't stir again tonight. And work on your father, my dear. I don't want to see you next surrounded by a ring of fire.'

With a little push, he released her and turned away. There was a rustle of leaves as he ducked through the hedge, then in one movement he was sprinting across the grass. For the last few yards he was in full moonlight, a tall dark figure dressed in riding-breeches and a black jerkin, then he vaulted over the gate into the lane, and was gone.

Trembling, she raised her hands to her burning cheeks, staring at the spot where he had disappeared, then ran across the cold wet grass to the steps outside the parlour. Only when she was safely on the veranda did she pause for a moment, trying to calm herself, shivering violently from the cold and from the shock of her encounter. The parlour was empty when she pushed in through the unlatched windows. Thankfully, she pulled them closed behind her and drew the heavy curtains before she flew across to the fireplace to inspect her face in the mirror. Her lips were swollen and bruised and there was a streak of black across her cheek. She dragged her handkerchief from her pocket and scrubbed frantically before twisting her hair back into some semblance of order, skewering it into place with her combs. Then she sank to the hearthrug and held out her hands to the smouldering logs. She was shaking uncontrollably.

It was there, five minutes later, that Owen and her father found her, their faces very grim as they entered the room. Behind them was George.

'So you are here,' Henry Vaughan said, advancing into the room. 'We have been looking for you, Stella. May I ask where you were? Close the door, please, George,' he added sharply. He had changed his jacket and tidied himself and now looked considerably more normal, but there was still a cold fury in his face which Stella had never seen there before.

She looked from one to the other of the three men and her heart sank, but resolutely she smiled at them as she rose and shook out her torn, damp skirts.

'I was in the garden, Papa, as I'm sure George told you, trying to escape his stupid accusations,' she said defiantly. 'The mist on the trees is so beautiful in the moonlight I must confess I stopped to watch it for a moment.' Her voice was demure. Surely they would see the imprint of his kisses on her mouth, read the trembling of her body? She turned back to the fire to hide her face.

Henry let out a snort of impatience. 'Moonlight! You have some explaining to do, my girl. And, it seems, on two counts. First, what is this that Owen has just seen fit to tell me about you trying to break off your betrothal this afternoon? I have never heard such nonsense!'

Stella spun round to look at Owen. He was untidy and dirty like George, and there was a seething bruise on his jaw. He met her eyes coldly, and after a moment she looked away, unable to bear the sight of his anger.

She sat down on her mother's chair, uncomfortably conscious that her thin slippers were soaked through, and faced her father, her grey eyes wide. 'I am certain I would not make Owen a good wife.'

'Well, I think you would,' her father snapped. 'And so does he, and you will forgive me if we presume to know better than you in this matter. The betrothal stands, and you are lucky that Owen is prepared to be so patient with you. The wedding will be at Christmas.'

Stella gasped. 'But, Papa—'

'Christmas, Stella.' He took up a stand in front of the fire, rubbing his hands together behind his back. 'I wish to hear no more about it. Now, as to this other matter, I shall dispose of it at once.' He turned to George. 'You accuse your sister of somehow warning the rioters of our intentions this evening.' He knitted his brows. 'You base this assumption on the fact that she released that fellow from my custody, presumably, or do you have other proof?' He did not look at Stella.

George stared uncomfortably at the floor. 'Father, it was a joke. I didn't really believe it. I was teasing her that she had fallen in love with Mother Rebecca when he took her into the mountains.' He shuffled his feet and at last glanced up at Stella's face. She had gone very pink.

'I hope it was a joke,' Henry went on grimly. 'Though if it

was, it was in exceedingly poor taste in the circumstances. If I thought that Stella, or anyone in this house, had in any way fraternised with the rioters, the consequences for them would be very serious indeed.'

Stella was sitting very still. Surreptitiously she glanced at her fiancé. He was glaring at George.

'That is a dreadful thing to suggest about your sister, when you knew she loved me,' he said under his breath.

'It doesn't sound as if she does love you,' retorted George.

'Silence!' Henry roared at his son. 'It would be more helpful if you were to concern yourself with our present troubles. Stella, you may go to your room. There is no need for you to remain downstairs.' He drummed his fingers on the arm of his chair. 'We must decide on our plans and post guards around this house until the dragoons arrive next week. He will not get away with what he did tonight. I shall find him if I have to look under every stone in the border counties!'

Stella did not wait to hear more. She fled towards her bedroom, closing the door thankfully behind her.

On the landing Eliza greeted her, her finger to her lips. 'I've given Mama some valerian root. She's sleeping now,' she whispered. 'Stella, I've got to talk to you.' She caught Stella's hand and pulled her into her own room. The flame of the single candle on the dressing-table streamed sideways in the draught, scattering wax on the table as she pulled the door shut, and leaned against it. Her eyes were brilliant with excitement as she surveyed her sister, and there was a gleam of triumph in her face. 'I saw you,' she said at last. 'I was watching from the window and I saw you with him.'

Stella gasped. She sat down heavily on the bed. 'Are you going to tell Papa?' she asked faintly.

Eliza moved away from the door and, crossing the room, sat down at the small writing-desk, deliberately arranging her skirts round her until they lay in neat exact folds. Stella waited, mastering her temper with difficulty, her eyes fixed steadily on her sister. 'Well?'

'I don't know. Probably not.' Eliza looked up at last. 'Was it he? Mother Rebecca?'

Stella narrowed her gaze sharply. 'You could see who it was, surely?'

Eliza shook her head. 'He was standing in the shadows. He wasn't wearing a skirt, but I suppose by then he had got rid of it.' She picked up a pen and idly traced a pattern on the desk top with the empty nib. 'I saw him kiss you,' she said at last in a small light voice.

Stella swallowed hard. 'I didn't know he was out there. I ran into the garden to avoid George—'

'Well, he obviously guessed you would find a way of seeing him. You didn't seem to object to being kissed.'

Stella blushed. 'If you had seen more clearly, Eliza, you would have realised that I objected very much. But he is so strong, I could not prevent him . . .' Her voice trailed away as she thought again about what had occurred in the garden. 'He held me so tightly. Oh Eliza—' Impulsively she ran to her sister and knelt beside her on the carpet. 'Please don't tell Papa. He would be so angry with me, and it was not my fault. The man was prying in the garden, he hadn't come to see me. I swear it.' She paused abruptly. 'I don't know why he was there,' she went on, her voice suddenly hushed. 'He must have followed them back for some reason . . .'

Eliza was watching her through narrowed eyes. 'Did you tell Papa he was here?' she asked.

Stella shook her head miserably.

'I see.' Eliza smiled slyly. 'So we know whose side you're on, don't we. Did you enjoy his kisses?'

'Eliza—' Stella turned to her in desperation. 'I've told you. He forced me. Please, don't say anything to anyone. they wouldn't understand.'

'No,' Eliza echoed. 'They wouldn't.'

Stiffly Stella rose, and crossing to the window threw back the curtain with a rattle. 'You won't tell Papa?' The chill from the glass struck into the room and she saw that there were pools of condensation on the window-sill.

'Of course not, I told you. We are sisters, after all, Stella.'

'Yes, we are sisters.' Stella turned her back on the window and stared at Eliza, who had not moved. 'You want something, Eliza, don't you?'

'Nothing very difficult.' Eliza put down the pen with elaborate care and, folding her hands in her lap, looked up at Stella at last. 'I do not intend to become a laughing-stock by allowing my younger sister to be married before me; I never want to hear myself described as an old maid. Now, I have no wish to come between you and Owen. I do not begrudge you your good fortune in securing such a match, and I should hate anything to come to his ears which might give him grounds for breaking off the engagement, so I know you will help me.' She lowered her eyelids, a provocative smile playing on her lips.

Stella gave a small laugh. 'There you are too late, sweet sister. I have already told Owen that I intend to break off the engagement!'

Eliza's eyes widened. 'Why? Not because of him!' she gestured towards the window and the garden beyond.

'No, not because of him. Because I do not love Owen sufficiently, and I do not like the threats he keeps making as to how he intends to change me when I am his wife.'

'Does Papa know?'

Stella gave a slow nod. 'He knows.'

'And he accepts your decision?'

'Well, no, not yet, but he will.'

Eliza laughed. 'He won't. You know that as well as I do. Owen would have to break the engagement and, if he did, there would be a dreadful scandal.' She paused significantly. 'And that would kill Mama.'

Stella took a deep breath. 'What do you want me to do, Eliza? I cannot conjure a husband out of the air for you.'

'You don't need to. I have decided on the man.' Eliza stood up at last and shook out her skirts. Then slowly she began to unbutton the bodice of her dress. 'It is late and we must go to bed. Help me with my gown. As I said, Stella, your part is not very difficult, for you seem to have such persuasive ways with gentlemen.'

Stella flinched at the sarcasm. 'You know I will support you, Eliza. Who is he?' she asked, helping her to pull the heavy material of the dress over her head. Eliza turned to face her, clad now only in her petticoat, and held out her hands for the dress. 'Cannot you guess?'

'Unless it is Sir Samuel Atkins—but I thought you disliked him—'

'No, no.' Impatiently Eliza threw the crushed pink silk over the back of a chair. 'Leave the gown for Megan. No, you already know who, Stella, someone quite new in the area. Someone handsome and clever, and, as Mama has discovered, very, very wealthy. It is Mr Vivian!'

Stella gave a faint gasp.

Her sister looked at her hard. 'Yes, another of your flirts. That is why I thought you could help me with my campaign.'

'But you hardly know him.' Stella whispered at last. Her heart had given an anguished lurch.

'That did not seem to stand in your way, sister, in Mr Griffiths's office.' Eliza's voice took on a harsh edge. 'Anyway, however well I do or do not know him now, I intend to know him a great deal better. When he calls, I shall rely on you to help me all you can.'

'But Eliza!' Stella was still staring at her sister, overwhelmed by the feeling of desolation which had swept over her. 'Have you no pride? You cannot make a man love you!'

'What has love to do with it? Do you think Owen loves you?' Eliza sat down in front of her oval mirror and began removing her hairpins. 'Oh, I'm not saying he does not have the highest regard for you, but the reality is that Papa has offered him a substantial marriage portion. Higher than any other family in the neighbourhood could manage.'

Stella gave a small smile. 'You sound very bitter, Eliza,' she said softly. 'So you think that if your dowry is great enough Mr Vivian will take you?'

'Naturally.'

'You do not place your own worth very high, then. When a man marries he should do so for love alone.'

Eliza laughed. 'Do you honestly think that Owen would marry you if you were a penniless maidservant from the mountains?' she asked acidly.

Their eyes met in the mirror. Slowly Stella shook her head. 'That is why I cannot marry him.'

'That is why you must marry him. Papa and Sir Robert will insist. It is a business contract, no more, no less. And that is why John Vivian will marry me. Papa will offer him terms that he cannot refuse. Because—' Eliza began to brush her hair with long, firm, strokes, 'you will make sure Papa knows what I want. He always listens to you.'

There was a long silence in the room, broken only by the distant sound of slipping hooves and a shouted command as Ianto busied himself in the stable yard bedding down the last of the horses. Eliza laid down the brush. 'It would be so tragic if he found out his favourite daughter was in league with criminals, wouldn't it?' she murmured sweetly. 'Poor Mama would never survive the disgrace.'

Stella stared down at her sister's triumphant face, stunned at her calculating coldness. What claim, after all, did she have on John Vivian when he detested her, and she . . . yes, she thought firmly, she detested him.

Then she gave a wry laugh. 'Very well, Eliza, I'll do all I can to promote your affairs with Mr Vivian. I can do no less,' she said at last.

She walked towards the door and paused, her hand on the door-knob, to glance back at her sister. 'I told you I thought Mr Vivian was a dangerous man to know,' she said softly. 'I still think so. Are you not afraid?'

Eliza turned on her chair. 'Why should I be,' she retorted. 'I shall make him the perfect wife.'

CHAPTER
NINE

STELLA SAT for a long time before her candlelit mirror that
night, listening to the howl of the wind which had risen in
the valley and was tearing through the orchards and the
fields beyond the garden. Dispassionately she studied her
reflection in the glass, scanning the large grey eyes fringed
with dark lashes, then dropping her stare to examine the
small bruise on her mouth which showed where Mother
Rebecca's kiss had hurt her. Slowly she began to unpin the
remnants of her heavy chignon, allowing the hair to fall free
almost to her waist, and began brushing it, counting the
strokes of her ivory-backed brush.

Her mind was a turmoil. It was so unfair that men were
allowed to control the destinies of women, she thought
stormily. Eliza was right. Men like her father and Owen
discussed her future as though she were a mere chattel,
talking of settlements and dowries without thought of love,
while others like the hated Mother Rebecca merely took
what they wanted with cynical force. In the mirror she saw a
tide of colour rising in her cheeks at the thought of him, and
she looked away angrily. How dare he touch her and kiss
her as he had! The man was an unprincipled monster! She
brushed furiously at her hair till the sparks flew. He was a
bully and a criminal and she bitterly regretted ever having
imagined she could talk to him.

Tears welled suddenly in her eyes. What was to become
of her? Surely she could not be forced to marry a man she
did not love? Her papa loved her, he wanted her happiness,
and yet he seemed unable to understand that she could have
changed her mind. And Mama? Eliza was right. It would
kill her mother if any breath of scandal touched either of
her daughters. She was trapped; trapped in a silken inexor-
able web of her own choosing, and there was no way out.
Owen's hard, unforgiving face swam before her for a

moment and the tears began to creep slowly down her cheeks.

'*John.*' The name was torn in an anguished whisper from her lips as she stared at herself in the mirror and her beautiful face, ravaged with misery, blurred as her lashes glittered with tears.

But John could not help her. He was as bad as the rest of them. He despised her and made fun of her beliefs. Eliza could—would—have him. He had, after all, shown more than a passing interest already in her sister, and she would rather die than ever let him suspect for a single second that her own heart had fallen under his spell.

She was jolted from her thoughts by the sounds of the grandfather clock striking one. Putting down her brush, she rose wearily and began undressing, and it was only then that she noticed that the brooch Owen had given her was missing. Her hand flew to the neck of her gown. She must have dropped it when she was struggling with Mother Rebecca in the dark.

She lay awake a long time tossing and turning, too exhausted to sleep, and the sky was already lightening in the east when at last she fell into an uneasy doze. When she woke it was morning. Her thoughts flew immediately to the brooch as she realised that it was already late and, with her fingers all thumbs in her haste, she dressed, pulling a warm merino wrap round her shoulders as she opened her bedroom door and listened. From the morning-room she could hear the sound of the piano, and knew that Miss Gwillam had already arrived to give Eliza her lesson. She tiptoed past the door and into the parlour and let herself out into the cold morning air.

In the daylight, the gardens on this side of the house looked small and painfully open to view, and she realised how easy it must have been for Eliza to see her from the upstairs window. Her cheeks burned at the very thought. She banished the memory furiously, her eyes on the ground as she retraced her steps of the night before, searching for the brooch, but the grass was long and unkempt beneath the hedges, and already a drift of pale ash leaves lay caught in the tangle of weeds. There was no sign of it. She shivered.

Owen would be so angry if she confessed that she had lost his betrothal gift—if he believed her at all.

A shout from the direction of the house attracted her attention, and she looked up to see her father standing on the veranda, beckoning. With a sinking heart she went towards him. 'Good morning, Papa.'

He ignored her greeting. 'What were you looking for, Stella?'

She blushed miserably, glancing past him into the room through the open windows, wondering if Owen were there. 'A comb, Papa,' she improvised quickly. 'I lost it last night and I wondered if I had dropped it in the grass.'

Her father snorted. 'You were lucky that was all you lost, it seems,' he muttered. 'Come in, child, come in,' and ushered her through the windows into his study.

She stopped short at the sight of the two figures standing by the fire place. One was Owen. The other was John Vivian.

Stella felt the hot colour flood into her cheeks as she stared from one to the other. The two men had been scrutinising a letter.

'Well, did she see anyone?' Owen turned to her. The bruise on his jaw was livid and ugly above his collar.

Henry Vaughan closed the double windows behind him and stood in front of them, looking at Stella thoughtfully. Muted in the silence, they could hear Eliza playing the lilting strains of a Mozart sonata.

Stella was trembling as she looked from Owen to her father, and back. 'Did I see anyone?' she repeated softly, trying to keep her voice steady. She was intensely conscious of John's sardonic gaze on her face.

'Last night,' John said quietly. 'I gather you went into the garden to enjoy the moonlight. Your father is wondering whether you saw the special messenger who brought this letter from your friend Mother Rebecca.'

'He's not my friend!' she retorted desperately. 'I detest him!' Unconsciously her hand had risen to her lips, still bruised against her pale face. Her eyes went to the piece of paper in Owen's hand. 'What does it say?' she said at last. Her mouth had gone dry. So that was why he had come last night. To deliver another letter, in person this time, to Magistrate Vaughan.

She could not bring herself to look at John. She knew he was still watching her and she was terrified he would read the guilt in her eyes.

'It contains the same nonsense as before,' Owen said tersely. 'I take it you saw no one in the garden last night?'

'Of course I didn't,' she murmured. She lifted her eyes cautiously to find John's amused gaze fixed on her face, as she had known she would. Furiously she turned away from him, pulling her shawl round her shoulders more tightly. 'You are an early visitor, Mr Vivian,' she said, striving to keep her voice from trembling. 'When you said you would call upon Mama, I hardly thought you would mean at breakfast-time.'

He bowed slightly in her direction. 'Nor, in spite of the temptations, did I intend so early a visit, Miss Stella,' he said. His eyes gleamed.

'I came for two reasons. One, to commiserate with your father upon last night's unpleasantness and to offer my help if it will be of service. And second, to beg for the company of one of your ladies, sir,' he inclined his head towards Henry. 'I am on my way to visit a poor female client who is in some distress, and it would comfort her immeasurably if I took Mrs Vaughan with me, or perhaps one of your daughters, if they would consider doing such a kindness. It is a matter of some delicacy, and the presence of a lady would give her strength to bear what I must tell her.'

Henry frowned. 'My wife is unwell, Vivian. Yesterday's events have proved too great a strain on her. And Eliza is engaged, as you can hear, with her music.' He hesitated.

Stella caught her breath in alarm as both men looked at her, a wave of panic rising in her breast. 'I cannot go with you,' she exclaimed before she could stop herself.

John raised an eyebrow. 'Not even, Miss Stella, to aid a member of the oppressed poor about whom you profess to care so much?'

She looked away stormily, aware of the gleam of triumph in his eye, as her father intervened. 'Of course you can go, Stella,' he said sternly. 'As my daughter, it is your duty to give help where you can.'

She looked at him desperately. 'But Papa—surely, Owen would not wish me to go—'

But it was no use. Owen stepped in with a stern smile. 'Your father is right, Stella. It is your duty to go. I am sure we can trust Mr Vivian to take good care of you. Megan can accompany you.'

But John frowned. 'I regret, but in a confidential matter such as this even the proprieties cannot allow me to take someone else. If she comes, she must come alone.'

Owen hesitated, looking at Henry, who shrugged, and then slapped Vivian on the shoulder. 'I can see no harm in it just this once, my boy. As you say, I'm sure we can trust John . . .'

And so it was that ten minutes later she found herself seated mutinously next to John Vivian in Toby Griffiths's trap, a basket of food and a bundle of cast-off clothing at her feet, as the solicitor whipped up the bay pony into a smart trot and bore her away from Bryn Glas.

She glanced across at him furiously. 'What is this, Mr Vivian? A ploy to test my sincerity?'

His presence so close to her was making her heart beat uncomfortably fast. She could feel the pressure of his knee against hers in the confined space of the trap, and she tried to draw away on the narrow seat. He did not take his eye off the lane as they negotiated a steep corner.

'I do not doubt your sincerity,' he said curtly. 'It is your idea of reality I sometimes query. You haven't asked me where we are going?'

'And where are we going?' She stared at him defiantly, wishing he were not so close. Beneath his hat his dark hair curled low on his neck, and she found herself aching to touch it. Furiously she clasped her hands beneath her cloak.

'To see Mrs Prosser. Mrs Dai Prosser.'

'Who is she?' She caught her breath as one of the wheels went into a pothole and she was almost thrown into his lap. He steadied her gravely, and for a moment she felt his eyes resting thoughtfully on her face.

'She is the wife of the man arrested by your father for helping to kidnap you; the wife of one of Mother Rebecca's right-hand men.'

Stella gave a little cry. 'But you can't take me there!'

'Why not, pray?' His eyes were like ice suddenly.

'Because—because, it would upset her, surely,' Stella stammered, tearing her gaze away from him.

'Why?'

'Because she must blame me for her husband's imprisonment. If he hadn't brought me home he wouldn't have been caught; he wouldn't have been shot! Stop the pony! Turn round. I do not want to go!' She leaned forward to catch the rein.

His hand came down on her wrist in an iron grip as he pushed her back in her seat.

'You will come with me, and you will see what it is really like, the poverty and the misery you so glibly seek to help. And you will speak to Janet Prosser and you will tell her you are sorry.' His voice had dropped to an angry whisper, and she stared at him.

'For a moment you sounded just like—' she stopped in mid-sentence. She had almost betrayed herself into admitting what Mother Rebecca had said to her. She stared at him again. 'Why do you care what I think,' she asked suddenly. 'You who are a newcomer to this part of the world. These people are at least my neighbours. They are nothing to you.'

'I am merely doing my job, Miss Vaughan.' He clicked his tongue at the pony as they reached the bridge over the Wye. The wheels rattled, echoing, across the boards and they glimpsed the broad shallows of the river beneath them. The trap swung right and, skirting through the quiet western streets of Hay with their neat grey houses, set off at a spanking pace on the Brecon road.

'I don't understand you,' she said at last. 'You despise me for trying to help people and yet you must be doing the same thing yourself. I can't believe that Mrs Prosser can afford a fashionable solicitor for her husband.'

His reply was ironic. 'So, you think I am fashionable, do you?'

She felt a surge of anger rise in her. 'I meant, Mr Vivian, that your services are probably expensive!'

He laughed. 'Oh, they are indeed!'

'So, how can Mrs Prosser afford you?' She raised her eyes to his accusingly. 'Or is that the way you make your money.

Will you delight in extorting every last penny from her by promising to help her husband, making her pay and scrimp and steal for the rest of her life?'

He jerked the pony to a halt. 'Is that what you think?' His voice was cold as ice.

'Yes, Mr Vivian, that is what I think,' she cried. 'It all makes sense suddenly. I think you are a vile hypocrite!' She tried to keep her voice steady as she saw the muscles at the angle of his jaw tighten.

'Well, you are wrong.' He looked at her with such fury that she quailed at the expression in his eyes. 'Dai Prosser's expenses for both myself and a barrister, should he need one, will be taken care of by, shall we say, an anonymous wealthy sympathiser. The firm will not lose and Janet Prosser will not have to pay a penny.'

She gasped. 'Mother Rebecca,' she breathed. 'He is a wealthy man.'

'How do you know he's wealthy?' The question cut like a whiplash across the sound of the impatient pony pawing the road.

She shook her head, shrinking away from him. 'I don't know. I guessed. Papa told me . . . Mrs Prosser must know. Why don't you ask her who gives her the money!'

He gave her a look of withering contempt. 'Mrs Prosser would never betray her husband's friends, Stella Vaughan, never!'

Picking up the whip, he set the pony in motion once more. They turned off the road and began to climb a narrow pitch, the wheels brushing against the high banks on either side which rose high above the pony's ears. Thick clusters of elderberries and rose hips trailed in the hedges, and blown hedge-parsley shook tiny white petals into drifts over their clothes and into the trap. Stella's pulse was beating fast. She did not understand this strange man next to her. The suppressed violence in him frightened her.

How could her treacherous body ache for him to touch her when every instinct she had been born with told her she should be afraid. She stole a glance at him as he coaxed the pony up the steep incline, intensely conscious of the unleashed power which radiated from every pore of his being, and found herself wishing with wistful longing that he would look at her, just once, with anything other than mocking dislike.

The pony drew up at last outside a single-storey stone cottage which stood on the high bank above the pitch. Three or four small children were playing outside in the dirt among some hens, and, as they watched, another small boy appeared, carrying two heavy wooden buckets of water from somewhere behind the house. He stopped to stare at them, then, setting the buckets down with such a thud that water slopped all over his bare feet, he ran into the cottage, shouting.

John looped the reins round the whip and vaulted over the side of the trap.

'Wait here,' he said curtly. 'There are private matters I wish to discuss with Mrs Prosser—then I will warn her that I have brought her a visitor.'

Stella watched with some apprehension as he strode up to the cottage door and ducked inside, followed by the chattering excited children. She was suddenly left completely alone. Beyond the bank the wooded hillside descended steeply towards the valley, while overhead the sky vaulted in a huge arch towards the mountains, deserted save for a lonely buzzard which rode the air currents in lazy circles, climbing ever higher until it was out of sight as she strained her eyes against the glare.

Five minutes later John reappeared in the doorway. He beckoned, and reluctantly she climbed down from the trap. She picked up the basket of food and the bundle of clothes and made her way slowly towards him.

The cottage was cramped and tiny, lit by only one small window. But in its light she saw Mrs Prosser, sitting in a rocking-chair by the smoking fire. There was a baby in her lap. The woman's eyes were red from weeping.

'You are welcome here, girl,' she said slowly. 'I want to thank you for what you tried to do for Dai. I know it was you that rescued him the first time he was caught. That was a brave act.'

Stella flashed a look at John, but he had seated himself on the edge on the table and was engrossed in whittling a stick for one of the small boys who crowded round his knees. Stella stared for a moment, watching his quiet patience as one of the children plied him with questions, registering the fact that the boys obviously knew him and liked him, before she turned back to Mrs Prosser with a shy smile.

'Have they let you see him?'

The woman shook her head, tears filling her eyes once more, and impulsively Stella knelt beside her, touching her hand. Then, gently, she took the baby into her arms and looked down at the sleeping face. 'He will be very proud of his father one day,' she said, cradling the tiny bundle. 'I'm sure Dai will be all right, Mrs Prosser. Mr Vivian is a clever man. He'll help him somehow. I know he will.'

Mrs Prosser's sad face broke into a smile. 'Yes, you're right, he'll help him somehow. He's given me his word to that,' she said.

They stayed some time in the cottage before John, consulting his watch, announced that they should leave. He did not speak to her until they were once more in the trap and heading back down the steep track towards the valley.

Then he glanced at her, a gleam in his eye. 'Your dress is filthy after sitting on the floor of that shack. Did you think it would help that poor woman to see you making a fool of yourself like that?' he said curtly.

Stella's eyes blazed. 'Don't you criticise me, John Vivian! You made me go there,' she cried. 'How I behaved when I was there is none of your business. If I want to talk to those children and play with them, that is my affair!' Her eyes narrowed. 'I seem to remember you yourself were making those boys a toy.'

She broke off, suddenly suspicious as she saw the hidden laughter in his eyes, and she felt her heart give an uncomfortable little lurch.

Desperately she turned away from him, staring up at the hillside, trying to compose herself. 'You are teasing me again, Mr Vivian,' she said stiffly.

'Of course I am,' he sounded unrepentant. 'You so easily fly to the attack!' His strong brown hands steadied the reins as a jack-rabbit bolted across the lane, making the pony dance and toss its head. Stella found herself watching his long supple fingers, staring at the dark hairs curling on the back of his wrists, and she felt a wave of longing sweep over her. Angrily she pushed the feeling away, brutally forcing herself to remember her pledge to her sister.

'You must have found it very annoying that Eliza could not come this morning,' she said in a tight little voice.

He glanced at her thoughtfully, his expression veiled. 'Not at all.' He clicked his tongue at the pony. 'This morning's excursion was for you alone. Had your sister been free to join us I would have taken her to see someone quite different. I have no shortage of poor clients from whom to extort my exorbitant fees.'

Her gaze flew to his, mortified, and was met by a look of humorous resignation. 'I don't think Eliza's presence would have comforted Janet Prosser,' he said gently.

'And mine did?' The question was torn from her unwillingly.

'Yours did.' He smiled at her. 'I owe you an apology. You really do care; I could see that.'

She felt the colour flood into her face. 'And you don't think I was doing it this time just to have myself singled out for attention,' she asked with a small smile. 'I suppose I should be flattered.'

He laughed. 'You should indeed. With the kind of attention you attract I should be terrified of being seen in your company.'

She could not help laughing. The thought of his being terrified of anything at all was too ridiculous.

Wistfully she looked down at her pale blue skirts, streaked with dust from the bare feet of the children who had climbed on her lap as she knelt on the muddy floor to play with them. 'It must be a relief to know that we shall soon be home, then, and you will be free of my company,' she said, unable to keep a sudden sadness out of her voice.

He drew the pony to a halt. Stella looked up in surprise. John was studying her face. The expression in his eyes was inscrutable. 'Does your engagement to Owen Morgan still stand?' he asked suddenly.

She blushed. 'Of course.'

'And you love him?' His voice was harsh.

'That is no business of yours,' she said tautly. She ached to tell him that she had never loved Owen, that her heart was his and that she was desperately seeking to end her betrothal, but she could say nothing. She was trapped.

'Miss Stella!' He reached across and put his hand on hers.
The touch of his fingers was like a brand, burning into her
skin. She stifled a little gasp as she tried to pull away from
him.

'Look at me. Can you look me in the eye and tell me you
love him?' he grated.

'Yes,' she cried desperately. 'I love him.'

He released her abruptly. 'I'm sorry. That is all I wanted
to know.' Picking up the whip he cracked it in the air over
the pony's ears, setting it into a brisk canter.

His expression was forbidding as she stole a glance at his
face, blinking away her tears. She could not guess at his
thoughts and it was with a tremor of fear that she realised he
was pulling the pony up once more as they turned into the
highway.

'What is it?' she cried, wretchedly. 'Surely there is no
need to stop again.'

He did not look at her. 'No need for you, perhaps,' he
said curtly. 'The pony, however, appears to be lame. I trust
it won't inconvenience you too greatly if I stop and examine
his feet.'

Without pausing for a reply, he swung himself out of the
trap and bent to pick up one of the pony's hooves.

Stella sat motionless for a moment, trying to control the
tears of mortification which were threatening to fall. Then,
unable to bear it any longer, she scrambled down to the
road. Her back to him, she fumbled in her reticule for a
kerchief and wiped her eyes.

John had taken the pony's foot on his knee and produced
a clasp-knife from his pocket. 'Hold his head, if you please,'
he said without looking up. 'There is a stone wedged here.'

She took the bridle obediently and gentled the animal
while John prised the stone loose. 'There.' He watched as
the pony tested its weight on the hoof. 'That should be all
right. I am obliged to you. I had forgotten you had such a
way with horses when they are frightened or distressed.'

Reminded so abruptly of their last encounter, Stella
blushed. She stared at him challengingly. 'I had hoped you
would not mention our last meeting, sir. It is something I
would rather forget,' she said with spirit.

He laughed. 'To forget the sight of a lady in such charming disarray would be hard,' he said mischievously. 'However, if it is your wish, I shall endeavour to do so—'

He broke off as a shout interrupted him, and they both looked round. Two riders were approaching at a canter, and almost at once Stella recognised her sister accompanied by Ianto.

Stella watched, her heart full of misgiving, as Eliza rode up, a picture in her rose-coloured habit on her immaculately groomed grey mare. The girl's face was sharp with anger as she saw Stella standing so close to John by the wheel of the trap.

'So. Papa thought you had come this way,' she said, dimpling prettily at John. 'When my music lesson was over, I thought I would ride to meet you. I hope you don't mind.'

John bowed, catching her rein as she stopped beside him. 'We are honoured,' he said. 'We were on our way back, when, as you see, the pony picked up a stone. I don't think he's lame, though.'

'I trust not.' Eliza looked hard at Stella. 'Has my sister been good company, sir?' she enquired with deceptive charm.

John smiled, easily. 'Indeed she has. I was very glad to have been able to take her with me. She proved a great comfort to my client.'

'Oh, she's a comforting sort of person.' Eliza loosed her foot from the stirrup and slid from her mount gracefully. 'As Mother Rebecca found last night.'

'*Eliza!*' Anguished, Stella caught her sister's arm. 'Please, there is no need to say anything.'

'No?' Eliza turned on her. 'I think you have forgotten our little agreement, Stella.'

She turned to John, who was watching them speculatively. 'There is something you should know about my sister, Mr Vivian,' she said.

He raised an eyebrow. 'Indeed,' he said smoothly. He was looking at her with shrewd attentiveness. Then he spun round and addressed Ianto, who was still mounted, hovering near them on George's cob. 'Take the mare and walk her up and down, if you please,' he said sharply, 'or she will take cold.'

'Now, Miss Vaughan,' he went on as Ianto retreated out

of earshot, dragging the unwilling grey behind him. 'What was it you wished to say?'

'Eliza,' Stella gasped. 'You cannot tell him—'

'I am sure that Mr Vivian will not pass this on to Papa, knowing the pain it would cause him, but I am equally certain he should know,' was the tart reply.

Stella felt herself go cold. She saw John's amused gaze rest on her for a moment, then he was once more looking at her sister.

'You mentioned Mother Rebecca,' he said quietly.

Eliza looked up at him, her soft blue eyes appealing. 'Stella saw him last night, in the garden,' she said triumphantly. 'They spent hours talking together, and then she let him kiss her.'

CHAPTER
TEN

STELLA'S HAND was on the trace, her knuckle white as she bit her lip miserably, waiting for his anger and his scorn to break over her head.

There was a moment's silence; then, when he spoke, it was to Eliza. 'Did she tell you this herself?' His voice was grave.

Eliza shook her head. 'She didn't have to. I saw them from my window in the moonlight.'

Stella, glancing up desperately, saw the sharpened interest in his face. He had not looked at her. His thoughtful gaze was still on her sister. 'And did you recognise him?' he asked softly.

Again Eliza shook her head. 'It was too far away. Why don't you ask her who it was?'

'I intend to.'

Why didn't he look at her? Why didn't he say anything to her? Stella could feel the pulse jumping in her throat.

'Just tell me one thing,' John went on, and Stella saw Eliza beginning to look uncomfortable beneath his intense concentration. 'How did you know it was Mother Rebecca?'

Eliza looked nonplussed for a moment. Then she smiled triumphantly. 'I guessed. And she admitted it. She's in love with him. That is why she's trying to break off her engagement to Owen Morgan!'

He looked at Stella then. His blue eyes narrowed. 'Is any of this true?' There was a hint of steel in his voice which made her quail. Beside her, the pony laid back its ears and rolled its eyes nervously; instinctively she soothed its neck, unable to tear her eyes away from the icy scrutiny which seemed to read her very soul.

In the distance she could hear the slow hoof-beats as Ianto returned, leading Eliza's mare. From the water-meadows the clear bubbling call of the curlew broke the silence. Ianto drew up discreetly about ten yards away, and she heard one of the horses snort and shake its bit.

Stepping away from the trap, she unconsciously raised her chin a little higher as she turned and beckoned Ianto forward. 'My sister likes to romance almost as much as I do, Mr Vivian,' she said, her voice tightly controlled. 'I can assure you I feel nothing but abhorrence for Mother Rebecca. Had I recognised him,' she hesitated, 'I would probably have told my father by now who he was.'

'Would you, now,' he said thoughtfully. 'I wonder.'

She couldn't breathe properly. It was as if a tight band constricted her chest as she moved towards the grey mare and raised her hand to its bridle. Her eyes were blind with tears. 'May I suggest,' she cried 'that you escort my sister home, sir. You obviously have a great deal to discuss with her. I shall ride back on my own.'

Ignoring her entangling petticoats, she threw herself up into the saddle. Conscious of John's hand reaching out to grab at the horse's bit, she wrenched the animal's head away and sent it thundering back up the road, leaving Ianto staring open-mouthed after her. She did not look back. Bending low over her neck, she whispered encouragement in the mare's ear, feeling the stride lengthen to full gallop, conscious of her pale blue skirts billowing crazily behind her as the scalding tears spilled over down her cheeks and mingled with the rippling mane.

Her only thought was to escape. To free herself from the cold despising stare of the man she knew she loved and who would think of her now with nothing but scorn and disgust.

The mare veered off the road, taking a sloping track which led gently up the hill and through a plantation of young oak trees, the leaves already gold beneath the misty sun. She was riding in the opposite direction from home, but she did not care. All she wanted was to be alone. She allowed the horse her head, letting the animal gallop through the fields, scattering sheep, while she clung like a burr to the saddle as the mare lengthened her stride to jump a brook; the small hooves scrabbled for a moment in the soft mud of the bank before she regained her footing and flew on.

Then, suddenly, Stella became aware of the sound of a second set of hooves thundering behind her. She glanced over her shoulder and saw that the chestnut cob was gaining on her, its rider bent low over its neck.

A spurt of anger knifed through her and she lashed the grey mare with the end of the rein. But it was no use. It was only moments before the cob drew alongside and she realised that it was John, and not Ianto, in the saddle.

'Pull up, you little fool,' he shouted at her. 'Do you want to be killed?'

'Leave me alone!' She dragged the mare round to the right and set off recklessly down the rough ground away from him, but he was beside her again in seconds. The mare's ears were pressed flat to her head as Stella's fear communicated itself to her and, the bit between her teeth, she bolted back down the steep rutted track which traversed the field, heading for the copse.

'Pull up, Stella!' John shouted again. The gap between the horses was closing once more. This time he leaned forward to try and grab the bridle, and Stella lashed furiously at his hand with the reins. She heard his exclamation as an angry weal appeared on his wrist, then, before she knew it, he had the reins of her horse, then his arm was around her and she was dragged bodily from the saddle and thrown, completely winded, in front of him across the withers of the cob as the mare, half crazed with fright, reared high in the air and gave a whistling scream of fury.

Beneath John's steadying hand the chestnut slowed to a walk and then stopped, blowing hard. Stella struggled feebly in John's grip, helpless in the undignified position until he should choose to release her, her bonnet gone, her hair hanging almost to the ground. John dismounted. Then his hands were on her waist and he lifted her down and set her on her feet. She pushed her hair out of her eyes and glared at him furiously. 'What did you do that for? If I choose to go for a ride it is none of your business. You might have killed us both, trying to stop me like that!'

He pulled the cob's rein over its neck and looped it to a stunted thorn tree. Then he turned, his hands on hips, and looked at her.

'I am not accustomed to people riding off in mid-conversation,' he said quietly. 'It is extremely ill-mannered. And may I remind you that I have told you not to ride anywhere alone at the moment. I do not expect advice like that to be ignored. You are a troublesome young woman. I was greatly tempted just now, when I held you across the saddle before me, to give you the spanking you deserve.'

Stella stepped back with a gasp. 'You wouldn't dare touch me!'

'I assure you I would, as no one in your family seems able to control you. Your headstrong behaviour is a danger to others as well as yourself. Now, may I ask why you felt it necessary to ride off in that childish manner in the first place. You cannot run away from the truth. Is that what you were trying to do?'

'You do not know what the truth is!' she cried stormily.

'Do you?' He put his hands on her shoulders, turning her to face him gently. 'You poor child. I wonder if you have any idea of what you've got yourself mixed up in?' He sighed in exasperation. 'Is it true that you've tried to break off your engagement?'

She nodded wretchedly.

'Then you are not in love with Owen Morgan?' He put his hand beneath her chin, gently raising her face so she was forced to look at him. 'Why did you lie to me earlier?'

'Because it was none of your business,' she whispered. His face so close to hers made her heart beat wildly, and her body was racked with longing as his fingers strayed idly to her cheek. 'And anyway Owen refuses to release me.' Her eyes filled with tears suddenly. 'We are to be married at Christmas.'

He swore under his breath. 'Your father knows how you feel about him?'

She nodded again. 'Please—' she hesitated, as she looked up into his stern face. 'Please don't tell them about last night. I didn't meet Mother Rebecca on purpose. He was hiding in the garden. He must have come to deliver that letter for Papa . . .'

'But you did kiss him.' John was watching her face through narrowed eyes as she stood before him, her long hair blowing across her face, her dress and cloak dis-

hevelled and streaked with dirt. She looked down, a
delicate blush mantling her cheeks. 'He forced me,' she said
so quietly he had to bend to catch the words. 'He is no
gentleman.'

He grinned suddenly. 'Did you expect him to be a
gentleman?' He raised his hand and gently brushed a strand
of her silky hair from her face. 'A man of his calling? A
rioter, an outlaw, an arsonist: a man of violence! And you
expected him to be a gentleman?'

'Don't laugh at me, John!' She pulled away from him, her
voice gaining in strength and dignity. She had used his first
name, but she did not notice as she went on, 'I was mistaken
in wanting to talk with him, I know that now. And I've paid
for it. He mocks me and derides me, just as you do, just as
Papa and George and Owen do.' She stared at him proudly.
'All I wanted to do was to help. Was that so very foolish?'
But her tears betrayed her, clinging to her lashes, spilling
down her cheeks, and suddenly his arms were round her
and he was holding her gently as she sobbed bitterly into his
shirt.

It was several moments before she realised what had
happened and tried to pull away, but he folded her more
closely against him, and after a half-hearted protest she
abandoned herself to the comfort of his embrace, snuggling
against him like a child, her arms creeping almost of their
own volition around his neck. He stared down at her
through half-shut eyes, which darkened to a shade of
indigo, then, with a muffled oath, he brought his mouth
down on hers. Her lips parted beneath his as with an eager
little cry she clung to him, her slim body pressed against his,
her hair a cloud of ebony silk blowing around them both as
the wind from the mountain brought the scent of sun-
warmed bracken and heather in a cool caress to surround
them.

Releasing her at long last, John stared down at her
enigmatically, his eyes still dark and inscrutable as he took
in her radiant face, her slightly parted lips, her long curved
lashes, still wet with tears. She was trembling slightly, not
daring to look up and meet his gaze.

'Mother Rebecca,' he said softly, 'has impeccable taste
when it comes to ladies!'

Her eyes flew to his, and met a look of triumphant mockery as he released her. He folded his arms and stood watching her as she gasped, backing away from him in horror and disbelief. 'What do you mean?' she whispered shakily. 'Why did you kiss me?' Humiliation and despair swept over her. 'Why did you hold me like that? You should not have done it!'

'You are right, Stella.' He looked anything but contrite. 'I shouldn't have done it. But neither, my dear, should you. Come, we must go back. Your father will want to know what has happened. I sent Ianto back in the trap with your sister.' He strode towards the cob. 'That pretty grey mare you snatched from Eliza will no doubt be back at home in her stable by now, so you will have to ride with me.'

'No!' She backed away from him. 'I am not going with you. Never.'

John turned towards her. 'You will come with me, Stella. I have wasted enough time on you this morning. Either you ride willingly or I put you across the saddle.' His voice was harsh as he brought the reins back over the cob's ears and led the animal up to her. 'So, which is it to be?'

She stared round desperately, looking for a means of escape, but his hand came down on her wrist and he pulled her against him. 'Well?' he said.

'John—' Her eyes pleading, she pushed him away. He did not attempt to restrain her. Suddenly he grinned. 'Don't tell me you are going to ask me to go hunting for your bonnet, Stella. You seem to have more than your share of misfortune with your hats and your horses!' His hands were on her waist before she could dodge him, and she found herself seated on the horse, looking down into his upturned face. 'I am afraid it will be more than obvious that you have sustained some kind of accident, my dear. A bonnet will not cover your sins this time,' he said as he pulled himself into the saddle in front of her. 'I suggest you hold on tightly and we will concentrate on getting you home.'

He chose the back roads and lanes, avoiding the town, fording the river near Glasbury, pushing the cob at a fast canter. She clung to him unwillingly, resting her cheek lightly against his back, every touch of his body a torment to her, reinforcing her burning humiliation.

Ianto was waiting for them in the yard. He frowned when he saw them, running to the cob's head. 'When the mare came home riderless, I thought Miss Stella must have fallen,' he said. 'Are you hurt, miss!'

John dismounted and turned to lift Stella down. 'She is only a little shaken,' he replied curtly. 'Where is Mr Vaughan?'

'Out, sir . . . The magistrate and Mr George rode out with Mr Morgan about an hour ago.'

Stella closed her eyes and breathed a little prayer of gratitude as John's hand steadied her elbow.

'Is Miss Eliza inside?' he asked.

'Yes, sir. She said you was to go straight in.'

Stella tried to free herself from his clasp, but he held her firmly as he guided her indoors. Eliza met them at the door of the parlour. Her eyes widened as she saw Stella's dishevelled appearance and tear-stained face. 'Oh, my Lord! Stella, did she throw you? Are you hurt, my dear?' Her anger forgotten, she flew to her sister as John led Stella to the sofa.

'Your sister has had a very lucky escape,' he said. 'The horse bolted, but there is no harm done. She is a little shocked, I think. But not hurt.' His eyes gleamed humorously as Stella raised her wan face to his.

John turned to Eliza. 'I think, Miss Vaughan, that the least said about this whole incident the better. We shall inform your father that you met us as you intended, and that we travelled back to the house together. I shall make sure that your groom understands and will say nothing. There is no need to upset your parents needlessly.' His expression grew stern. 'Just as there is no need for either of us to mention Stella's activities in the garden last night.' He studied Eliza's face. 'I know so loyal a sister would not wish to cause unhappiness unnecessarily.' He smiled, and Stella, watching from the sofa, saw Eliza smile back, radiant suddenly beneath his charm. He moved towards her and took her hand. 'Perhaps, Miss Vaughan, after I have called on you and your mother properly, one afternoon you would do me the honour of coming driving with me? In something a little more up to the mark than the firm's pony trap?' He raised Eliza's hand and brushed it with his lips.

Anguished, Stella tore her eyes away, unable to watch as he took his leave of her sister. Then he was standing before the sofa. She did not look up. Clenching her hands in her lap, she felt her cheeks warming as he looked down at her in silence.

'Take care of yourself, Stella Vaughan,' he said quietly. 'And remember, no more riding alone.'

With a small bow to each of them, he left the room.

Eliza was jubilant. 'Did you see him kiss my hand? And he intends to take me driving!' She pirouetted around the sofa. 'You made a complete fool of yourself, Stella!'

'I know,' Stella whispered through dry lips. She glanced up at her sister's happy face and forced herself to smile. 'But I'm getting used to doing that.' She pulled herself to her feet and made her way towards the door. 'Forgive me, Eliza, but I think I am going to lie down for a bit, I feel a little shaken.'

Blindly she made her way to her bedroom and threw herself down on the bed, her face pressed into the pillow. Through the window, she heard the distant scrape of hooves and then the rattle of wheels as the trap swept out of the yard and turned into the lane. In a moment the sound of hooves had died away, and John had gone.

The next few days passed in a haze of misery for Stella. She seldom saw her father or George, and Owen, much to her relief, had returned to Radnor, where some business on his father's estate needed his urgent attention. Pleading a headache, she kept to her room as much as possible, relieved that Eliza seemed content for the time being to leave matters as they were.

Her mother, however, was not so easily distracted. She had noted Stella's pale face and red-rimmed eyes with concern, convinced that the girl was pining for Owen, and finally insisted that Stella came downstairs to the parlour each morning to listen to Eliza reading while she took a hot restorative tisane to bring the colour back to her cheeks.

It was a Thursday morning that Stella was sitting wearily stitching at the lace collar of one of her gowns as Eliza read to them, when she happened to glance out of the window. It was misty, with the promise of some heat later, and the tall trees along the lane stood up to their waists in milky drifting whiteness. She could just make out the figure of one of the gardeners raking the wet clinging leaves off the lawn as the visibility cleared slightly, pierced by a ray of hazy sun. She watched him idly for a few minutes and, as she did so, caught sight of a rider cantering across the field beyond him, his horse breast high in the drifting mist. Something about the set of his shoulders made her throat constrict suddenly and she narrowed her eyes, trying to see more clearly, but the mist had thickened once more and he disappeared from sight. Minutes later, the door opened and the housemaid Peggy appeared with a note for Mrs Vaughan. Margaret read it carefully and then looked up in delight. 'Girls! This is from Lady Morgan. She is to call on us this afternoon!' She rose and moved across to Stella. 'My dear, you shall wear your slate blue, I think. It becomes you so well. And, of course, you must put on the brooch Owen gave you. She will certainly wish to see it.' Her gaze travelled to her elder daughter, who had stopped reading and was sitting motionless at the table. 'You should put on your prettiest gown, too, dear,' she said, her eyes softening a little as she saw the wistfulness of Eliza's expression.

Eliza was about to make a retort when there was a second knock on the door, and Peggy reappeared. She dropped a small curtsy.

'There's Mr Vivian called, ma'am. He wants to know if you are at home.'

On the window-seat, Stella was motionless. Her mouth went dry and her heart began to beat irregularly as she watched her mother peering quickly into the mirror and patting her lace cap into place.

'Show him in, Peggy, then bring some refreshment,' Margaret commanded, a little flustered as she turned back to the maid. She glanced at Stella, whose face had grown white as alabaster, and she frowned. 'Put your work away, Stella, do, and arrange these cushions.' She twitched the embroidered table-cloth into place, and threw a quick critical look around the room. Stella did not hear her. She was staring at the french doors. They had provided her with a way of escape before, but it was already too late. Peggy had reappeared in the doorway, and behind her stood John.

Margaret bustled forward. 'Mr Vivian, how very good of you to call,' she greeted him effusively.

Stella rose unsteadily to her feet, composing herself with an effort, but he did not look at her as he bowed first over Margaret's hand and then over Eliza's, greeting the latter with an especial warmth which sent a shaft of anguish into Stella's heart. Only then did he seem to notice her, half-hidden as she was in the curtained bay, and he stepped forward, holding out his hand with distant politeness. 'Miss Stella. How are you?'

She did not look up as his lips brushed her fingers, snatching her hand away, desperately trying to school her features into serene indifference, but he was already turning back to her mother, leaving her without a second glance.

'Forgive me for not calling on you sooner, Mrs Vaughan,' he said. 'We have been so busy at the office, but I made sure that at the very first opportunity I would come and visit you.'

He took his place next to Eliza on the sofa while Stella stiffly resumed her own hidden seat in the window, able to watch him unseen from her vantage-point. He was dressed in an immaculately cut coat and peg-top trousers, his boots showing no trace of mud or dust from his ride to the house. Her gaze strayed to his face, and she watched the animated features as he talked to Eliza, the intense blue of his eyes, caressing the girl as he talked, the mobile mouth which had so briefly and so devastatingly taken hers; the strong hands lying loosely linked upon his knee.

Then she realised suddenly that Eliza was staring at her, and she dragged her eyes away from John's face, glad to be able to rise, as Peggy returned with a tray, to clear a space for it on the table and busy herself with the glasses.

John glanced at her indifferently as she passed him to return to her seat. Then he turned to Margaret.

'My dear Mrs Vaughan. I did make a promise some time ago to take Miss Vaughan for a drive one afternoon.' He smiled down at Eliza. 'I wonder if you would permit it? These autumn days are so beautiful and I have the loan of an open carriage.'

'But of course! How delightful!' Margaret smiled triumphantly at her elder daughter. Then she collected herself
visibly. 'But, of course, I cannot allow Eliza to drive out
alone with so handsome a gentleman unchaperoned!' She
simpered at him ingratiatingly. 'Stella must accompany
you.'

'Mama!' Eliza broke out in protest, but Margaret was
adamant.

'I am sure Mr Vivian understands. I know Stella drove
with him the other day, but Stella is affianced and went with
Owen's knowledge and consent. I cannot allow you to do
the same. My goodness,' she sounded quite breathless.
'What would the county think!'

John glanced at Stella, and she thought she caught a
gleam of amusement in his eye. 'It would be the more
delightful for me to escort both the Miss Vaughans,' he said
gallantly. 'I shall look forward to it. Now, tell me, Mrs
Vaughan. You have had no more trouble, I trust, from
Rebecca and her daughters?'

Stella stiffened, clutching her hands together in her lap to
stop them trembling. Surely he would not betray her now?
But his attention was on Margaret, who had blanched at his
question. 'Thank the Lord, no. But my husband is beside
himself with worry in the effort to find the scoundrel.' She
shook her head sadly. 'You know the wretch has threatened
to burn this house,' she reached for her vinaigrette. 'My
nerves are all to pieces about it!'

'I saw one of his letters,' John observed grimly. 'Michaelmas, I think he said. The town will be distracted, of course,
with the fair, and he thinks to strike then. Has Mr Vaughan
had any further thoughts on defending the house?'

Margaret shrugged. 'We are to have the dragoons, but
you know that. And I believe some other militiamen are to
lie in wait in the fields around to try and entrap the man, but
I must confess I am terrified.' She fumbled for her handkerchief and held it to her eyes. 'I have begged Henry to allow
me to take the girls away—'

John nodded soberly. 'I think that would be wise. I'll
mention to him that the idea has my support. And now,' he
rose abruptly, 'forgive me, but I have another call to make.
Perhaps I could send round a note early next week to

suggest a day for our drive. Your servant, Mrs Vaughan; ladies.' And with that he withdrew.

There was a moment's silence as the door closed behind him, then Eliza and her mother began to chatter at once. Neither noticed Stella's silence as she slowly picked up her sewing once more and stared down at the lace collar with unseeing eyes. Only later, as Eliza was about to leave the room, did the girl approach her sister and stand before her, her eyes narrowed. She glanced at Margaret to make sure she would not overhear, then she declared, 'You are not coming on the drive too, Stella, do you hear? At the last minute you are going to be indisposed and I shall go alone!'

CHAPTER
ELEVEN

LADY MORGAN arrived promptly at three o'clock in her glossy barouche with her husband's coat of arms emblazoned on the doors. Descending with great dignity before the front door at Bryn Glas, she swept into the long drawing-room in a rustling taffeta afternoon gown of deep magenta.

The cheek she offered Stella was ice cold. 'So, you are to be my daughter, sweet child,' she murmured, looking Stella up and down before motioning her to sit beside her on the heavily upholstered sofa. 'How charming. I'm sure we shall be friends. My son speaks of you endlessly, as I am sure you know. And tells me what a perfect match you will be for him. And this is your sister?' She raised a lorgnette and surveyed Eliza, who had lowered herself gingerly into a buttoned chair beside her mother. 'And when are we to hear about your betrothal, miss? Can't leave it too long, you know, you being the elder gel! I was married and a mother by the time I was eighteen. It won't do at all to have your younger sister off before you; won't do at all!'

Stella's heart sank at her future mother-in-law's lack of tact as Eliza blushed an unbecoming crimson. 'I hope to announce something very soon myself, Lady Morgan,' she stammered defensively, throwing a pleading glance at her mother.

'Indeed?' Lady Morgan leaned forward in her seat, her face alert. 'Why, my dear Mrs Vaughan, you never told me that Eliza has a beau as well. But how exciting. May I know who it is?'

Margaret looked at her archly, her eyes sparkling. 'Well,' she said doubtfully. 'This must be completely between ourselves, dear Lady Morgan,' she said dropping her voice almost to a whisper. 'Even Mr Vaughan doesn't know as yet, but we have great hopes of Mr Vivian, Toby

Griffiths's new partner in Hay.'

Lady Morgan's mouth dropped open. 'John Vivian? The Earl of Ambleston's nephew? Well, I must say, you do surprise me. Not, of course, that he isn't about the most eligible bachelor in the whole of Wales, in some ways, but his reputation, my dear! It doesn't bear thinking about!'

There was a moment's intense silence, during which Stella's eyes anxiously met those of her sister. Eliza was sitting bolt upright, her cheeks still startlingly pink.

'What reputation?' she managed to whisper at last.

'Oh, my poor child. Didn't you know? He does the strangest things. You know of course that he is in some kind of employment—a solicitor, I believe. Well, over the last year he has been helping these dreadful Rebecca people when they've been arrested, arranging their defence, giving their families money, helping them in all sorts of ways. It is really quite disgraceful. Poor Lord Ambleston is, I believe, quite distracted by the whole affair. John is quite brilliant, so he manages to do all this quite legally, almost using the law against itself, or so I've heard.' She shrugged expansively.

Eliza had gone pale. 'He is a very caring man,' she eventually managed to say. 'I am sure he would not—could not—work for them unless he thought their cause was just.' She refused to meet Stella's eye.

Stella could hardly breathe. John believed in the Rebecca cause, just as she did. It was his money which would help Dai Prosser! Shaken, she dragged her attention back to Lady Morgan who was speaking once more, her voice lowered confidentially. 'My dear Mrs Vaughan, you said that Eliza's father does not yet know of the attachment? I must warn you that my husband, Sir Robert, would never countenance any plans of this sort for one of our daughters.' She shifted her bulk comfortably on the sofa. 'Although, of course, the fortune and the prospect of a title would militate in John's favour, I must agree. And fancy you, Eliza, winning him! He has, you know, quite apart from everything else, the reputation of being a veritable misogynist! The number of hearts he has broken is countless, yet his name has never been linked with that of any particular woman! But this is exciting. Tell me, how long have you known him?'

Margaret Vaughan had risen to her feet and, walking swiftly to the bell, she pulled it. 'Not long,' she replied over her shoulder. 'But there was an instant attraction. Eliza has so many admirers, of course, but I should certainly favour this one,' she added defiantly, 'should she decide to encourage him, whatever his political views may be. Ah, Megan, would you bring the tray now, please? Stella?' She turned to her younger daughter, anxious to divert attention from Eliza, who was looking dangerously near to tears. 'My dear, you are not wearing that beautiful brooch which Owen gave you. I'm sure Lady Morgan would have liked to see it.'

It was Stella's turn to blush as she dragged her thoughts away from John. She had searched the lawns and paths on several occasions, but to no avail. The brooch was nowhere to be found. 'Mama, the pin was loose,' she murmured. 'I was afraid I should lose it, so I asked Perry to take it back to the jeweller to be tightened.' She glanced uncomfortably at Lady Morgan. 'I said nothing to Owen in case he was upset, and I so hoped to have it back soon.'

It wasn't entirely a lie. The moment she, or one of the gardeners whose help she had enlisted, found the brooch, she would indeed send it back to have the clasp tightened.

The visit did not last long. Lady Morgan, it appeared, was on her way to dine at Llowes, but before she left she came back to the subject of John Vivian. 'I've been thinking about that gentleman,' she said, as she got up and began to draw on her gloves. 'If you wish, I shall write to his grandmother Lady Ambleston to enquire about John's prospects. As I recollect it, he is next in line for the title now that his poor father is dead, God rest his soul, and the earl a widower too, of course. And John is extremely wealthy in his own right.' She sighed loudly. 'Oh, it would be so delightful if he has at last decided to settle down! Perhaps it will distract from this foolishness of his over the Rebecca riots.' She offered her cheek first to Eliza and then to Stella, 'Then we could have a double wedding at Christmas. Would not that be heavenly!'

When Margaret Vaughan went up to Stella's room that evening she found the girl lying on her bed, her face flushed and feverish with crying. She sat down and felt her forehead with a cool hand, unable to conceal the worried frown on her face.

'What is it, Stella?' she asked gently. 'Can you not tell me, child?'

Stella turned her head away on the pillow, unable to prevent the tears from flowing once more. 'Nothing, Mama. I feel a little unwell, that is all.'

'Is it something to do with Owen?' Margaret's grey eyes moved thoughtfully over her daughter's face. 'I have feared for some time that maybe you were not as happy as you should be about the match.'

Stella felt a sudden blaze of hope. Sitting up, she stared at her mother, her hands gripping her fingers tightly. 'Mama, would you be very sad if I said I didn't want to marry Owen?'

But the naked shock and disappointment in her mother's face confirmed everything Eliza had said. She scrambled to her knees on the quilt and put her arms round Margaret's neck hastily. 'No, Mama. Don't look so sad, please. I didn't mean it. I do want to marry Owen. It is just that Christmas seems so soon . . .' Her voice trailed away as she tried desperately to hold back the tears which threatened to overwhelm her once again.

Margaret smiled with relief. 'It's natural, sweetheart, to be a little afraid. But Owen's a good man. And the connection is so important for your father. You do see that, don't you?' She looked pleadingly at Stella. Then she gave a little laugh. 'You know, I had begun to wonder if you were falling a little in love with Mr Vivian. Thank goodness there is no question of that. Imagine, all this time the man had been defending the rioters! And never a word about it!' She sniffed. 'You would think Toby Griffiths would have mentioned it to your father. Really, I am not at all sure now whether he would do for Eliza, even if he would have her. He sounds as though he is not entirely a steady sort of gentleman.' She stood up with a sigh and shook out her skirts thoughtfully. 'Not that we shall see him again for a while. Your father has agreed that I should take you and Eliza away next week. We shall remain with our cousins in Hereford until after Michaelmas, when this whole terrible threat from the Rebeccas is over. After that I shall think again about Eliza and Mr Vivian.'

Stella watched her mother close the door behind her, listening to the light swish of her skirts as she walked away down the landing. Then she lay back on the bed and put her arm over her eyes.

The news that John disliked women had come as no surprise. That he sympathised with the Rebeccas was harder to credit, when everything he had said and done had led her to believe the opposite. Or had that, too, been merely part of his mockery of her? She turned to her pillows and punched them miserably with her fist. No. She would not care if they never saw him again.

She must not care. For her future belonged to Owen.

Owen himself appeared at the weekend. The bright cold weather had broken, and a westerly gale lashed up the valleys, tearing leaves from the trees and drenching the world with a penetrating wall of rain. Stella was glad that the weather prevented them from walking together in the garden, or riding, but it was obvious that Owen was determined to speak to her alone. At last, before dinner, he cornered her and led her into her father's study, shutting the door firmly behind him.

'I asked your papa if I might borrow this room, Stella, for a quick word with you,' he said, catching her hand and pressing it ardently to his lips. 'I have been looking for the opportunity to speak to you all day.'

She forced herself to smile. 'But, Owen, we have been together all day.'

'With your mama and your sister and George. Stella, there is something I want to ask you.' He frowned unhappily.

She managed to free her hand and walked over to the fire, drawing her thin cashmere shawl more closely round her shoulders as a gust of wind down the chimney blew a puff of smoke back into the room.

'What is it?' she said.

'Why did you tell my mother that you had sent the brooch I gave you away for repair?'

She turned and looked at him, a catch of fear in her

throat. 'She asked to see it.'

'And you could not show it to her because you did not have it.'

'I explained to her what had happened—'

'That the pin was loose. She told me. That much was true, Stella. But you hadn't sent it away. You had dropped it in the garden.'

She gasped. 'How do you know?'

'Because I found it.' He groped in the pocket of his ivory satin waistcoat and produced a wisp of twisted paper and held it out to her.

She unwrapped it with shaking hands. The brooch was caked with mud.

It was a while before she plucked up the courage to look into his face. 'I have been looking everywhere, Owen, and I asked all the servants and the gardeners, everyone, to search for me. Where did you find it?'

'When, would be a more pertinent question.' He walked across to her father's desk and sat on the corner of it, still looking at her gravely. 'Do you remember you said that you had lost your comb in the garden? It struck me then that it was strange to be so worried about an ordinary tortoiseshell comb. I had noticed your hair at dinner, you see, and then I remembered that, when I saw you in the parlour after all the unfortunate business that night, the brooch had gone from your gown and the silk was torn as though it had been pulled off. I went out to search, and by chance I found it.'

'But why didn't you tell me?' Her heart had begun to thud as she stared at the dulled encrusted ornament in her hand.

'I wanted to see if you were going to tell me you had lost it. And I wanted to work out in my own mind the significance of where I found it.'

She looked up, startled. 'Where did you find it?'

'Trodden into the earth beneath the old ash tree out there. Trodden into the footprint of a man's riding-boot.'

Catching her breath, she felt her colour rising. 'One of the gardeners, perhaps, or George—'

'Perhaps, Stella. You must know. I found your footprints there too, and plenty of his with them. You two must have spoken, I think, for some time.'

He slipped off the desk and walked stiffly over to the cabinet in the corner. Opening it, he withdrew a decanter and a glass and poured himself a small brandy. 'Forgive me, Stella, but this is very painful for me. You must realise that I have to draw my own conclusions from the evidence I saw. I am not going to ask to whom you spoke in the garden, or why. Under the circumstances I would rather not know, but I must . . .'—he took a sip from the glass and closed his eyes for a moment, 'I must,' he said again, 'have your assurance that you will not repeat your assignation.'

Stella could feel herself trembling all over as she forced herself to meet his troubled gaze. 'You have that assurance, Owen. But it was not an assignation, I swear it. I didn't know anyone was out there—'

'No,' he interrupted. 'Don't tell me, Stella, please. I don't want to know anything, *anything*, about it. Come, let us join the others in the drawing-room.' He put down the glass. 'If I might have the brooch back, I shall have it repaired and cleaned for you and then perhaps you can show it to Mama the next time you see her.' He gave her a thin smile and ushered her to the door.

Dinner was served promptly, and Stella, seated between her brother and Owen, found herself glancing apprehensively at the circle of candlelit faces around the table. George, Eliza, Owen—all knew now, or guessed, whom it was she had met in the garden that night. How was it possible that her father remained in ignorance of it? She scanned Henry Vaughan's face as he bent over his plate, but his expression was relaxed and jovial as he regaled them with an account of a poaching case over which he had presided that morning.

It was only after the gentlemen had joined the ladies for tea, much later, that George broached the subject she had been dreading.

'Mother Rebecca's been pretty quiet lately, Owen. Do you reckon, like Papa, that it wasn't after all locally-inspired trouble, or do you think she's saving up her strength to come here?'

Owen's eyes strayed to Stella's face. 'I hope for all your sakes that it is the former. When do your dragoons take up guard?'

'Michaelmas Day.' George rose to throw another log on the fire. 'If he comes, we'll be ready for him. I just wonder whether we have anything to fear now. It may well be that he found too much opposition here and decided to move back west.'

'Let us hope you are right.' Owen leaned back in his chair, flinging his arm across its back. 'Hark at that wind and rain. Perhaps the chap just likes to keep his petticoats dry!' The general shout of laughter that greeted his remark almost drowned the sound of a knock at the door.

Perry, his face white, peered round it before stepping hesitantly into the room.

'Mr Vaughan, I wonder if I might have a word, sir. Outside,' he said. He was plainly agitated.

Henry opened his mouth to protest, then, with a second glance at his butler's face, he stood up. There was complete silence in the room as the door closed behind them.

Then George cleared his throat. 'Some crisis in the servants' hall, no doubt,' he said. 'Mama, has cook been having the vapours again?'

Margaret was standing, anxiously twisting her handkerchief between her fingers. 'If she had, Perry would deal with it,' she said. 'Besides, he would hardly interrupt our evening to bother Henry about it—' She broke off as her husband reappeared in the doorway. 'What is it?' she whispered. 'What has happened?'

Henry Vaughan's face was grey as he stared tight-lipped around the room. 'Owen,' he said at last. 'It appears that your prediction that Rebecca likes to keep her feet dry is lamentably wrong. She has been out tonight. The toll-house on the Brecon Road has been burned to the ground . . .' He paused, with a glance at his wife. 'My dear, I'm sorry, but you'll have to know. It appears that the toll-keeper and his son were both most brutally murdered.'

CHAPTER
TWELVE

FOR A MOMENT, Stella thought she was going to faint. She was vaguely conscious of her mother lowering herself into a chair by the fire, her face immobile with shock, then of Eliza bending over the swooning figure, a vinaigrette in her hand, chafing Margaret's wrists. No one was paying any attention to her as she gripped the arm of the sofa, her nails tearing at the soft brocade, her eyes fixed on her father's face.

'How did Perry hear?' George had risen to his feet, his tanned cheeks white.

'A message from Glynn Williams. They went straight to him for help, as he was nearest. The dragoons are on their way and also reinforcements from Hay. Perry says there is a general outcry against the murder. The toll-keeper was a popular fellow, and witnesses say he was gunned down in cold blood by Rebecca's own hand.'

Eliza straightened, letting her mother's wrist fall. Her eyes met Stella's steadily, and they were full of anger. 'Well,' she said, 'what have you to say about this?'

'I?' Stella stammered.

'Yes, you, who support the cause of these poor defence-less rioters.' Her voice was heavy with irony. 'You, Stella, who find Mother Rebecca such a romantic hero. What do you say now?' She left her mother's side and walked slowly forward until she was standing immediately in front of Stella, her eyes blazing: 'I think the time has come, Stella, for you to make a decision, don't you? Just whose side are you on?'

'Eliza, that is enough!' Henry Vaughan roared at his elder daughter. 'Leave your sister alone. She knows nothing of any of this.'

'Nothing!' Eliza retorted. 'She knows a great deal!'

'Eliza, please.' Stella jumped up, seizing her sister's arm.

'Remember our agreement. Remember what we said—'

Eliza snatched her arm away. 'I don't believe what you are saying, Stella! You would still protect him, knowing that he is a murderer, a cold-blooded murderer?'

'Eliza!' Henry stepped forward threateningly, but his daughter swung round on him.

'Ask her! Ask her what she knows, Papa. Oh, I know she's always been your darling, and your favourite, but she's been lying to you. Ask her the name of Mother Rebecca!'

There was a stunned silence. Dimly, Stella was aware that Owen had moved to her side. She stared round desperately at the circle of accusing faces.

'I don't know,' she cried. 'I don't know who he is.'

· 'You do know, Stella. You must know,' Eliza persisted coldly. 'You spent long enough in his arms in the garden. I can't believe you can kiss a man on the lips and not know his identity!'

Margaret's small shocked cry of protest was drowned by a roar from her husband.

'Eliza, you will withdraw that remark!'

'Why?' White-lipped, Eliza stood over her sister, her fists clenched, as Stella shrank back on the sofa. 'Why, when it's the truth? My sister is a flirt, Papa, and it's time you recognised the fact.' Her eyes sparkled with tears. 'No man is safe from her. It's time you knew it too, Owen, before you tie yourself to someone who is no better than a . . . a . . . loose woman!' And in a sudden burst of sobbing she ran to her mother and, falling on her knees, buried her face in Margaret's lap. Stunned to silence, Margaret rested a white beringed hand gently on the girl's hair.

Stella had not dared to raise her eyes. She could feel Owen close beside her, holding his breath, and she tensed, waiting for him to explode with anger.

When he spoke at last, however, his voice was calm. 'Eliza appears to be somewhat overwrought, Mrs Vaughan. Perhaps it would be better if she were to leave us and retire to her room.'

He put his hand gently on Stella's shoulder.

She stiffened, and at last looked at him.

'Yes, yes, of course.' Margaret bent forward and shook

Eliza gently. 'Go up, dear. Do. Go up and call Megan to give you a draught.'

'It's not I who need physicking, Mama,' Eliza retorted. 'Perhaps Stella should have something to bring her to her senses!'

'I think you should go, Eliza,' Owen repeated gently. 'What I have to say will only distress you further.'

'Owen, if you have something to tell us, please do so,' Henry Vaughan snapped, his unfailing courtesy worn thin at last. 'This whole business has gone on long enough. If my daughter—either of my daughters—knows anything, I wish to be appraised of it. Now.'

Stella felt the gentle pressure of Owen's fingers on her shoulders and drew back further beneath them.

'I believe I know the identity of Mother Rebecca,' he said slowly. 'And I regret to say that I have reason to suspect that Stella knows as well. If she is not prepared to tell you, I am.'

Stella tried to rise. 'I don't know,' she protested in anguish, but Owen pushed her back on the sofa. Then, releasing her, he walked over to the fire and turned to face the others. 'I believe it is our friend John Vivian.' His voice was very low.

There was a long silence in the room, then Eliza let out a scream. 'That's not true. It's not . . . It's not.' Tears were flooding down her cheeks. 'He wouldn't . . . He couldn't . . .' Stumbling to her feet, she ran towards the door.

'No, it's not true,' Stella echoed her. She rose and stared at Owen, clear-eyed. 'It is not true, Owen. I would have known—'

Henry Vaughan shook his head. 'No, Owen. I admit he's implicated, and pretty deeply, from what I hear from Toby Griffiths, but he's kept strictly within the law. He works for these people, but he hasn't sunk so far as to ride with them.'

'I think he has,' Owen repeated quietly. 'And although it pains me greatly to say so, I think Stella warned him the other day of the trap we set for them at the toll.'

'No!' she cried. 'No! I saw John, but it was by accident, you know it was. He's not Mother Rebecca, I swear it. He's not!'

Owen stared at her coldly. 'I wonder how sure you can be of that.'

'You slut!' Eliza screamed at her suddenly. 'No wonder you were so anxious I shouldn't have him. You had been making love to him! You wanted him for yourself! Pretending you didn't know who was kissing you, pretending you were blindfolded. Oh, I *hate* you!'

'Eliza!' Henry thundered at her. 'It is not Vivian! I refuse to believe it. Damn it, the man was here, he offered to help!' He shook his head. 'But this conjecture hardly matters. We'll have this Rebecca soon enough and then the whole world will know the thieving murderer's identity for certain. Oh, go to your room, girl, if you can't stop snivelling!' He rounded on Eliza.

Stella had not moved. She was staring miserably at Owen.

'You're wrong,' she whispered faintly. 'It's not John. It's not. He would not kill.'

George had been standing open-mouthed at his father's side, but now suddenly his arms were round her. 'Poor little sister.' He turned to Owen. 'I don't believe it is John Vivian, either. That's a mad suggestion. He was with us at the Williamses' that night the Rebeccas took Stella. That gives him an absolute alibi. I'm sure he has a dozen others. I can guess your motive for trying to implicate him,' he glanced down at Stella, 'but you're wrong. I'd swear it.'

Owen shrugged, throwing himself down in a chair. 'All right. I'm sorry. The man is obviously above suspicion, so forget it. As your father says, there is little point, anyway, in speculation. We'll wait until we have him in chains, then no disguise will hide him.'

'And we'll have him in chains tonight!' Henry reached for his cup, set hastily on the mantelpiece when he had left the room, drained the cold tea, and looked round.

'George, Owen. We must ride out now and give assistance. The more men who hunt these fiends down, the sooner we'll have them behind bars. Margaret, my dear, forgive us, but you can see that you'll be perfectly safe here. George and Owen and I will ride at once to join the search.'

Margaret was shaking visibly. 'But Henry, the danger! They have already killed . . .'

'We shall be perfectly safe, woman. The fellow is out-numbered a hundred to one with the police and the soldiery.' He looked over his shoulder and lowered his voice. 'Take care of the girls, my dear. I shall speak to Stella later.' And with that he strode out of the room, followed by Owen and George. The former had not so much as glanced at Stella again.

The three women stood in complete silence after the men had left, listening to the rattle of the rain against the window. Then, suddenly, Eliza broke out into noisy sobs once more. 'How could you, Stella? How could you! You let a murderer touch you!'

Stella looked at her sister numbly, without seeing her. Mother Rebecca, who had held her in his arms and talked to her of justice, who had laughed, and stroked her hair, Mother Rebecca, so righteously committed to his cause, was nothing but a murderer and a thief. And just how sure was she that it was not John Vivian? She thought of the touch of his lips, his hands on her body, the deep, husky voice; and she shivered violently.

For a long moment she stood there, listening to Eliza's sobs, then, woodenly, she began to move towards the door.

Neither woman made any attempt to stop her as she went out and closed the door gently. The bedtime candles were ready at the foot of the stairs as usual, and automatically taking one, she lit it, and began to mount towards her bedroom. But she knew already that she would not be safe there. She did not have the key to her door and Eliza would be bound to follow her. Hardly realising where she was going, she turned away towards the servants' attics and the long-disused nursery wing. There she took refuge at last in the dusty day nursery, where the windows, bare of curtains now, threw the reflections of her candle back across the floor and up the walls to the sloping ceiling which was crossed and looped with spiders' webs. Up here, beneath the roof, she could hear the batter and splutter of the rain as it poured down the slates and gurgled into the gutters, driven by a gusty wind. She shivered violently, nearly dropping the candle, but knowing that Eliza would not think to look for her there, she stayed where she was. Setting the candlestick down on the scrubbed oak nursery table, she wandered across the room, pulling her thin shawl more closely around her shoulders.

In the corner stood the old chipped rocking-horse which had taught all three of them the first faltering rudiments of riding. She touched the cold wooden neck gently. His mane had nearly all gone, leaving only wisps of faded hair, and his once-beautiful red bridle had cracked and bleached in the sun to a pale beige. She pushed him gently, and was startled by the movement and the loud anguished squeaking as he bucked back and forth, his shadow huge and real against the wall.

She remained there for a long time, her mind a whirl of images. Mother Rebecca, John Vivian, Owen—the three figures merging and separating through the mist of her tears. Miserably, she slumped to the floor at the horse's feet, leaning against the huge high-curved rocker, and closed her eyes.

A distant roll of thunder woke her. The guttering candle had burned down to a stub. Almost too stiff to move, she pulled herself to her feet, collected the dying candle, and let herself out of the cold nursery. Shivering uncontrollably, she made her way down the steep flight of stairs towards her room. The corridor was in darkness and the house completely silent as, cautiously, she opened her door. Then she stopped dead. A branch of candles burned brightly on the chest by the window, and her father was seated in a chair by a blazing fire. There was a glass of brandy on the mantelpiece before him. Taking in the scene at a glance, Stella hesitated in the doorway, but it was too late to retreat. Her father had swung to face her, his eyes dark with anger.

'About time! I've been waiting an hour to speak to you,' he roared. 'I never thought a child of mine would betray my trust, betray everything I stand for, as you have done. I am amazed by your foolishness. Completely amazed!'

Stella had not moved. In her hand the candle-flame went out in a trail of acrid smoke.

'Papa, I told you. I do not know who he is,' she said listlessly.

'No!' He stood up, towering over her. 'Yet you meet him in the garden, and allow him to maul you like some common . . .' he restrained himself with difficulty. 'Stella,

Stella. How could you be so foolish?' He gazed at her in angry despair. 'Have you learned now that your good Rebecca is nothing but a vile criminal, or do you still hanker after him?'

She shrugged miserably. There was no point in arguing. He would not believe she had not encouraged him. 'I've learned, Papa.'

'Good. Now,' he glared at her with renewed ferocity, 'I'm giving you one more chance. Are you prepared to show me their hideout in the mountains?'

'I don't know where it is. I was blindfolded. I never saw the way there,' she cried. 'Papa. I swear to you—'

'And I don't suppose you've been out of the house for the last few hours either?'

She frowned, puzzled by the question. 'Papa? I don't understand. No.'

'You understand well enough. You went to try and warn him; him or one of his followers!'

'Papa—'

'What did you say to him? "Half the county is hunting for you, Mother dear!"' he mimicked cruelly. 'I'm surprised he hadn't guessed that already.'

'Papa, I haven't been outside—'

'You rode out shortly after us. Perry saw you on a horse—'

'Not I, Papa. I swear it.' She was trembling violently. 'I've been up in the nursery—'

'The nursery!' he exploded. He thumped the table with the flat of his hand. 'Stella, my patience is exhausted. You were seen leaving. On Cariad.'

She could feel little snatches of panic mounting in her throat as she stared at him. 'Papa, you must believe me—'

'I am sorry, Stella, but I can no longer believe anything you say. Somehow this man has gained control of your head as well as your heart. I thought you had seen sense when you realised that he was nothing but a vile murderer, but it appears even that cannot sway your allegiance to him. I very much doubt now whether I should even attempt to save you from the consequences of your actions.' He sighed loudly and picked up his glass. 'You will remain in your room, Stella, until we have them all behind bars. Then and only then shall I decide what to do with you.' He reached into the pocket of his coat and produced his house-keys. 'For now, I suggest you go to bed.' Without another word he turned on his heel and strode from the room, pulling the door behind him. She was not even surprised to hear the sound of the lock.

Staring round through a haze of tears, Stella did not move for several minutes. Her father had left the candelabrum, and its light and that of the brightly burning fire gave the room an almost cheerful appearance, but she did not see it. She saw nothing as she moved towards the grate and sank to her knees before it, holding out her chilled hands to the flames. Then, miserably, she began to cry.

She dozed off eventually, her head cradled on her arms on the seat of the velvet chair by the fire. When she awoke she was cramped and cold; the fire had burned down and the candles were smoking. She stared at them, overwhelmed with unhappiness, as she stretched out her stiff arms. Then she heard again the slight sound from the door that must have awakened her. A quiet scratching from the keyhole, and then at last the faint rattle as the key slipped home and turned. She scrambled to her feet apprehensively as the latch moved, and she watched the door swing open. A small figure slipped silently into the room.

'Megan?' Stella gasped. 'What is it?'

The girl raised her finger to her lips. 'Bring your wrap, Miss Stella, and come down quickly,' she whispered.

'But why?' Stella stared at her puzzled, her heart beating rapidly as she scrutinised the girl's pale, frightened face.

'It's Mr Owen, he wants you to come down and speak to him, Miss, secret-like.' The girl glanced over her shoulder. 'He's worried about your Papa thinking you're with the Rebeccas. He didn't want to come upstairs to see you, that wouldn't be proper, so he said he'd wait out back. You must come quick!' She was in a fever of impatience.

Hope flooded through Stella, and she felt her heart lighten. 'Where is my father?' She gathered up a thick shawl and flung it round her shoulders. Then she hesitated.

'He's gone away back to the town with Mr George. Oh, please hurry!' Megan's voice cracked with anxiety. 'Mr Owen is waiting.'

Stella felt a quick surge of joyful relief. Owen, at least, still cared, still believed in her in spite of everything. He would know it wasn't she who had ridden out on Cariad; she would make him believe her, make him understand. Holding her breath, she tiptoed out into the corridor and waited while Megan carefully relocked the door. The girl appeared to be holding her father's key-ring and, as Stella watched, she slipped it out of sight beneath her apron; then she picked up the candlestick that had been put down outside the door and began to hurry towards the back stairs.

The kitchens were in darkness, save for the glowing range, and Stella did not at once see the two men standing in the shadows by the door. They were both muffled in scarves and dressed in dark trousers and jackets. When she did see them, she stopped with a little gasp of fear, but Megan had closed the door behind her and was standing, her back to it, the candle in her hand. 'This is Miss Stella,' she said quietly to the men. Her voice had become suddenly hard.

One of them stepped forward. He was grinning. 'So. Magistrate Vaughan's beautiful daughter. You are coming with us, miss. Quickly now and quietly.'

Stella backed away. 'What do you mean? Where's Owen?'

'Owen, is it?' The man chuckled. 'He's ten miles from here by now, girl.'

Stella found she was breathing in tight little gasps, her heart beating wildly with fear. 'I don't understand you. I'm not going with you. I'm no use to you.'

'Oh, I think you will be. I think you're going to be very useful.'

From behind her, Megan made a little sound of impatience in her throat. 'For the Lord's sake hurry, Lloyd, will you? Someone might come.'

Stella turned on her. 'Megan, how could you—' It was all she managed to say. The two men stepped forward and, while one held her fast, the other forced a woollen scarf into her mouth to prevent her screaming. She felt a rope tightening around her arms and then she was lifted off her feet. Through her terror she heard a low exchange of words as the second man spoke to Megan, and the sound of a quick kiss, then she was outside in the icy rain with them, and the door had closed silently on the warm kitchen. The last thing she heard was the heavy bolt being shot back into its slot.

She was carried at a run across the yard and out into the lane. There was no sound from the dogs, and the stables seemed deserted. The man in whose arms she lay carried her effortlessly, only stopping when they reached the gate, over which the other man vaulted, then she was passed to him and lowered gently to the ground. Two horses were tethered in the intense darkness in the lee of a hazel copse.

The ground was wet and muddy, and the wind drove the rain through her shawl, soaking her to the skin. The wool in her mouth sickened and choked her, and already her arms were deadened from the tight rope which had been wound around her waist, pinioning her. Half-fainting, she felt herself lifted on to a saddle in front of the taller of the two men. An arm locked around her, and the horse set off at a canter down the field as another distant roll of thunder rumbled around the horizon. The rain lashing her face, blinding her, as it stung her eyes and ran down her cheeks to mingle with her hot tears. Neither man spoke, nor did they slow down until they reached the river. The level of the Wye had risen, and the brown tide swirled around the horses' hocks as they forded it, loose reined, in the teeth of the gale. The crossing seemed to take for ever, but at last they were safely across and riding up the hillside towards the woods which nestled in the folded foothills of the mountain.

The wind roared through the trees, funnelling up the slopes with vicious speed, and the horses pecked resentfully as they made their way up the dark slippery pathways. Stella had no doubt where they were taking her, but she had ceased to care. Her terror had rendered her almost unconscious and she slumped helplessly against the man's shoulder, her eyes closed, oblivious of the cold and the wet and the roar of the wind, or the changing note of it when they left the woods and rode on to the bare mountainside where the few stunted thorn trees bent before it as dark tortured landmarks in the black of the night.

The horses stopped at last at the gate in the stone wall which bounded the small shepherd's house where she had been brought before, although she did not recognise it. The second man dismounted and led his horse through, then he pulled Stella down from the saddle, supporting her when she would have fallen. 'Put the horses in the shelter, by there,' he shouted to his companion. 'I'll take the girl in.' The wind whipped the words from his lips and tore them away into the dark.

He swung Stella to face him and lifted her in his arms as, opening her eyes at last, she stared terrified around her.

'So, you've woken up!' he said gruffly as he began striding through the small muddy yard. 'Just as well, I'd say.'

Reaching the door in the lime-washed wall, he kicked it open, and ducking his head beneath the low lintel he carried her inside.

The silence and warmth of the room was intense after the whine of the icy wind. As the man set her on her feet, she just had time to see that they were alone, before he pushed her towards the fire. 'Warm up, girl, while you can,' he said, not unkindly, and gave her a grin. Then he turned, and let himself out once more into the dark.

With her arms still bound, and trembling with fear, she had taken only two steps into the room before her legs collapsed beneath her and she found herself falling to her knees on the bare flagstones, her sobs muffled by the choking gag.

At that moment, the door beside the huge chimney opened and John Vivian strode into the room. His face was a white mask of anger.

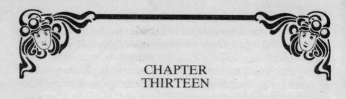

CHAPTER
THIRTEEN

'Good evening, Stella,' he said softly. 'Still riding impetuously into the mountains, I see, in spite of my warnings.'

He smiled grimly as he saw the anger flare in her eyes and, arms folded, he stood looking down at her, for a moment, without speaking. Then he laughed out loud. 'What a blessed thing is a silent woman! I'm surprised some sort of bridle is not issued with every wedding-ring in church!' He reached into his belt and pulled out a knife. Ignoring the look of terror which crossed her face and the impotent scream which rose, but was stifled in her throat, he stooped behind her, with his fist clenched round the handle of the knife.

She closed her eyes and waited, but the expected blow did not come. He merely slid the blade beneath the rope which bound her, and with one sharp flick severed it. Then he unknotted the scarf behind her head and pulled away the gag.

As she gasped for breath, painfully rubbing her arms to restore the circulation, he went back to his position before the fire. He, too, was soaked to the skin, his hair glistening with rain. He wore trousers and boots and a white linen shirt, open to the waist, which showed a broad chest covered with black curly hair. As he replaced the knife in his belt, she raised her eyes stormily to his face, anger overcoming her fear.

'I didn't believe that you were Rebecca—I should have known better!' she cried. She struggled to her feet and took a step towards him, shaking out her soaking skirts. 'And you are nothing but a common murderer as well! But, of course, a man of your sort would be capable of anything!'

He folded his arms. His smile had vanished. 'And what is a man of my sort?' he asked grimly.

'A . . .' She hesitated, unable to find the words. 'A two-faced, cynical impostor. Pretending to be an honest man, when all the time . . .' She stopped breathlessly,

'When all the time I was an outlaw and a rebel,' he prompted. 'And are you not afraid of me, Stella, knowing of what I am capable? Don't you wonder why I have had you brought here once more?'

She felt herself go pale, but she managed to keep her voice steady. 'Nothing would surprise me,' she said defiantly. 'But you won't dare to hurt me. Too many people know who you are.'

'Ah yes, Owen Morgan again. It seems to me that my reasons for disliking that gentleman increase hourly. How fortunate that you managed to persuade him that his suspicions were ridiculous.' He grinned maliciously. 'And how sad for you. You must not underestimate me, Stella. I dare anything for my cause. If I needed to set an example by hanging you from your father's stable clock, make no mistake about it, I would do so. I've had you brought here to make use of you, and use you I will.'

She gasped as a fresh shock of fear hit her. 'You are going to kill me, then?' she managed to whisper.

He was staring at her thoughtfully. 'No, I'm not going to kill you,' he said after a long pause, his expression softening slightly. 'You are too valuable. I intend to use you to persuade your father to help us. The thought of what might be about to happen to you will be enough to make him rethink his attitude. And in that he will have the considered help of John Vivian, that respected if misguided solicitor.' He smiled grimly once more. 'Your father does not believe that I could be so vile as to be a Rebecca, and you will not be there to disabuse him. I shall be the shocked and sympathetic go-between, the carrier of the message from the sincere but desperate leader of the men who hold his daughter.'

'But you can't keep me here!' She looked round wildly. 'They'll find me. If you let me go, I'll talk to Papa. I promise—'

'You promise!' he broke in. 'You've had your chance to persuade him, Stella, and you failed. Now you will stay here and I shall do the persuading. I'm very good at that, remember.'

She blushed violently as his gaze slid over her body, remembering his intimate caresses. Furiously, she turned away from him, hugging her wet shawl to her, mortified by her body's shameless response as she felt the quick flare of desire through her fear.

'Go and persuade him, then,' she said, biting back her tears of anger and humiliation. 'See what he says. Just so long as you leave me alone!'

Her gown and shawl were heavy with clinging moisture, and she was beginning to shake with cold as the water dripped round her feet on the flags. She longed to approach the fire, but he stood between her and the warmth, watching her through narrowed eyes. She was infuriated to see laughter in his face.

'Come to the fire, Stella,' he commanded. 'It will serve no purpose to either of us if you contract an inflammation of the lungs.' He turned and pushed a smouldering log back into the hearth with his foot. A shower of sparks lit the blackened stones of the chimney, and she felt a wave of heat reach out to her chilled bones.

'Thank you, but I am all right here,' she said with as much dignity as she could muster.

'You are far from all right,' he said. He strode across to a low wooden chest and, throwing back the lid, produced a couple of old blankets. 'May I suggest you remove your dress and wrap yourself in these. And take off those ridiculous slippers and put your feet on the fender. Here, take this chair.' He pulled forward the chair in which he had been sitting the first time she had met him as Rebecca, standing it temptingly near the warm blaze.

She hesitated. She had no desire to freeze to death, but the thought of approaching him made her throat constrict with fear. Cautiously she held out her hand for one of the blankets and, dropping her shawl, pulled the rough wool round her gratefully.

He laughed out loud. 'You once told me, Stella, that your sister was a paragon of virtue. From the way you clutch that blanket round you, I would say you are trying to outshine her in modesty. Which is very foolish when you are soaked to the skin.' He took a step towards her and pulled the blanket away. Then, spinning her round, he began to unfasten her dress. With a cry of alarm she began to struggle, violently, but it was no use. He held her easily and she heard the delicate fabric rip under his impatient fingers. Beneath the low-necked gown she wore nothing but a fine camisole trimmed with lace, for her slim figure had no need of corsets. Turning her to face him once more, he pulled the silk from her shoulders, and with it the undergarment, leaving her half-naked as she stood before him in the firelight, clutching desperately at the ruined blue flounces, the flickering shadows playing over her pale skin, emphasising the gentle roundness of her breasts, and the vulnerable slender throat.

He stared at her for a long moment, then uttering a low groan deep in his throat, he drew her into his arms, crushing her breasts against his chest as his lips sought hers. She did not struggle; she did not think. The knowledge that this man was an outlaw and a murderer and her captor all vanished as her body melted against his, her lips parting submissively beneath the violence of his kisses, his hands on the naked skin of her back caressing fire into her veins as his fingers traced her spine. Her legs grew weak as she clung to him, and as if sensing her surrender, he lowered her gently to the blanket before the fire, leaning over her, his blue eyes dark with passion as he surveyed her face, his hands gently moving over her breasts. Then his lips were on hers once more, and with an inarticulate little cry she threw her arms around him, feeling his weight crushing the breath from her body.

On the fire a wet log split with a violent explosion, sending sparks soaring up the chimney. John looked up with an oath. Then, abruptly, he drew away from her and stood up, looking down at the flawless creamy skin of the near-naked girl on the floor at his feet. Stooping, he picked up the spare blanket from the chair and threw it to her. 'Cover yourself,' he said curtly as, dazed, she struggled to sit up.

He turned away as she pulled the blanket round her shoulders and, rising shakily to her feet, huddled miserably into the chair by the fire.

'My apologies,' he said abruptly. 'When I removed your dress I expected to find you safely encased in whalebone, as are most of your sex. I should have known that even in dressing you defy the accepted rules.'

Her face flamed. 'You had no business to touch my dress!' she retorted, trying to suppress the sharp sense of disappointment which swept over her.

'Perhaps not, but it seemed important to me that my hostage remain in good health. You are no use if you die of a chill.' He strode towards the door in the wall next to the chimney. 'My men were eating some hot soup earlier. I shall see if there is any left for you.'

The second he was out of sight she jumped to her feet. Hugging the blanket around her, she flew across the floor to the outer door, and dragged it open. The candles guttered and the fire flared viciously as the wind and rain blew into the room, and she stared for a moment out at the cold darkness, her heart failing her as she thought of the bleak loneliness of the mountain.

'Shut the door, Stella, and come back to the fire.' The laconic voice behind her made her spin round, clutching the blanket to her throat. John was standing in the inner doorway, a steaming bowl in his hand. He set it down on the hearth and then came towards her, firmly closing the door against the rain before taking her arm and propelling her back to the chair. 'I suggest you drink this while it is still hot. I assure you it is not poisoned, though my reputation might seem to suggest it.' He handed her the bowl, and she cupped her hands around it obediently and raised it to her lips, conscious that her cheeks were pink with anger and resentment.

He watched her drink. 'Not up to the standards of the kitchens at Bryn Glas, I presume,' he said coldly, when she set it down after only a few sips.

'It's very good,' she retorted. 'I would expect nothing less of a rich man and the nephew of an earl who masquerades as a friend to the poor! No doubt you feed your "daughters" on the richest of food and wine.'

'Oh, so that's the way the wind blows.' He laughed quietly. 'You think my birth and position exempt me from sincerity?'

'You thought mine did!' She picked up the bowl again. Its warmth brought comfort to her hands and, clutching it, she could hide her trembling. But she did not drink. She was watching him surreptitiously as the firelight played across his face, highlighting the cheekbones, showing the strain and fatigue around his eyes, and she could not restrain a wave of tenderness towards him. Angrily she pushed it aside, watching as he stood looking down into the fire.

'Are you going to keep me here?' she asked at last.

He looked up from his reverie, 'I am. I am going to see your father as soon as it is light, Stella.' He folded his arms wearily. 'Once the good John Vivian has delivered the message from the dastardly Mother Rebecca, and your father knows the "lady's" plans for you, I feel he will soon see reason. And if he does not, then Rebecca plans to distract him further with a little reminder of her promise. It may not be Michaelmas quite yet, but I have an engagement with your father I intend to keep without delay. It is one that will, I feel sure, occupy him to the exclusion of all else save his daughter's disappearance.'

Stella stared at him in horror. Then, setting down the bowl with a jerk which slopped the contents on to the flags, she stood up. 'You don't mean—you wouldn't burn Bryn Glas?' Her face was ashen with fear.

'Your father is determined to see me hanged, Stella.'

'That is the punishment for murder!' she whispered.

His face hardened. 'So. You agree with him that I deserve to die, do you?'

Her colour flared beneath the whip of his scorn. 'I once told you that I thought hanging too good for you,' she said. 'I still believe it.'

'So,' he laughed, 'I merit drawing and quartering as well, do I? How lucky for me, then, that we live in an enlightened society!' He paused. 'Tell me, does John Vivian deserve the rope as well as Mother Rebecca?' He reached for her wrist and dragged her to him.

Clutching the blanket to her, she faced him defiantly. 'Don't make fun of me, John. They are bound to catch you.'

'I very much doubt that.' He pulled her against him until his face was only inches from hers. 'But if they do, it shall be my last request that you have a front-row view of my hanging.' His lips on hers were demanding, but this time she fought against him, pushing at him with all her strength.

'Let me go! I believed in what you were doing! I thought
you were right and that my father was wrong. But you plan
to burn our house just for revenge!' She dashed tears from
her eyes. 'And you are a common thief and a murderer. Oh,
yes, I hope they catch you, John Vivian. You deserve it!'

He released her so sharply that she staggered and nearly
fell. His face was white and angry. 'Then you had better
continue to believe the worst of me, Stella,' he said softly,
'because it is a side of me you are going to see often.'

'You wouldn't dare hurt me!' she cried.

'I think you will find, Stella, that I dare anything,' he said
grimly. 'As a murderer and a thief, what have I to lose?' She
clutched the blanket more tightly around her, staring at his
dark face.

He moved to the door, stopping to pick up his leather
jerkin and caped cloak, sodden with rain. He put them on,
and turned to look at her once, then dragged the door open
and ducked out into the darkness, closing it behind him
with a crash. The sudden sweet smell of rain filled the room.

It was a long time before she summoned up the strength
to try the door after him, but now it was locked firmly from
the outside, as she had known it would be. She was a
prisoner.

Clutching the blanket round her, she tiptoed to the other
door and listened. No sound came from the next room so,
plucking up courage, she lifted the latch and pushed. The
door opened with a protesting squeak into the dark kitchen
of the cottage. It was quite empty. Turning to collect the
candle, she ventured in and looked round.

On the table lay the remnants of a hastily abandoned
meal, bread and cold mutton, and a half-empty jug of ale
and several dirty earthenware bowls, such as the one from
which she had drunk. The fire had burned low and was
smoking badly in the wind, and over it hung the heavy iron
pot on its sway, the savoury broth still steaming gently
round the ladle. She sniffed at it with a sudden wave of
distaste as she thought of the food, then, turning her back
on it, set out to explore the room more thoroughly.

Here, too, there was one door, out to the back of the
cottage this time, but it was firmly locked, and a small
leaded window which appeared to have been nailed up. At

the far side stood a cold slab with the leg of mutton covered by a piece of muslin. Beside it lay dishes of cream and butter and a jug of milk. Not touching anything, she went on with her search, but the room revealed nothing that could help her. Even the drawer of the table which held several battered spoons produced no knife which she could use to try to force the window.

A small steep staircase led up beside the chimney, and cautiously she mounted it, holding her breath as she peered into the room upstairs. It was completely empty save for a few wisps of hay and a couple of buckets. Obviously no one lived in the cottage. As far as she knew, she was the only human being for miles.

Shivering, she descended the stairs again, guarding the candle-flame with her hand, and retraced her steps to the first room, where she sat down once more before the fire and drew her feet up painfully beneath her, trying to warm them by wrapping them in the blanket. Whatever the Rebeccas were doing, she could not stop them. If they attacked her beloved home, it would be without warning.

When she opened her eyes again the candle had gone out, but she could see a faint light at the window. Stiffly she began to move, straightening her legs and stretching her cramped, bruised arms. The cottage had grown very cold. The fire had burned out, and with an exclamation of dismay she fell on her knees before it and blew on the ashes, the way Peggy did in the morning, in her bedroom. They glowed feebly for a moment and then died. She looked round frantically for some fuel but there was nothing she could use, only her own shoes in the hearth where she had left them. Those, at least, were now dry and warm and gratefully she slipped them on. She found her torn dress which had dried in a maze of creases, and pulled it on; then, groping her way to the kitchen door, she found the fire there still glowed faintly. By its light she found a box of kindling and, feeding it inexpertly, she managed at last to coax it into a blaze. It would soon be full light outside and until then she could just see to make her way around the kitchen. The rain still poured down the window-panes and thundered on the roof slates, and she could hear the mountain wind moaning gently in the chimney.

Her spirits rose a little as the broth reheated. Refusing to think about what might be happening down in the valley, she broke herself a wedge of bread and began determinedly to chew a piece of mutton. That and a bowl of steaming broth would restore her strength for whatever was to come. As soon as she could see properly she was going to search once more for a means of escape. She had no intention of being there when John Vivian returned, with his threats and his promises and his insolent caresses which sent such unwelcome emotions flooding through her body.

But, search as she could, she could find nothing which would shift either of the doors or the windows, and after one fleeting thought that she might try and climb up the broad chimney, she gave up trying. Instead, she huddled by the kitchen fire, staring glumly at the dwindling logs in the basket.

From the back window she could see the firewood and peats stacked in the small rain-swept yard, but they might as well have been on the moon for all the help they would be in keeping her warm. Beyond the stone wall round the yard the mountainside swept gently upwards, bleak and deserted; the only life that she could see was a herd of bedraggled ponies, their heads low as they moved slowly up the ridge in the distance and disappeared into the cloud which lay along the mountain top.

She had no way of knowing the time, but it must have been well after noon when at last she heard the sound of a horse's hooves clattering over the stones in the muddy yard. She listened for a moment, holding her breath, then rose and went to the window, her heart thudding with fear.

A figure appeared briefly in her line of vision, anonymous beneath a pulled-down old hat and the sodden sack draped around his shoulders. Then she lost sight of him as he tramped round to the front of the cottage. Minutes later she heard the sound of a key in the lock.

She did not know the man who appeared in the kitchen doorway, stooping below the low lintel. He was wizened and toothless with piercing brown eyes as he surveyed her with a faint grin.

'Kept warm, did you, girl?' he asked, glancing at the nest of blankets in the chair by the fire.

'Yes, thank you.' Stiffly she moved away from the window, watching him warily as she drew the rug closer round her shoulders to cover her torn bodice.

'That's good. It gets cold on the mountain at night.' He stooped to the fire and stirred it vigorously. 'I was sent to see you have logs and water. It will likely be night before Mother Rebecca and her daughters return.' He smiled at her. 'I'm Evan. Cook-general to the troops, the Mother calls me!'

Stella found herself relaxing a little. The man seemed friendly enough. 'Where have they gone?' she asked nervously. 'I thought you rode only at night?'

'We ride when we need,' he replied. 'Last night we visited the lock-up at Hay, and rescued Dai Prosser while all the authorities were in such a fluster looking for Rebecca!' He gave a cackle of laughter as he picked up the empty log-basket and swung it on to his shoulder. 'You'll be needing some more logs, likely.'

Emboldened by his kind face, Stella ran to him and put her hand on his arm. 'Please, please, let me go!' she stammered. 'Don't make me stay here!' She clutched at him desperately.

Startled, he put down the basket and backed away from her.

'There's nothing I can do, girl. You have to stay. I have my orders.'

'He said he was going to burn my home.' Tears filled her eyes suddenly. 'Please, please, I have to warn them. Don't you see . . .'

'Bryn Glas, is it?' He went to the hearth once more. 'It is men like Magistrate Vaughan as need having their eyes opened, girl.' He picked up the heavy black kettle from the hearth and rested it for a moment on the table as he surveyed her white face. 'We're burning soon,' he said at last, relenting, 'but it's not your father's fine house we're going after. Mother Rebecca is soft in the head, if you ask me, but she says we're to leave Bryn Glas alone for the time being. For your sake.' He could not keep the scorn out of his voice.

She stared at him in disbelief before a feeling of intense relief swept over her, and she sank on to the chair. 'Thank

God.' She could not keep the sob of gratitude from her voice. 'But why? Why did he change his mind?'

'I told you, girl. He did it for you.'

She blushed, stung by the scorn in his voice. 'I can't think why,' she retorted, 'he owes me nothing.'

'No.' Evan considered her thoughtfully. 'You are a pretty enough girl, but he doesn't usually dangle after petticoats. Likely it is part of his plan, in holding you here. A hostage, see.' The grim glance he gave her sent an icy whisper of fear down her spine.

'What does he mean to do with me, then?' she whispered at last, her elation gone.

He shrugged. 'He doesn't tell me all his plans, girl.'

'And you don't care?' she cried desperately. 'You take orders from a man who commits arson and now,' she bit her lip trying to keep the terror from her voice, 'and now, cold-blooded murder!'

He glared at her, his eyes suddenly round. 'John is no murderer, girl!' he exclaimed. 'What do you think he's doing now? After freeing Dai we spent the rest of the night hunting for the men who did that job at the toll. It was common thieves who took the strong-box and then killed Bob Ellis and his boy, not us. They were wearing skirts to throw suspicion on the daughters, and they burned the toll-house to cover their tracks. It's happened before in the west, but they are not going to get away with it here. We'll find them and they'll discover their mistake!'

Stella exclaimed, 'But why didn't John tell me? Why didn't he explain that it wasn't he?'

'Likely he expected you to believe in him without,' he retorted.

He reached into his breeches pocket and fished out a key with which he opened the back door. Leaving it open, he took the kettle out to the rain-water barrel and brought it back full and hung it on the sway above the fire, in place of the soup-pot. Then he went out again to fetch some logs which he fed to the fire.

She stared at him unseeing, her mind a turmoil of uncertainty. John wasn't a murderer. Her every instinct had been right. He wasn't a thief. He was still the man she had respected as the leader of a desperate cause, and he was, she reminded herself with a little jolt, John Vivian. 'Do you think his identity has been guessed yet?' she asked at last.

'No. Why should they? He'll go to his office today, I expect, same as usual. Only he'll have this little piece of insurance up his sleeve, won't he now?' He chuckled.

'Insurance?'

'You, girl. If Owen Morgan starts talking, he can be stopped, can't he?' He threw another log on the fire, and grunted with satisfaction as it blazed up. 'If he spreads his wicked lies about nice respectable Mr Vivian, the word might get back to him that something terrible will happen to his little lady!'

Stella swallowed. 'And will something terrible happen to me?'

He glanced at her swiftly. 'I daresay it might!'

'Then I'll find a way to escape!' She moved towards the door defiantly.

'I shouldn't, girl.' Evan had padded his hand with a cloth and leant forward to lift the heavy kettle from the sway. 'It'll only make it harder for you. You'd not get off the mountain. And if you give too much trouble I'll have to find somewhere else to keep you. Or put a chain round that pretty ankle, like a tether for a beast. There now,' he smiled at her, 'a nice hot drink is what we want. It'll put some roses back into your cheeks.'

Stella was in no doubt that he meant his threat. She retreated to her chair and pulled the blanket more closely round her, tucking her feet out of sight with a shiver.

'When is John coming back here?' she asked softly.

'Tonight.' Evan was intent on stirring the hot liquid in the mugs. 'We meet here at moonrise.' He turned to her. 'Lucky we were warned that Owen Morgan suspected the truth, isn't it?'

'How were you warned?' she asked listlessly. 'John seemed to know everything that we had said—'

He gave a sly grin. 'Someone in your house is on our side, I dare say!'

She frowned, dragging her mind back from her present predicament to the drawing-room at Bryn Glas. Who could have known? Only Perry could have overheard—. She paused, her father's voice coming back to her suddenly.

Perry saw a woman on a horse—on Cariad—

'Megan?' she stammered. 'Megan took my mare and rode out to warn him?'

'Who else? She's been walking out with one of the boys for months now. What more natural than that she should warn us? Mr Perry told them in the kitchens what was afoot, so she wore one of your cloaks, and took your horse from the stables and rode to the Swan to find Lloyd. The message was taken to John and he ordered then that two men be sent back to fetch you. Touched, he was, that you stood up for him the way you did.' He added the last sentence with a certain admiration in his voice. He produced a knife and began to hack at the loaf of bread on the table.

'It is important to him, his position in the town. It gives him the chance to save daughters all over Wales when they are caught and brought up before the beak.' He slapped the slice of mutton on the bread and handed it to her. She took it, but did not attempt to eat. 'So he has to take no chance. He'll use you to persuade your father to speak for the Rebeccas now. And if your Owen Morgan threatens to talk out of turn, he can keep him quiet as well. A double insurance, see; just by keeping you to hand. You'd better pray, girl, that your father agrees to help.' Once again his grim speculative glance sent a shiver down her spine.

He stayed with her about an hour, then, making sure the log-basket was full, he left her alone once more. She watched from the window as he led his muddy pony out of the shed, and mounted, riding off to disappear almost at once into the mist of rain which still shrouded the hillside, and only when he was out of sight did she turn away and at last allow her tears to fall.

It was full dark before she heard hooves again. She was sitting huddled by the fire in the kitchen, not daring to light the last candle-stump, watching the leaping shadows of the burning logs running up the rough walls. This time unmistakably she heard the sound of several horses, and the subdued voices in the yard announced the arrival of more than one man.

She rose fearfully, pulling the rug around her, and waited, facing the door. When it opened, four men appeared, one of them holding a storm-lantern. They stared at her in silence as they filed in, and then began to busy themselves about the kitchen. Within minutes it was full of light and the fire was roaring up the chimney. No one spoke to her and she recognised none of them. There was nothing to do but stand helplessly by as they moved around her, wondering fearfully when John would appear. Only when the room was ready to their satisfaction did one of them approach her.

'I think you would be more comfortable next door, Miss Vaughan,' he said politely. 'We've lit a fire for you there.'

It was cold in the other room, despite the fire, and there was only one candle on the table. Huddling into her blanket, she sank miserably into the chair, staring at the door as she heard a sudden roar of laughter from behind it and then the steady companionable hum of conversation as the men could relax without her.

Her heart was beating unsteadily. Any moment now, John would return. Perhaps he was there already, laughing with his men.

He might not be a murderer, but he was unscrupulous and dangerous, and he cared nothing for her. She was a useful pawn in his game, no more. But what did he intend to do with her then?

She clenched her fists to stop herself from crying as she slipped to her knees before the fire, trying to get nearer the heat.

The door in the corner opened, and John walked in as she was listlessly stirring the smouldering logs. His mud-splashed trousers and shirt were once more covered by the long black cloak which he took off and flung carelessly on the table, making the candle-flame leap and fade.

'I trust you were able to entertain yourself in my absence,' he said harshly.

Her mouth had gone dry with fear, but she squared her shoulders, still kneeling before the fire.

'Why did you let me believe you had killed those men?' she asked softly, without turning.

He raised an eyebrow. 'Should it matter to me what you believe?'

'Perhaps not to you, Mr Vivian, but it matters to me. The man who spoke so grandly and of such high ideals about the cause of Rebecca would not have killed.'

'He would, Stella.' His voice was grim as he looked down at her. 'Make no mistake about that. Not willingly, not easily, but if the cause demanded it, he would. What he would not do is rob and murder.' He began to pace up and down, his hands clasped, his jaw set. 'I must find these men before they repeat their crimes and my reputation is for ever tainted. Only then can Rebecca ride once more in her own right.'

He stopped behind her, and she turned. 'We have had a busy night. You heard from Evan, I gather. A man rescued. A letter delivered.' He grinned mischievously. 'To your distraught papa, no less. Now I return to my house to don once more the sober identity of John Vivian, and then I shall make it my business to commiserate with your family on your abduction.'

She was scarcely able to contain the impotent fury which filled her.

'You find that amusing? The idea that my father and mother will be beside themselves with worry?'

'Indeed I do. And let us not forget the noble Mr Morgan, whose soul burns to make you its helpmeet!'

'I should not mock Owen, if I were you, Mr Vivian,' she whispered. 'It is likely to be Owen who will prove your downfall, remember. He, of all of us, saw through you.'

A frown crossed his face. 'True. I shall have to beware of him. But I don't think he is any real threat. Not,' he reached down lazily and, catching her wrist, pulled her to her feet, 'while I have you here.'

She was conscious of the strength of the lean brown hands which held her so effortlessly and the treacherous longing which swept over her, driving her to abandon herself to his kisses, but she resisted furiously, pushing her fists against his chest. 'It is so easy, is it not, to get your way by force,' she said icily. 'Whether it's a defenceless toll-keeper, or a woman. You will enjoy seeing my mother suffer, won't you?'

He stared down at her, his face harsh. 'No, Stella. I shall not enjoy that. Your mother is a good woman and it is unfortunate that her husband is obdurate.' He drew her close against him. 'A trait you appear to have inherited.'

Her furious protest was stifled as his mouth came down angrily on hers, and she felt the now familiar sense of surrender sweep over her, depriving her of the will to resist.

Was it minutes or was it hours later that he released her and looked down at her, a smile on his face. He reached up and touched her lip with the tip of his finger and she tasted the salt tang of blood. 'I've hurt you, Stella,' he said, and there was a new gentleness in his tone. He folded her close to him again. 'Why don't you admit you are in love with me, you silly child? You are, aren't you?' His eyes were dark with passion as they held hers, and she felt herself drowning in his gaze. She wanted to deny it, to repulse him, but every fibre of her being ached to surrender to him and confess the truth. This time his lips were gentle, caressing, exploring her face, her throat, nibbling her ear. She had begun to tremble. She closed her eyes slowly.

'I love you,' The words were torn from her lips in anguish.

He smiled again, and there was triumph in his face as he pushed her away from him.

Seeing it, she felt a quick surge of misgiving, searching his face for reassurance. But there was none. He was turning away from her already. 'Then I look forward all the more to our next encounter, Stella,' he said softly. 'Perhaps then I shall be able to devote the time to you which you deserve. But now I have to go. The daughters ride tonight without their Mother, and none will be more appalled to hear their latest exploits than John Vivian, as he sips tea with Miss Eliza at Bryn Glas and plans to take her driving.'

He laughed out loud at Stella's expression. 'Poor Stella. And you not there to act as chaperon!'

He picked up his cloak, fastening it with a swirl around his shoulders. 'You will find clothes for you in the kitchen, as that dress is no longer decent. Put them on as soon as we have gone,' he commanded. 'Then sleep. I shall return at first light. And then perhaps I shall have an hour or two to spend in your company. You have the makings of a passionate woman, once you have stopped playing at being a spoiled and ignorant child. It is going to be a pleasure to instruct you!' And with a laugh, he was gone.

She did not move. Behind the kitchen door his voice was

muffled by the heavy oak, and chair-legs scraped the floor.
Then she heard the sound of several pairs of feet crossing
the flags as he led his men outside, and the back door closed
behind them, the sound of the turning key echoing through
the sudden silence.

Long after the sound of hooves had died away she was
still standing, stunned with anger and humiliation where he
had left her in the middle of the floor. He had kissed her and
forced her to confess she loved him, and then he had gone
to Eliza.

CHAPTER
FOURTEEN

WHEN SHE awoke, the sun was streaming through the window. It touched the corner of the table and fell diagonally across the floor to the white ash in the fireplace. The room was bitterly cold. Dazed, she looked around, her misery and loneliness returning as she remembered the happenings of the night before, then stiffly she climbed to her feet and went to the window in sudden panic. Surely they should have returned by now? The mountain rose before her, grey and mossy green, streaked with the gold of the rain-flattened bracken. Across its shoulder trailed streaks of the mist which still filled the valley below with milky whiteness. The only moving thing in sight was the tiny speck of a circling buzzard high in the sky above the cottage. She watched it for several minutes, then resolutely she turned away and went into the kitchen to stir up the embers of the fire.

On the table she found a bag containing a skirt and blouse. She pulled them out cautiously, expecting the huge torn garments sported by Rebecca's daughters. But both were neat and clean, and near enough her size to fit comfortably. Thankfully she shed the torn blue gown and put them on. Immediately, she felt better.

The mist had cleared completely from the river valley before at last she saw the six horsemen cantering in single file across the mountainside. She watched, holding her breath slightly, until they were close enough to recognise. John was not with them.

She waited uncertainly as the men rode into the small yard and dismounted, then, as they filed into the kitchen, she looked from one to the other, searching their faces for some sign. They were all grey with exhaustion and there was a faint muttering of anger from one or two of them as they threw themselves down on the chairs round the table.

It was Dai Prosser who approached her, his arm heavily bandaged, his face solemn. 'We got the bastards,' he said, his voice hoarse with fatigue. 'The ones pretending to be us, with their pretty skirts still in their saddle-bags.' He spat on the floor.

Stella stared at him nervously. 'What did you do with them?'

Dai laughed. 'Oh, don't fret, girl. We didn't hang them ourselves. Law-abiding we are—are we not Sisters?' There were a few grim smiles in the silence. 'We took them to Magistrate Williams, see, and we persuaded him to see the truth of the matter.'

'Fersuaded?' she repeated in a whisper.

'Most men is persuadable, looking down the barrel of a gun. And anyway one of the bastards made a full confession. He's been taken up for murder.'

Behind him, Evan was stirring the fire, feeding twigs and branches from the basket by the hearth to the reluctant flames beneath the kettle.

'And John?' Stella forced herself to say the name. 'Did he go to see my father?'

Dai glanced round uncomfortably. 'Well, he did and he didn't, as you might say.'

'I'll tell her.' Evan threw down the poker and turned to face her, his wizened face heavy with gloom. 'He went to Bryn Glas all toffed up in his best coat and trousers, but our Megan stopped him in the lane. Waiting, she was, to meet Lloyd. She threw herself at his horse. "Don't go in there," she says. "That Mr Morgan has finally got them convinced that you are Mother Rebecca and Miss Eliza has been creating something unbelievable because her sister", that's you, miss, "has run off with the man she loves!" They didn't believe that you'd been taken by force. They think you joined us voluntary.' He paused and stared at her white face. Then he winked at her slyly. 'They all know you are in love with John, girl.'

Stella felt herself blushing crimson. Every man was staring at her now. 'But where is he? Where is John? I must go home. Surely you can see that. I must. Oh, please—'

Dai elbowed Evan out of the way. He had a mug of steaming tea in his hand. 'Here, girl. Drink this and sit quiet. Don't you see, you can't go back. If you return, you will be arrested.'

She gasped at him in horror. 'I don't believe you.'

'It's true, girl.' He spoke more gently. 'Your father has disowned you and your fine fiancé has broken off your engagement.' He smiled grimly round at his companions. 'It appears that, whether you like it or not, your future lies with us, girl—'

'And what about John—all his plans . . .'

He frowned and shook his head. 'He's on the run. When he went back to his lodgings the dragoons were waiting. No, no—' At her gasp of terror, he raised his hand. 'They didn't catch him. He gave them the slip. We're not sure where he is now, but he'll come . . .'

Stella had subsided on to the wooden chair by the hearth. Her head was spinning. Her mama, George, Eliza, Owen— they all thought of her as a rebel. They had rejected her and turned her out for ever. She felt her eyes fill with tears and she blinked them back angrily. These men were not going to see her cry. She straightened her shoulders. 'What am I going to do?' she said.

Dai surveyed her solemnly. 'You're going to help us. And you're going to help John.'

Her mouth was dry with fear as, with a heavy shawl pulled close round her head and shoulders, she made her way up the dark drive. She had never met Sir Ivor Davies nor any of his family, but she knew him by reputation. He was a cruel, harsh man who had made himself universally feared in the countryside. And he was powerful.

A streak of pale moonlight opened at her feet across the drive and she hesitated for a moment, then looked up at the house which loomed ahead of her. The huge roofs and pinnacles clustered menacingly against the star-strewn sky and she could see the pale threads of smoke rising from innumerable chimneys. The windows were dark.

All day they had waited for word from John. The men had rolled themselves in blankets by the hearth to sleep, while two at a time they had ridden down to the valley to seek for news. But there was little. They reported that the dragoons were still quartering the countryside, although the murderers who had pretended to be Rebeccas had been taken to Brecon. In Hay the offices of Toby Griffiths were closed. There was no word of Mother Rebecca, nor of the respected solicitor John Vivian, who was now wanted for questioning. The atmosphere was tense.

'You'll help us, won't you, girl?' Evan had said as it grew dark. 'This was the most important raid John planned, and if they are holding him somewhere on suspicion it'll maybe help convince them he's innocent.' He looked at her hard. 'You'll not only help save his life, there'll be people in the house you'll save. People who might be burned alive . . .'

She had agreed to do it, of course. What had she anyway to lose?

Taking a deep breath, she forced herself to walk steadily on, looking neither to left nor right, but kept her eyes fixed on the house and on the bare bright area in front where the drive swept into an elegant circle around a stone fountain. She had to cross that space.

She glanced up at the huge front door and pulled her shawl more tightly around her head. Then resolutely she walked on, her thin shoes almost soundless on the gravel, and began to mount the flight of steps.

The pealing of the bell was greeted immediately by the furious deep-throated barking of a dog. She heard the scrape of its claws on the floor, and felt the panels shake as the animal hurled itself bodily at the wood which separated him from his prey. She gasped with fear but stood her ground, and, sure enough, almost at once a harsh voice called it off. The claws retreated and instead she heard the grating of bolts and locks.

The door was pulled open by a smartly-attired butler, who held a candelabrum high in his hand as he peered out. He looked at her in astonishment.

Stella took a step forward. 'Please,' she faltered. The tremor in her voice was real, for she had begun to shake with terror. 'Please, you must help me. I must see Lady Davies—' Say just enough, Dai had said, for them to know you are a lady. You must attract the attention of the entire house, not just the servants. 'You must take me to her.' With great presence of mind she took another stumbling step, half-staggered, and, as the butler reached out a white-gloved hand to her arm, she flung her hands out wildly as if to save herself, and grabbed once more at the ornate bell-pull. Peal after peal rang through the house as she sank to her knees, watching through half-shut eyes the effect her entry was creating. The deafening summons of the bell, coupled with the butler's cry of alarm, brought a rush of light into the cavernous hall behind them as door after door was flung open and more than a dozen people appeared, peering at her figure as it subsided on to the door-mat in the semblance of a dead faint. The hubbub of voices closed over her, and she felt the sudden warmth as a candle was held close to her face.

'Who the devil is it, Johnson?' a gruff voice enquired. 'What is wrong with her?'

'She was asking for her ladyship,' the man replied; then from somewhere behind him a woman spoke. 'What does it matter who she is, she's ill. Don't leave her lying there in the cold. Pick her up, someone—'

'No, wait, we must know who she is, what she wants—'

'For goodness sake get the door closed. There's a gale blowing out there.'

'Someone stop that damn dog barking—'

Stella, her eyes closed, was holding her breath as the voices swirled round her. They must not move her. If they tried to, she must cling to the door and scream; anything to make sure that every person in the house was brought down to the hall, to be sure that no one was asleep high in the bedrooms, or closeted in some lonely corner in one of the distant wings.

She became aware that someone was kneeling beside her now, and she smelled the bitter aroma of burnt feathers tickling her nose. Burnt feathers, or was it something else? Her eyes fluttered open for an instant and, to her consternation, she found she was looking straight into the face of another woman, a young pretty woman, of about her own age.

'There, my dear, are you better?' Stella saw rather than heard the words framed by the girl's lips, for the noise around her was overwhelming, and she felt a sudden pang of sadness for what was about to happen. The girl was kneeling close beside her, bending so close that Stella was aware of the faint lavender scent she was wearing. She stole a look past her at the crowd which had gathered, and saw with a certain satisfaction that not only the house-guests were there, but the servants too. As long as there was no one asleep upstairs, no children—but Dai had assured her there were no children.

The cry of 'Fire' came so suddenly, so unexpectedly, that even Stella was startled. The terror in the voice that shouted and the panic that greeted it were overwhelming. All round her, people were in tumult, and for a moment she thought she was going to be trampled underfoot. She had to get away now. She had to slip unnoticed into the dark, her duty done, the household assembled in the hall whence they could escape, unharmed, while the house burned, but something had gone wrong; the girl was still kneeling with her, her kind face full of concern.

'You poor dear, don't distress yourself,' she was saying as Stella tried to rise. 'Papa and the servants will take care of it. You must not be afraid. We will look after you.'

Stella pushed herself up to her knees and raised a dazed hand to her face. 'I'm all right,' she said. 'I can stand up.' But the girl was holding her arm, trying to prevent her from rising, the girl who was Sir Ivor's daughter.

Stella's legs were trembling so much that the stagger she gave as she rose to her feet was real. She clung to the door for a moment, feeling the supporting hand steady beneath her elbow as she gathered her strength. Behind them she could smell smoke now and, more frightening still there was a roar of flame. The other women had streamed past them outside, a screaming, cackling mass of silk and chiffon, while the men of the house ran to and fro with buckets.

'I . . . I must go. I shouldn't have come,' Stella stammered, pulling her arm away from the girl. 'Please, let me go!' But the girl was clinging to her, refusing to release her arm. 'Stop, you mustn't go. You're not well.'

Panic-stricken, Stella began to struggle in earnest. 'Let me go! I have to, don't you see!' At last she broke free and, hurrying down the steps on to the gravel where the clustered women ignored her, their faces upturned in horror as flames leaped from an upstairs window, she ran past them, not looking back, and plunged frantically into the thick rhododendrons which banked the drive.

The branches caught at her skirt and legs, whipping at her arms, stinging her face, and too late she realised she had lost her shawl. All she knew was that she must escape and make her way back to the gates, where she would find the others waiting for her. She could hear shouting behind her in the distance and, glancing over her shoulder, she saw the livid glow in the sky. She stopped running, her breath coming in short gasps, and stared for a long time in horror, then, pulling herself together, she looked round her, trying to regain her sense of direction. She must find the main gates again or she would become lost in the acres of woods which surrounded Sir Ivor's home.

She set off once more, more slowly this time, keeping the glow of the burning house behind her left shoulder as she tried to make her way back in what she thought was the right direction, but the woods were growing thicker here; her nostrils were full of the sharp sweet smell of rotting logs, and she stumbled frequently over the fallen powdery branches which had collapsed into the undergrowth. Almost beneath her feet a pheasant rose, calling hysterically as it floundered up into the trees, and she stopped again, shaking with fright.

She was completely lost. The drive should have been there before this, for she had run a long way, but the woods were thicker than ever, and reluctantly, weary beyond caring, she decided to try and retrace her steps. If she approached the house cautiously and then began to circle, surely she would be bound to cross the drive? Once there, she could creep back through the shadows and find the entrance.

From the shelter of the trees she saw that the fire had taken a firm hold on only one wing of the house. There, flames licked from the windows and acrid smoke poured into a sky which was spangled with sparks. The rest of the place was dark. Dozens of figures milled around the burning building and still, on the open lawns, huddled the bedraggled ladies clinging to one another in their evening dresses.

A shadowy figure loomed next to Stella in the dark, his blackened face relieved only by the gleam of his eyes. He grinned at her. 'You did well, girl,' he murmured. 'There's been no one hurt. Now get you back, out of the way.'

She was clinging to the trunk of a tree for support, her exhaustion and fear draining her strength to nothing, but she could not drag her eyes away from the sight before her where the tall twisted chimneys of the house stood out black against the orange smoky pall. The man beside her had slipped away into the dark, but still she did not move.

There was something fearful and exciting in the force of the flames, and she stared fascinated. She heard a shout of warning in the distance and saw the small helpless figures stop and draw back, their buckets useless against the inferno, as with an ear-splitting roar part of the roof caved in, shooting smoke and flame upwards.

It was several minutes before Stella noticed a new feature in the crowd of distant figures. The flames showed up two men in blue informs, then another, their black chacos clearly silhouetted against the flames, and she saw the flicker of light catching and glinting on the blade of a fixed bayonet. She caught her breath in fear. The dragoons! How was it possible that they had arrived so quickly? She glanced round in fright, looking for any tell-tale signs of shabby skirts and shawls flitting among the trees, but there was no sign of any of Rebecca's daughters in the shadows. The parkland round the house was empty.

Only then did she realise her own danger. Peeping from the shelter of her tree she had not noticed the file of uniformed men moving systematically out from the house, but when at last she saw them, she whirled and ran once more towards the deepest shadows.

The man who caught her must have been standing watching her for some time. She had not heard him creep up behind her, neither had she seen him silently beckon to a companion, pointing at her as she pressed close against the tree. The two men exchanged nods and were advancing purposefully towards her when she turned suddenly and ran towards them.

'I've got him. I've got the bastard!' one of them shouted as he flung himself on her. All the breath was knocked out of her body as he bore her, full length, to the ground, twisting her arm viciously behind her.

She felt her face pushed into the cold wet earth, and gasping with pain, she lay still. The man got up and pulled her roughly with him, not relinquishing his iron grip on her arm. 'Call the officer, Jim,' he grunted. 'It's only a little one, but, by God, we'll make him talk, fancy wig and all!' As he spoke he took a firm grip on her hair and pulled.

Stella screamed. The blinding agony tearing at her scalp and the torture of her twisted arm knifed through her body until she was one searing mass of pain, but somehow she did not faint. There was to be no escape that way from the horror around her.

The sound of her scream brought an instant response from her captor. He released her so abruptly that she almost fell. 'Good gawd almighty, it's a real woman!' he stammered. 'Jim, it's a real bleedin' woman!'

The two men stared at her, then the first resumed his grip, more gently, but just as firmly, on her arm. 'Can't be helped. She's one of them, all right. I've been watching her skulking in the shadows, and another one with her, if I'm not mistaken, a few minutes before I caught her.'

Half dragging, half carrying her, they brought her out of the darkness into the light of the gravel in front of the house, where an officer was talking with Sir Ivor and two of his men. They all fell silent as Stella was brought before them, and she saw Sir Ivor's face darken with rage.

'So she was with them. Sent to distract us while they set their fire!' He approached her wrathfully and she found herself cowering, but the two dragoons were holding her fast and she was forced to wait, head held high, as the man thrust his face furiously into hers.

'Just who are you?' He fired the words at her with venom.

She bit her lip and turned away as best she could to avoid the full blast of his hot brandy-smelling breath, determined not to speak, while behind him the huddled women had noticed the scene and begun to draw near curiously, staring at her filthy torn gown and dishevelled hair.

Miserably Stella became aware of the approach of the girl who had been kind to her, her sweet face concerned as she put her hand on her father's arm. 'Oh, Papa, let her go, poor thing. She can have had nothing to do with all this.' As she turned to gesture towards the burning house, Stella saw that her face was streaked with tears, and she felt a terrible pang of regret, knowing so clearly how she herself would have felt had it been Bryn Glas which, after all, had been put to the flame.

'She's part of it, all right,' one of the dragoons holding her commented tersely. 'Don't be fooled, miss. Don't waste your sympathy.'

Sir Ivor moved away, his face still hard and unyielding. 'Take her away,' he said. 'We'll interrogate her later, and I want the rest of them rounded up, too. I'm too busy to see to it now,' and he turned back to the fire without giving her another glance, as Stella was dragged away.

Her last sight was of Sir Ivor's daughter standing watching her, her gentle face registering first disbelief, then horror, and then finally disgust.

CHAPTER
FIFTEEN

HER IMMEDIATE reaction was one of relief that she was alone in the cell. She could hear the oaths and screams of the other prisoners through the door, and smell the stench of the prison air, but her own dungeon, lit by a small barred window high above her head, was completely empty except for the pile of straw in the corner which, she assumed, must be her bed. She stood in the middle of the floor, dazed with fear and disbelief, for a long time after the gaoler had pulled the heavy door to behind her and locked it. Then, in despair, she sank on to the straw. She had no idea where she was. Hay or Brecon, she supposed. The window was too high to see out of, save for a square of greying sky, and apart from the distant rumble of wheels over cobbles, she could hear nothing from the street. Her ears were too full of the noises of the gaol, and she put up her hands to try and block them out. In her misery, she did not cry. It seemed she had no more tears. There was nothing left that she could do.

Slowly the grey window-shaped patch of sky lightened until it turned to blue, but the cell stayed dark. It was bitterly cold; the stone floor ran with moisture, and she was white and stiff with cold before she heard a key in the lock once more. The gaoler had returned, a bowl in his hands and a dirty grey rug over his arm.

'As soon as you give your name we'll contact your family, and no doubt they'll bring you all the comforts of home,' he said, not unkindly, as he handed her the bowl. He flung the blanket down on the straw. 'Well, are you going to tell me?'

Clutching the bowl to her breast, grateful for the luke-warm feel of it at least, she smelled its contents cautiously. There was a faint odour of peppery cabbage and little else, but she raised it to her lips and drank. Then she looked at the man, who was standing, hands on hips, watching her.

She shook her head. 'I am no one,' she said softly. 'No one at all.'

It was less than an hour later, however, that the man returned. With him was Glynn Williams, her father's colleague on the bench. Clutching the rug around her shoulders, Stella stood up, the colour rising in her face as he turned to the gaoler. 'Leave us till I call,' he said, curtly, and the man with a slight bow withdrew, jingling his bunch of keys.

'So it is you,' Glynn started without preamble. 'We guessed it might be when we heard that they had picked up a woman at the scene of the fire. Are you hurt?' His face was grim.

She shook her head miserably, not daring to trust her voice.

'First, you had better know the exact nature of the charges which they intend bringing against you,' he went on in business-like tones. 'It has been decided that you are the person known as Mother Rebecca locally.' He paused and glanced at her sharply as he heard her quick intake of breath. 'There are a number of further charges, of which the gravest is arson.' He stopped again, watching her closely. 'Stella, my dear, you do realise the gravity of the situation? The charges are being brought by Sir Ivor himself, and his brother, who is Lord Lieutenant of the county in which you were apprehended. Your friends will, of course, do everything in their power to help you, but I must warn you that, at present, things look grave, very grave indeed.'

'My friends?' she said at last, her voice husky. 'Not Papa?'

Glynn sighed. 'I'm sure he will, of course, Stella. He doesn't know yet for certain that it is you they have in custody.' He looked uncomfortable.

Stella turned away to stand below the window. She was shivering uncontrollably. 'He has disowned me, is that not true?' she asked bleakly.

When there was no reply, she turned to look at him, her grey eyes wide. 'Do not spare me the truth, please. I would rather know the worst. Owen, too, has forsaken me, I believe.' She clutched at the blanket for comfort.

A look of intense sorrow swept across his features. 'You must try to be brave, Stella. We'll do all we can to get you out of here, never fear. And meanwhile I shall arrange to have some small items sent in for you to make life easier.' His gaze swept the small cell with undisguised disgust.

There was little more that he could say to reassure her, and soon afterwards he took his leave, clasping her hand for a moment with a sympathy that brought tears to her eyes. When he had gone, she subsided once more on the pile of straw, her aching head a turmoil of jumbled thoughts.

The horror of her situation was so overwhelming that she could not bring herself fully to understand it. She stared blindly at the wall on the opposite side of the cell, her eyes tracing the crudely carved lettering of a previous occupant's name without even seeing it, and allowed herself to cling to the one ray of hope which pierced her misery.

John must still be free. And, as long as he was free, surely he would find a way, somehow, of rescuing her, as he had rescued Dai.

That afternoon, as Glynn had promised, a small iron bedstead was carried into the cell, with blankets and pillows and, bundled up with it, a change of clothing. She recognised with a pang of misery her lavender wool gown and the warm shawl which usually lay on her bed at home, and wondered who had selected them for her. Not Eliza, certainly. Perhaps Mama—or Megan? At five, a hot meal was brought to her—from the hostelry down the road, the turnkey informed her—and to her surprise she found she could eat a little. Her newly-acquired luxuries included candles, so when the window grew dark she was able to light the cell, huddling fully dressed on the bed beneath the blankets.

When, next day, she heard the key rattling in the lock, it came as no surprise. The gaoler, obviously well bribed by Glynn, had returned two or three times with small items for her. On the first occasion it had been the candles, then a mug of spiced ale, which she sipped occasionally, although she disliked it, for the sake of the warmth it spread through her veins. This time, however, he was not alone. A tall figure loomed behind him in the doorway. She stared incredulously, then, scrambling off the bed, threw herself towards him. 'Owen? Is it really you? I never thought I'd see you again!'

He held her for a moment, then gently pushed her away, his face very serious as he sat down beside her on the bedstead and began slowly to draw off his gloves.

'I am very sorry to see you in here, Stella.'

She hung her head. 'I have been foolish, Owen, and I'm sad if it has hurt you.'

'Of course it has hurt—and shocked—me!' His jaw tightened imperceptibly. 'You realise that there can be no more talk of an engagement between us?'

Nodding, she stole a glance at his face, but he was not looking at her. His whole attention was fixed on the glove he was folding between his fingers.

'We are, of course, doing all we can to help you,' he went on, 'but things look very grave because this ridiculous claim has been put forward that you are the brains and inspiration behind the rioting! Your views, unfortunately, have never been restrained. There is hardly a soul in the county who does not know about your radical thinking, whereas Mr Vivian,' he paused as if unable to bring himself even to discuss the man, 'has always taken extreme care to cover his tracks and advertise himself as the most sensible of men.' He looked up at her suddenly. 'You do realise that you have been most expertly used, and you do not, I hope, look for a rescue from him? He has taken leave of absence from Griffiths—perfectly legitimately, the old man hastens to assure me—and returned home to Pembrokeshire—for the shooting.' He could not keep the sarcasm out of his voice. 'While his followers have sunk back in to the bogs and hills they came from, to return, no doubt, only long enough to watch you being taken down to the Bristol packet in chains on your way to the colonies!'

Stella shrank away from him. 'They would not sentence me to transportation?' she faltered. 'Papa would not let them—'

'Your Papa can do very little, Stella, even if he chooses to,' he went on more gently. 'Sir Ivor will be satisfied with nothing less than your conviction, and he has enormous power. Whoever decided to burn his house made the biggest mistake of his life. The publicity!'

'It was the publicity he—we—wanted,' Stella interrupted wearily. 'It seemed the only way to draw enough attention to the plight of these people and to get some action in London.' She stood up slowly, hugging her shawl around her shoulders, and began to pace up and down the cell. 'It was good of you to come, Owen.' Her eyes filled with tears suddenly as she looked up into his solemn face, and, unable to restrain herself, she threw herself sobbing into his arms.

He held her tightly, his face buried in her hair, rocking her gently to and fro as if she were a child, without speaking, then at last he pushed her away from him. He groped for a handkerchief and pressed it into her hands.

'How long have you been in love with him?' he whispered.

Stella's face was wet with tears. 'Since the first time I saw him.'

Owen gave a grim smile. 'The evening of our engagement. So. I never stood a chance. When did you realise who he was?'

She buried her face in his handkerchief.

'I didn't,' she whispered brokenly. 'I didn't know.'

But her body had known. Her heart had recognised him, and had refused to deny her love, long before her lips acknowledged his name.

She looked up at Owen again. 'I'm sorry,' she cried. 'I didn't mean it to happen.' She clung to his hand tightly. 'Will they really send me to the colonies?'

He looked down at her frightened face, and swallowed.

'You will go before the assize for trial,' he said gently. He sighed. 'I have no way of knowing how the sentence will go. We must pray they are lenient. I'll do all I can to help you, my dear. It may be that we can get you released into your father's custody, but I'm not too hopeful at the moment. Sir Ivor has so far vetoed any attempts at getting you released on bail, as the only other "daughter" of Rebecca captured was rescued the other night from Hay lock-up, as I'm sure you know.' He stood up, releasing himself as she tried to cling to him. 'I'll come back as soon as I have any news.' His voice became brisk suddenly. 'Tell me, have you any money?'

She shook her head.

'Then take this.' He reached into his pocket for a bag of coins. 'Your gaoler has proved himself a very venal man. I doubt if there is much he could not be bribed to do. But take care. His allegiance is fickle, and Sir Ivor's coffers are no doubt bottomless, so don't trust him.'

With that, he rapped for the door to be opened, and vanished into the dark, stinking passage outside.

Stella wept for a long time after she had extinguished the candle that night, muffling her sobs in the cold pillow, as Owen's words whirled in her brain and one sentence returned again to torment her. 'Mr Vivian has taken leave of absence and returned home for the shooting . . .' John had gone. And with him every shred of hope.

Why had she ever thought he would save her, when he had shown again and again that he despised her? He had forced her to admit she loved him, but he had never said he loved her in return.

It was not, after all, as if she were one of his followers, one of his 'daughters', whom he would go to such lengths to save. She was just a woman, the daughter of one of his enemies, who had meddled in his affairs. A woman who had been used as a dupe and a scapegoat, while he and his friends had gone free.

Exhausted by her sobbing, watching the pale dawn lighten imperceptibly behind the bars of the window, she lay quiet at last. Her only consolation lay in the fact that he was still free, and she knew she would do nothing to implicate him further, even if it meant she could not save herself. She loved him too much.

Only when the first cautious thin notes of a robin crept in at the window did she finally fall asleep.

She had no visitors the next day, but the gaoler proved as amenable as Owen had suggested he would, procuring hot food, a second candlestick and writing materials in exchange for a few of the precious coins.

On the following morning, her brother came.

'Stella, you are a prize idiot!' he said amiably, as he stared round at the cell.

'Can they—are they doing anything to get me out?' she begged. 'Oh, George, I'm so frightened.'

He looked uncomfortable. 'Papa will come round to it,

Stella, I know he will, but just for the moment he's not being very helpful. You've embarrassed him dreadfully, old girl. He's the laughing-stock of the whole country. They've even written about you in *The Times*!' He threw himself down on the bed and then, grimacing, felt in his coat pocket. 'Here, Mama has sent you this, by the way. A pomander to ward off gaol fever!'

She took it with tears in her eyes, and the spicy fragrance cheered her a little.

'Owen came to see me,' she managed to say through her stifled sobs. 'That was good of him.'

George looked sceptical. 'I'm glad. He's been at Bryn Glas most of the time since—since you left. You know he's broken the engagement?' He glanced at her nervously.

'I know.' She tried to smile. 'It was I who broke it off first, George—or tried to, remember? It's for the best.'

He sighed with relief. 'I'm glad you feel that way, because he's awfully thick with Eliza suddenly.'

There was a long silence. George glanced at her, trying to read her expression, but her face was hidden by her loosely knotted hair and her nose was once more buried in the pomander. He sighed. Poor Stella. He doubted if she had even realised the danger she was in.

The visit from Megan three days later was a total surprise. She had despaired of seeing any more faces from home and, thin and exhausted from crying, she could barely rise from the bed when the gaoler, with a saucy smile, ushered her visitor in. Megan carried a covered basket in her arm.

'I've brought some things from your Mama, Miss Stella,' she said nervously, as the man pulled the door closed behind her and locked it. 'Mr Vaughan won't let her come herself to see you. See here, she's sent calves' foot jelly and cheese and bread rolls from the kitchens—'

'Is it true, Megan, that Mr Vivian has gone?' Stella interrupted her in an anguished whisper, ignoring the basket with its white linen napkin as she caught at Megan's arm.

'Hush!' The girl pointed at the door in an agony of fear. She bit her lip and stepped further into the cell, glancing at

Stella under the heavy hood she wore. 'I do have a message for you,' she murmured.

Stella's heart stopped still and she stared at Megan, not daring to speak.

'I was told to say that you are not to worry,' said the girl, almost inaudibly. She paused.

'Is that all?' Stella's voice choked in dismay.

Megan nodded violently, her eyes still on the door.

'But . . .' The hope was already dying in Stella's heart. 'Who told you to say that?'

Megan's chin jutted. 'I was just told,' she repeated stubbornly. 'I'm not saying any more.'

Stella sank down miserably on the bed. There was a long silence in the cell as the two girls looked at one another with strained suspicion. Then Stella noticed the basket which Megan had set on the floor.

'Will you tell Mama how pleased I am with all her gifts,' she said at last, with an effort. 'Tell her she must not try and come here, it would be too terrible for her. And tell her I am sorry to have caused her so much anxiety. I never meant to hurt her.'

'She knows that, miss,' Megan turned and looked at the door uncomfortably. 'Will he let me out again?'

'Of course. You have only to knock.' Stella laughed ruefully. 'If only it were as easy for me!'

As soon as the girl had gone, Stella had opened the basket, feverishly searching for some sign from John, but there was nothing. Disappointed, she slumped back on the bed and gazed at the locked door through which Megan had vanished into the outside world.

The next few days were interminable. In her imagination, she built a thousand dreams around Megan's cryptic message and, every time the door opened, her heart leapt with hope; on each occasion it was the same greasy face of her gaoler. No visitors came to lighten her loneliness, and slowly her optimism died. If the message had indeed been from John, perhaps all he had ever intended was to mock her from a safe distance.

She glanced at the rough table which yet more of her precious coins had procured. On it lay a letter from Glynn Williams, full of encouragement and reassurance, but unable to hide the fact that as far as he could tell nothing could prevent her being hauled before the next assize.

Sleepless night followed sleepless night, while during the days she spent long hours standing on the rickety chair which had accompanied the table, peering out of the window from which she could just see a long high wall of grey stone, swathed in scarlet leaves. Day after day she watched as a pair of wrens played and danced amongst the fluttering foliage, dodging the spinning seeds of the sycamore which grew somewhere behind the wall.

Then, when it grew dark, she would lie watching the silhouette of the two highest branches of that tree appear before the crescent moon as it slid across the window.

October slipped away and she lost count of the weeks. No more visitors came and she grew thinner and more listless, spending the days as well as the nights lying on the cold bed in a half-dreaming daze. She hated the night most, for after dark the prison was full of noises: the groans and sobs of the other prisoners of whom she had never caught so much as a glimpse, much to her relief; the regular tramp of feet patrolling up and down the corridor, the light of the lantern showing for an instant below the door; the scampering of paws across the floor, accompanied by a frenzied squeaking which made her cower in terror beneath her blanket; the quavering hoot of a distant owl.

And when she heard the key in the lock, soon after the distant clock which measured her lonely hours struck midnight, she supposed it was part of her dream. Raucous snores reverberated through the building and somewhere someone spat, hawking, on to the floor.

She watched the door open, the wedge of flickering light widening across the ceiling, and in sudden terror she sat upright, clutching the blanket to her chin.

'Who is it?' she gasped, as a black figure appeared in the doorway, holding the lantern high, staring around the cell.

'Sssh!' The figure put his finger to his lips. 'Quiet, girl! Do you want everyone to know we're here! Come on, quickly. We've no time to spare.'

She threw herself from the bed, her heart beating with sudden excitement as she recognised the voice of Megan's beau, Lloyd Pugh from Glasbury. She slept in her clothes

every night for warmth in the icy cell, so there was no need
to dress. Trembling with nerves, she groped for her shoes in
the shadowy darkness and slipped them on as, putting his
darkened lantern on the table, he went back to the door and
peered out. She wrapped her shawl round her head and
shoulders and tiptoed to his side.

'I'm ready,' she breathed.

He nodded, his finger to his lips. 'The guards are trussed
up in another cell,' he whispered, 'but someone will raise
the alarm any minute. Come quickly and don't make a
sound—there are more in the guard-room.' Taking the
lantern, he led her from the cell and locked it behind him.

Then he turned down a dank passage lined with heavy
bolted doors like the one from which she had been freed,
and she found herself following him through what seemed
like miles of echoing stone corridors until at last they were
at the main doors of her prison. There, two more figures
awaited them in the shadows. She stared at them, recognising at once Dai Prosser and the wizened face of Evan. Both
men smiled and nodded a greeting, but already they were
easing open the small pass-door which led through the
enormous iron-bonded gates to the prison. Stella ducked
through after them and found herself in the quiet street.
She stared round, half-fainting with excitement, expecting
to see John waiting in the shadows, but the street was
deserted. There was no one else in sight.

'This way,' Lloyd muttered, and, dragging her with him,
he began to run. Her thin, worn, shoes slipped on the frosty
ground and she felt her feet bruise against the stones, but
she did not care. Nothing mattered as long as she was free at
last.

They ran until she thought she could run no more,
dodging through a network of narrow streets, until they
came to a darkened inn. Four horses were waiting for them,
tethered in the shadows beneath some trees in the yard. No
one spoke as Lloyd lifted her into one of the saddles and
handed her the reins before swinging himself up on to
another horse as the other two mounted grimly behind
them. The clatter of hooves in the yard seemed deafening to
Stella, and she glanced apprehensively at the darkened
windows of the inn, but no lights appeared, no dogs barked,

and soon they were out on the mud road.

Almost at once Lloyd urged them into a canter in the starlight. Stella forgot everything in the sudden exhilaration of breathing the cold free air which caressed her face and feeling the lengthening strides of the horse beneath her. Ahead she could see the black outline of the mountains against the starlight, and already she could smell the sweet scent of the bog myrtle and gorse on the wind.

They seemed to ride for hours, and the horses were lathered and blowing by the time they at last reined in. There was no sign of pursuit. The lanes and fields were silent and the sky twinkling with stars as Lloyd dismounted and came to her side. He grinned at her.

'Tired?'

She had a stitch, and her legs and back ached from the unaccustomed exercise, but she shook her head determinedly. 'I could ride for ever.'

Throwing back his head, he laughed grimly. 'That is just as well, girl, for you have a very long ride ahead.'

'How far?' She looked at him with a sudden shiver as he raised his hands to her waist and lifted her down, but he did not answer. Behind him, Dai Prosser was already leading the exhausted horses away into the bushes, and within seconds he and Evan had reappeared with two fresh mounts.

'You should hurry, Lloyd, boy,' Dai whispered from the shadows. 'Sir Ivor is not going to lose his prey without making a great deal of noise about it.'

'Where's John?' Suddenly she could hold back the question no longer. She saw Dai and Evan glance at each other, then Dai chuckled. 'You'll see him soon enough, girl. He's waiting on the way. There's a price on his head now, see, and the threat of the noose if he's caught, so we stopped him coming himself to the prison for you.' He stooped to test the girths of her horse and Stella was lifted once more into the saddle. Above them, wisps of angry black cloud were beginning to streak the starry sky, and she felt a cold wind tease her hair. Lloyd felt it too. She saw him look up as he mounted.

'The wind is changing at last,' he muttered, as he turned his horse back on to the track. 'We'll need to ride fast.' He raised his hand in farewell to their two companions, then he set off again at breakneck speed, with Stella behind him, heading for the south.

They rode all night in silence as their solid mounts covered the miles. Every now and then Stella stole a glance at her companion, but he did not respond, concentrating on guiding his horse through the narrow muddy lanes and across the open hillsides, never increasing the pace beyond a trot, but never allowing her to slow them down or stop. Her tiredness had given way to a kind of numb daze in which she rode now without consciousness of the slowly lightening sky or the heavy clouds which gathered in the east, smothering the frosty stars, carrying a cruel sleet which spat down on them, soaking through her shawl and dress. It was not until the faint dawn light began to creep across the hillside near them that Lloyd reined in at last, and looked at her, his strained face relaxing into a tired smile.

'Not much further,' he said.

She looked at him numbly, almost too cold to speak, then she took a brief glance over her shoulder at the deserted road which stretched behind them into the murky darkness. 'Are you sure we haven't been followed?' Her hands on the reins were stiff with cold, and her whole body ached with the bite of the wind.

He shook his head and laughed grimly. 'If we were, the others would have distracted them or warned us somehow. There's an inn ahead where we can lie up for a bit. The owner is a sympathiser with our cause. Only a few more minutes, girl and we'll be there.' He urged his tired horse into a trot again.

She bit her lip doggedly as a sharp stitch dragged at her side, her eyes focused somewhere between the horse's ears, even the pain of the cold deadened now to wary numbness.

The exhilaration had gone; the desperate hope of seeing John again. All that remained was the determination to stay in the saddle, as her horse automatically followed its companion off the road and into the quiet yard of a low stone-built roadside inn. The place was deserted, the shutters closed against the chilly dawn.

Lloyd slid from his saddle and came to stand beside her, shaking the sleet from his head as he grinned up at her. For a moment she could not move, then, slowly and gratefully, she allowed him to help her dismount. She staggered as her feet touched the ground, conscious of a sleepy groom who had emerged yawning from his bed to take their horses, then, his arm around her shoulders, Lloyd was half-carrying, half-guiding her into the inn.

In a dream she allowed herself to be shown upstairs at once to a pleasant long room, furnished with a large bed covered by a quilt of many colours, and warmed by the fire which roared up the chimney. On a rug before the hearth stood a hip bath.

The innkeeper's wife had followed her up the stairs carrying a heavy jug full of steaming water, and behind her came two sturdy girls, who appeared to be her daughters, with buckets of clean scented water. Emptying them into the bath, the woman helped Stella to remove the sodden shawl from her hair. Stella's fingers were too numb with cold to help and she stood there, shaking, as with gentle hands the woman unbound her hair and washed it, then wrapping a warm towel around her head, helped Stella remove the rest of her clothes so she could step into the bath.

The water was like heaven against her skin, warm and soft and cleansing after the filth of the prison, thawing the agony of tiredness and cold from her bones, and she lay back in ecstasy. More water was brought to rinse her clean, then the girls tiptoed away, leaving the innkeeper's wife who was draping the towel to warm on the chair near the fire.

The woman smiled gently at Stella, noting the dark rings beneath the eyes and the chalky pallor of the girl's face. 'I'll fetch you some soup, shall I, my dear?' she asked shyly. 'The gentleman said you would want food and warmth.' She picked up Stella's discarded garments and held them at arm's length. 'I'll dispose of these, my dear, and come back with the soup in a few minutes, shall I?'

Drowsily Stella nodded, luxuriating in the soft scented water, watching the drops running down her ankle as she stretched out a toe towards the fire, her head resting comfortably against the high tin back of the bath.

Behind her, the door opened once more. But instead of the rustle of starched petticoats, she heard the tread of male riding-boots. She turned in fright, reaching forward for the towel to cover herself, but another hand was there first, snatching it up from its resting-place, and it was whisked out of reach.

'Allow me.' John Vivian was standing beside her, his amused gaze travelling slowly over her naked body.

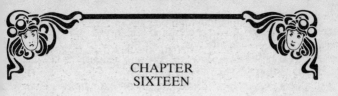

CHAPTER
SIXTEEN

TRANSFIXED, STELLA cowered back in the bath, blushing violently as she looked up at him, her heart pounding. He was holding the towel just out of her reach.

'You've become too thin, Stella,' he said severely. 'It doesn't suit you, my dear. I shall prescribe a course of fine cooking and strong French wine to bring the colour back to your cheeks.'

'Give me that towel, and you need not look at me, sir!' She reached out her hand again, but he stepped back, shaking his head mischievously. 'Now, Stella, aren't you going to say Please?'

'Please!' Anguished, she had hugged her arms around herself, trying to hide herself from him, painfully conscious that the sight of him, so tall and handsome in his riding clothes, filled her with unbearable longing. She looked away from him miserably, remembering her wet hair, skewered to the top of her head with some pins from the dresser, and her painfully thin body which must be ugly to him now, and she felt her eyes fill with tears.

'Please, John. The water is getting cold!' she said pitifully.

He laughed gently. Then the towel, warm and soft was round her shoulders, completely enveloping her, and he was helping her to her feet, lifting her bodily from the bath. He carried her to the bed and laid her on the quilt as a tentative knock sounded at the door.

Leaving her, he strode to open it.

'You may remove the bath,' she heard him instruct the landlady, 'and then bring my wife some soup.'

The woman and her girls scurried round the room, emptying the bath and removing it, tidying away the towels and making up the fire, then, with a quick bob to John, they withdrew.

Stella was watching from the bed, trying desperately to compose herself as she pulled the towel more securely around her.

'You called me your wife!' she said furiously as he turned towards her.

John raised an eyebrow. 'Purely for expedience, I assure you, Stella.' He silenced her with a quick gesture. 'This is no time for petty proprieties. Your freedom is at stake, and my life is in danger every moment I remain in this country. As long as we are here, I intend to keep an eye on you.' His voice was grim suddenly as he turned back to the door at the sound of a knock. He opened it and took a tray from the innkeeper's wife. Then he shut it firmly behind her, turning the key. He came back to the bed. On the tray was a bowl of fragrant steaming broth and fresh bread with creamy butter.

Stella stared at it, everything forgotten but the fact that she was desperately hungry. She heard John laugh again as he laid the tray across her knees. 'Go on. Eat,' he said softly. He sat on the bed beside her and watched her in the lamplight as she reached for the soup and sipped it.

She glanced at him, pushing a strand of long wet hair from her eyes. 'I had forgotten what real food tasted like,' she said apologetically. 'They used to bring me something from the tavern once a day, but it was always cold and greasy.' She shuddered at the memory. 'I couldn't eat the prison food they brought round in the evening.'

He frowned, his expression darkening. 'Then eat now, Stella.' He touched her hand gently, then stood up, walking to the window. She watched him as she ate. He lifted the corner of the curtain and, pushing the shutter open a crack, peered out. Outside it was beginning to grow light. 'The countryside is quiet still,' he reported over his shoulder. 'And the sleet and snow should hamper any pursuit. It will be safe, I think, to rest here today. We'll move on tonight.'

She pulled the thick towel more closely round her as she shivered slightly in the draught from the window. 'Where will you take me?' she asked. Her exhaustion was returning, and she could feel the insistent dull ache pulling once more at her limbs.

'To Bristol.' He pulled the shutter closed and let the

curtain fall back into place. 'We are to catch the next packet to France.'

She stared at him, bewildered. 'To France?'

His face softened a little as he saw her distress. 'You are one of us, now, Stella, remember? A criminal on the run. Neither your father, nor anyone else, can save you through the courts. And that brilliant young solicitor, John Vivian, who might have been able to help you,' he smiled grimly, 'has been discredited and outlawed so there is but one way out. To fly. And I am taking you to the only place where you will be safe from the law. France.'

She gasped faintly. 'But I thought—'

'What did you think, Stella?' he asked sharply. 'That you could stroll happily around Hay and run home to your tea parties and your dances? Perhaps one day you may, but for the moment you have to disappear.'

She was still gazing at him. 'But I don't know anyone in France,' she said piteously.

He laughed. 'We shall have to remedy that situation, then, shall we not?'

'And you? Your cause. The poor people. The tolls,' she went on, pushing aside her tray. 'You are leaving all that?'

'No. I am not leaving all that. I shall return. But I think, Stella, that our cause may be won. A petition was drawn up some weeks ago and sent to the young queen in London. As we thought, when the facts were put to her direct, she took notice of her people's plight. She has appointed a Royal Commission to investigate the situation.'

She glanced at him with grudging admiration, and saw the quiet triumph in his face. 'So, your tactics worked,' she said. 'While I was in gaol taking the blame and the name of Mother Rebecca. That was a clever idea. Using me like that.' She could not keep the sudden wistfulness out of her tone.

His expression darkened. 'It was unforgivable of my men to use you as they did. Did you really imagine that I should have allowed it, had I known?'

'You allowed me to wait weeks and weeks in that cell while you went shooting in Pembrokeshire, or so I hear.' Her voice was still gently reproachful.

He snorted. 'Shooting! Who told you that, pray? Up till

now I would have needed an army complete with heavy artillery to break you free. We thought up all kinds of ideas, but in the end only one seemed feasible. To wait until most of the soldiery were withdrawn to combat another riot at the far end of the county, then take those that were left by surprise. It takes time to organise a riot in another man's area, it seems.' He laughed bitterly. 'I do not allow others, Stella, to take the blame for my activities, any more than I allow men to impersonate me as a cover for their crimes. If I did, I would hardly have risked all to free you.'

Stella bit her lip, hurt by his tone, the quick colour flaring in her cheeks. 'I'm sorry that you should have had so much trouble on my behalf.' She struggled to her knees on the bed, pulling the towel round her tightly. 'But, I assure you, there is no need to trouble yourself further. You have done enough by freeing me. I can go on my own way!'

He narrowed his eyes, looking her up and down. 'And I do not get any thanks, Stella? Do you not owe me something for saving your pretty ankles from the chains of the transport ships?'

She stared at him furiously, suddenly full of misgiving. 'I owe you nothing! It was your fault I was dragged into this!'

'My fault?' He took a step towards her, looking down on her as she knelt before him on the bed. 'Was it my fault you involved yourself in affairs you did not understand? Was it my fault you demanded to see Mother Rebecca?' His voice was dangerously quiet.

She shrank away from him. 'Your men brought me to you by force!' she retorted defiantly.

'And while you were with me you admitted that you loved me.' The softness of his voice disarmed her completely, as his eyes held hers. 'Was that a lie then, Stella?'

Trembling, she looked up at him, unable to take her eyes from his, seeing the intensity of his gaze, knowing that he could read her very soul. A pulse had begun to beat violently in her throat and she was acutely conscious suddenly of her nakedness beneath the towel. Her lips had gone dry. She opened her mouth to claim the lie, to tell him that she had never loved him, to send him away for ever, but the words would not come, and tears filled her eyes as she slumped down on the quilt, all her defences gone.

In one stride he was beside her, sitting on the edge of the bed, his arms round her, strong and comforting. 'Stella,' he breathed. 'Don't cry, my darling. Oh God, I didn't mean to make you cry!' He drew her against him, crushing her against his chest, his mouth seeking out the sensitive nape of her neck beneath her heavy damp hair. Raising her face to his, he stared at her for a long moment, then he was kissing her eyes, her cheeks, and the soft hollows of her throat with low sensuous intensity. At last she felt his lips on hers and slowly the fire began to flare once again through her veins as, gently, he pushed her back beneath him on the soft bed and her arms crept around his neck. The towel slipped unnoticed from her body as he bent to kiss her breast and she heard herself gasp with shameless joy. Her eyes flew open and for a second she saw the expression of the man who leaned over her, recognising the dark passion in the handsome tanned face, so strong and determined above her own.

Her anger, her fear, her exhaustion, all were swept away on the rising tide of her desire. She had no thought of turning back. Warmth and excitement such as she had never dreamed possible flooded through her as she watched, half-fainting, while he drew away to pull off his shirt and then his trousers. Then he was standing before her, and she glimpsed the lithe muscular body before he turned and blew out the lamp. He lay beside her on the bed, his arms round her, his body against hers, claiming hers with hungry urgency, driving her to the heights of ecstasy until the world exploded in stars.

She lay awake a long time in his arms, staring at the crack of daylight which seeped through the shutters and lay like an arrow on the floor, mocking the darkness of the room. Then, at last, lulled by the steady beating of his heart, she relaxed into a deep dreamless sleep.

When she awoke, the arrow of light had gone. The shutters were open, and the room was shaded only by the thin curtains which were still pulled across the windows, and she was alone in the bed beneath the warm quilt. She sat up, staring round wildly.

In a moment he was beside her. He had pulled on his trousers and boots, and the linen shirt was already in his hand. He smiled down, touching her hair lightly with lean brown fingers.

'Did you sleep well?'

Memory flooded back and she felt the warm colour creeping up her cheeks. She did not dare to look at him.

Throwing aside the shirt, he sat down on the bed, pulling her against his naked chest. 'Darling Stella.' His mouth was on her hair. Then his hand was beneath her chin, impelling her to look at him. His eyes were dancing. 'You realise you are going to have to marry me now. Oh my God, Stella!' He pulled her roughly into his arms. 'If you knew how much I have missed you, my darling. I must have become used to having you around, with your preaching and your lecturing and interfering and your fiery temper!' He chuckled at the speechless indignation which spread across her face, and kissed her again quickly. 'Heaven only knows why I love you, but I did the first time I saw you on the arm of that ass Morgan. He was never right for you. I was so determined to warn you off your passion for the Rebeccas. I was so angry that you thought it a romantic game—then I saw you, and I was lost.' He kissed her again, more deeply this time, pushing her back against the pillows so that her long silky hair fanned out around her on the bleached linen.

'I thought you loved Eliza,' she said faintly at last. Her head whirled with joy. Her heart danced so much with happiness she could scarcely speak.

He laughed. 'Most of what you think about me, my sweet innocent, is wrong.'

He drew away from her reluctantly. 'Stella. We should leave soon. We have first to reach Bristol, where my grandmother has a house. We shall be safe there until the boat sails. But the wind changed last night. We should not have to wait long.'

'Your grandmother?' She sat up, suddenly sober, pulling the quilt up to her chin.

'The Dowager Lady Ambleston. She has a large house at Clifton, which is most opportune when her grandson needs to leave the country in a hurry.'

'You mean, she knows about your . . . your activities?'

'Of course she knows. And approves. Here, darling.' He bent suddenly and fished under the bed. 'I brought clothes with me for you. I had the landlady burn everything you were wearing yesterday.' He produced a large flat dress-box and laid it on the bed. 'My grandmother chose these for you while we planned your rescue. I hope they fit.' He smiled. 'We'll buy more clothes for you in Paris. Now, no more talking. Get dressed. Then we'll eat before we leave.'

He went to the window and peered out. Then he frowned. She saw the muscles of his shoulders tense as, swiftly, he began to pull on his shirt.

'What is it? What's wrong?' She scrambled to her knees, clutching the quilt around her shoulders as she felt a whisper of fear run down her spine.

'I don't know.' He turned and grinned. 'Nothing, I'm sure. Get dressed, my darling, quickly. I'll be back in five minutes.' He blew her a kiss, then he let himself soundlessly out of the door.

With shaking hands she tore off the ribbons which fastened the box, lifted the lid and peered inside. Folded among the swathes of tissue-paper was a pretty pale yellow muslin gown, a fine embroidered chemise, drawers trimmed with Brussels lace, slippers, stockings, an exquisite fine wool shawl and, beneath them all, a rich fur-lined cloak. She gasped with excitement and pleasure, then slipped from the warm bed.

The small mirror on the table showed her slim pale figure, the rose-tipped breasts still marked with the violence of his kisses, her long silken hair flying tangled down her back. She bit her lip, staring at her face. Her eyes were bright and excited; her skin, the prison pallor already gone, was flushed and radiant. It was no longer the face of a girl. It was the face of a woman.

Realising suddenly how cold the room was now the fire had died, she shivered and turned with excitement to the clothes. Lady Ambleston might have chosen them, but only John could so perfectly have judged her size. Smiling to herself, she dressed quickly, pulling on the soft gown, the pale primrose colour of which suited her to perfection. She managed to disguise her thinness by pulling the sash tightly around her waist. In the bottom of the box she found an ivory-backed brush and comb and set to work before the mirror to brush her hair into order, catching it up and knotting it at the nape of her neck in a becoming modest style. Then, throwing the shawl round her shoulders, she twirled before the mirror and stuck out her tongue at her reflection which showed her a modest young lady in the latest, if not the most showy, fashion, a young woman who lived a world away from the horror of prisons and violence and terror.

She ran to the window and glanced out. The stable yard below was deserted, swept with sleet, no sign of life in the cold bleak outbuildings. She shivered involuntarily and turned away. Then she made her way to the door and pulled it open.

There was a soldier standing on the landing. At her horrified gasp he swung towards her, raising his musket. Then, seeing it was a woman, he lowered it again and grinned insolently. 'Good evening, miss.'

She clutched at the doorknob, her heart jumping with fear, staring at him in disbelief. 'What is it?' she managed to whisper at last. 'What is happening? Why are you here?'

'Nothing you need worry about.' With a glance over his shoulder at the stairs, he came towards her. 'If I might suggest you go back into your room, miss. We're looking for a couple of felons who are hiding out in the inn. They'll be under arrest very soon, and we'll be on our way.' There was a shout from downstairs and he went back to his post. Stella shot back into her room and slammed the door, locking it fast. Her throat constricted with fear as she flew to the window and looked out. In the yard was a troop of armed men. There was no sign of John or Lloyd Pugh; no sound from below in the body of the inn. Only the disciplined men standing in ranks, facing the building, their bayonets fixed in the pouring rain.

She shrank back behind the curtain, her heart pounding, her eyes full of tears. 'John. Oh, John,' she whispered in anguish. But John did not come.

Somewhere a door slammed, and she heard the tramp of feet on the stairs. They approached her room, hesitated, and then went past. She flattened herself against the wall and cautiously peered out once more. The men outside had not moved. They all appeared to be watching the house.

The footsteps on the landing returned, and she heard

them descend the stairs. Complete silence followed. Holding her breath, she tiptoed to the door and, cautiously unlocking it, peeped out. The guard had gone. The landing was deserted. Gathering up her pale yellow skirts, she tiptoed to the head of the stairs and peered over the banisters.

Three uniformed officers were standing in the hall below and, with them, the landlady and her two girls. The faces of all three women were chalk white, and all were sobbing quietly. Beside them stood a tall florid man with wispy hair who sported a dirty white apron over his clothes, and seemed to be the landlord of the inn. His eyes, staring with fear in the pasty flesh of his face, were fixed, as were those of all the others, on the open doors of the tap-room. No one spoke.

Her hands clutching the banisters till her knuckles showed white, Stella leaned over further to see what they were all watching with such intensity. Two men were busy in the tap-room levering the panelling from the wall. As she watched, it gave way with a splintering crash, and with a cry of triumph both men disappeared into the black cavity behind, pistols ready in their hands.

The small frightened cry of the landlady told Stella the worst almost before it had happened, and as if she were in a hideous dream she watched as John was dragged from the hole. Still dressed in his shirtsleeves, he stood proudly between his two captors and faced the men in the hall. 'Your servant, sirs.' He bowed gravely.

'So, John Vivian. We have you at last.' One of the officers stepped forward. 'A pretty dance you've led us, and no mistake.' He snapped his fingers at one of the men guarding John, and within seconds the man had produced a set of shackles and was chaining John's wrists behind his back.

Stella, half-faint with terror, still clutched at the banisters, but no one looked up. All eyes were fixed on the tall man standing so proudly before them. She watched helplessly as John was led out into the rain. Two soldiers closed in on the landlord and dragged him out behind John. Then the front door closed, leaving the innkeeper's wife and her two girls sobbing hysterically into their aprons.

Dazed, not really knowing what she was doing, Stella went back to her room. She did not bother to close the door nor to hide as she went to the window and stood looking out.

She watched as the troop sprang to attention. She saw John brought out, still walking proudly erect. No one had to drag him, as they did the shambling, gibbering landlord. John was hoisted on to a horse, his hands still tightly fastened at his back, then the troop mounted, and they all began to ride out of the yard.

Only once did John glance up and, just for a second, she thought she saw him smile as he looked at her window.

Then he was gone.

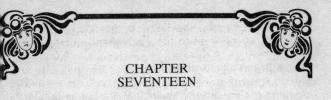

CHAPTER
SEVENTEEN

SHE STOOD for a long time gazing out at the empty stable yard, numb with shock, and only the sound of a tentative knock on the open door brought her back to her senses. She turned listlessly and stared. Lloyd stood there in the doorway, neatly attired in sober black, his wild hair brushed, his boots polished. He touched his forelock as she turned, his face a study of misery.

'You know what has happened, miss?'

She nodded dumbly.

He shrugged. 'They'll be taking him to Gloucester, likely. He told me I was to take care of you, girl. Take you to his father's old mam, he said I was to.' He straightened his jacket self-consciously.

Stella looked at him in despair. 'Why didn't they take me?' she asked. 'I actually spoke to one of them. Or you. Why didn't they take you? I don't understand.'

'I had changed already, see, when they came. They were looking for a wild countryman, they said, and a girl in rags.' He grinned for the first time. 'Never suspected you for a second, miss, dressed like that, I dare say.'

In spite of herself, she smiled as she saw the admiration in his sad eyes.

'No, I don't think they did.' She bit her lip. 'Lloyd. What will they do to him?'

'I don't know, miss.' She saw there were tears in the man's eyes. 'Hold him for trial, I suppose.' He wiped the back of his hand across his face. 'They'll take him back to Brecon, and once he's there . . . So many have sworn to see him hang . . .' His voice broke.

'They can't. They can't hang him!' she whispered in agony. 'They can't. We have got to help him.'

Lloyd shrugged. 'It was always John as did the helping, girl. He did the planning. We just did what we were told.'

He sat down abruptly on a chair by the door. 'If only Dai were here. And Evan and the boys.' He wiped his nose on his sleeve. Then he stiffened his shoulders suddenly. 'Still, I have my orders. John brought a carriage here for you, and he said I'd to take you to Bristol. I've harnessed the pony and it's waiting downstairs. Do you have something warm to wear? It's a long drive and the sleet is falling again.'

Numbly Stella picked up the fur-lined cloak and wrapped it round her. Then, with a quick glance at the room where, only hours before, she had lain so ecstatically in John's arms, she followed Lloyd down the stairs.

The landlady was standing in the hall, tears running down her cheeks. Impulsively Stella reached out to take her hands. 'I am so sorry,' she stammered. 'Your husband.'

The woman shook her head wordlessly and Stella ached to be of comfort to her. But what comfort could she give when her own heart was breaking? Her eyes filled with tears and the woman swam before her suddenly as she turned away, obedient to Lloyd's touch on her elbow, and followed him out into the icy rain.

A modest carriage drawn by a pretty black pony was waiting, ready harnessed, before the inn. Handing her into it, Lloyd gave her arm a small squeeze. 'Don't fret about her too much,' he said quietly. 'John paid them well for what they did. They knew the risks—and the landlord will likely get off with a year or two in prison.'

He put up the steps and shut the door. Then, with a brave attempt at a wink at her through the window, he went to climb onto the box.

Stella fell back against the leather squabs, unable to restrain her tears any longer. She wept until she could weep no more, then, as it grew dark, lulled by the monotonous motion of the carriage she began to doze fitfully, jerked awake now and again by a jolt as a wheel went into a deeper than usual pothole. Each time she woke, the tears returned, and muffled in the soft fur-lined cloak she would close her eyes and think of John. They stopped for tolls and bridges. They stopped at wayside inns to feed and water the pony. Lloyd brought food to the carriage, but she could touch little and sat staring out of the window at the flickering carriage lamps, seeing only John's face, so strong and proud as they took him from the inn, imagining him by now somewhere in a cell like hers, defeated and in chains. And tears rose in her eyes again and spilled down her cheeks as she lay back on the upholstered seat and abandoned herself to despair.

She had been restlessly asleep for some hours when the carriage at last turned off the road between a pair of tall stone pillars into a raked gravel drive. She sat up stiffly and peered out. It was nearly light. The rain had cleared, and bars of yellow- and green-flecked cloud streaked the sky to the east.

The carriage followed a curving drive for some half a mile, then drew to a halt outside an imposing grey stone mansion.

Somewhere in the distance Stella heard the yapping of dogs, as Lloyd lowered himself from the driver's seat and came to open the door.

Weary beyond belief, Stella forced herself to climb down from the carriage as the large white-painted door of the house swung open and a butler stepped out, a lamp in his hand. He did not seem surprised at his early morning visitor, but Stella saw at once that his sharp eyes were looking past her towards the carriage, searching for someone else.

Biting her lip, she climbed the steps towards him, conscious that Lloyd was at her elbow. Then, behind the butler, she saw an elderly woman—tall, elegant, in a dove-grey wrapper, with white hair piled high on her head beneath a night-cap adorned with pink silk ribbons. The Dowager Countess of Ambleston gave Stella one anguished look and then held out her hands.

'Oh, my dear child. What happened?'

Stella struggled for a moment to speak, but it was no use. Tears overwhelmed her and, sobbing uncontrollably, she found herself being held in the woman's arms.

Behind her, Lloyd briefly recounted what had happened, as Lady Ambleston stroked Stella's hair. Then Lloyd and the butler had gone, the front door was shut and Stella found herself before a blazing fire while the countess herself chafed her cold hands.

The woman smiled at her kindly. 'John would not want

you to cry so, my dear,' she said gently. 'He has told me so often of your courage and spirit.'

Stella stared up at her through her tears. 'He spoke of me?'

'Incessantly.' Lady Ambleston laughed sadly. 'He's been staying with me these last few weeks while laying plans for your rescue.' She put a gentle hand beneath Stella's chin and turned her face to the light. 'My grandson does not fall in love easily. But I can see why he loves you. I was, I must confess, a little astonished when he told me the girl he loved was in prison. And even more so when he told me you were in prison because of him. Then he told me the whole story. He intends to marry you, you know. He told me he would marry you even if he had to follow you to the Antipodes to do it.' She gripped Stella's hands tightly. 'Will you do the same for him, my dear?'

Stella nodded numbly, the tears still slipping down her pale cheeks. 'I would go to the ends of the earth for him,' she gulped.

The countess gave a short bark of laughter. 'I gather Van Diemen's land is exactly that,' she said crisply. 'But I trust it will not turn out that way. It is the wrong time of year for sea voyages, in my opinion.' She walked to the hearth and pulled the bell. Then she turned. 'They have threatened to hang John, my dear. I think you know that.'

Stella felt the clutch of fear, an icy hand on her heart, as she stared at the countess's face. 'But they couldn't . . .' she whispered, brokenly.

'They could. But they won't,' Lady Ambleston retorted. 'Ah, Bellwood.' She greeted the butler who answered her summons. 'A cup of warm chocolate for Miss Vaughan, then you will call Summers to take her up to bed. She can have the blue guest-room.'

She waited for the man to close the door, then she turned back to Stella. 'Don't despair, my dear,' she said taking the girl into her arms. 'I have every confidence that the situation can be saved. Pugh tells me that he overheard John's captors saying they would take him on to Gloucester, rather than cross the mountains again with the weather deteriorating. John and I discussed the possibility of his capture, and he made certain provisions which I shall act on without delay.' She smiled. 'It would be a marvellous piece of luck, my dear, if he is still at Gloucester. Pray for that, and I think you will find that we can save my grandson's neck. Now, you go and rest. You look worn out and I have urgent letters to write to put matters in train. Later we shall talk again.'

The room to which Stella was shown was large and elegant with long windows opening out on a balcony. From one of them Stella could see the sun swimming red out of the thick mist over the river.

She allowed herself to be undressed by the countess's maid and, swathed in a silk wrapper, she sat wearily before a huge gilded mirror while her hair was brushed and braided into loose plaits on her shoulders. Then at last she was allowed to climb into the huge feather-bed where, worn out with exhaustion and despair and clinging to a slender thread of hope, she slipped into the blessed oblivion of sleep.

It was late afternoon when she awoke, and Summers was once more in the room, deftly making up the fire which had burned low.

'Are you rested, miss?' she asked kindly, noting with disapproval the huge purple shadows beneath the girl's eyes. 'Her ladyship would like you to join her in the salon as soon as you feel strong enough.'

She helped Stella to dress, then she led the way downstairs. The countess was sitting at a writing-desk in the shadowy salon, scribbling intently by the light of a many branched candelabrum. She smiled as Stella entered the room, and throwing down her pen, held out her hands.

'We have news, my dear. We know where they are holding him and it is as I had hoped. He is still at Gloucester, where feeling is not nearly so strong against him as it is around Brecon. They plan to take him back there, of course, but the weather is still on our side. The roads get worse by the minute. While we must negotiate mud and sleet down here, already there is snow in the mountains, which will deter them from trying to move him at least till morning.' She shivered. 'By then, I trust he will be free.'

Stella stared at her, her eyes suddenly alight with hope. 'But how?'

The countess took Stella's hands and squeezed them tightly. 'The Ambleston name, my dear, coupled with not inconsiderable sums of money in the right quarter, will see to it that he has the opportunity to escape. Lloyd Pugh and two of my most trusted servants are already on their way with fast horses and weapons. He should be with us by morning, God willing.'

Stella gasped. 'I thought . . . I never dared hope . . . I thought I should never see him again.'

'Rubbish, child.' The countess smiled comfortably. 'He has to come back. Quite apart from anything else, I wish to see him safely married to you without delay. From what John let slip of his behaviour towards you in Wales, and from the account Pugh gave me of your stay in the inn where I understand John had you admitted as his wife, I think that the ceremony should be performed as soon as possible, don't you?'

Stella blushed. 'I assure you, Lady Ambleston, he does not have to marry me—' she flared defensively. Then she saw the laughter, so like John's, in the countess's eyes, and she looked down ashamed.

The countess patted her affectionately. 'You forget, my dear, I know John a great deal better than you do. He would take no argument in this matter, I am sure. And neither shall I. So I am assuming that he will be back with us by tomorrow. There is a chapel here, and I have already spoken to the bishop and obtained a special licence. One of his chaplains has arrived and he will perform the ceremony.' She kissed Stella on the cheek, then she sat down. 'Now, be so good as to ring the bell, my dear. We shall dine early, I think, then perhaps we can divert ourselves at the card-table for a while. If you don't know any two-handed games, I shall instruct you. It will help the time to pass.'

Stella lay awake a long time, staring at the glowing embers of the fire that night, watching the pale flicker of light on the plaster decorations of the ceiling and the faint movement of the heavy embroidered curtains in the draught. It was raining once more, and she could hear the moan of the wind amongst the tall chimneys of the house.

Where was John now? Had Lloyd reached him with the two armed grooms and the fast horses, or were the roads already impassable, even on the lower ground. Or had he already been taken from the prison in Gloucester to await his trial in Brecon in chains. Once there, no amount of bribery or planning would free him.

She turned her head miserably on the pillow. Suppose the countess was wrong in her optimism? Suppose his gaolers would not be bribed? Suppose they were not as uninterested in his capture as she thought?

Feverishly she moved her head from side to side. She did not think about the wedding at all.

After a while she dragged herself out of bed and went to the windows to peer out between the curtains. Rain, heavy with sleet, ran down the panes of glass next to her cheek and she could feel the chill reverberation of the wind as it screamed up the Severn estuary laden with cold Atlantic salt. The night was violent and very cold.

Shivering, she let the curtain fall and climbed back into the bed, huddling herself into the warm covers. There was nothing she could do but wait and pray.

When she awoke again, the sun was streaming in through the windows. She looked towards them, puzzled, wondering who had flung back the curtains. Then she saw him. Freshly shaven, in a spotless white shirt and embroidered dressing-gown, John was standing before the fire watching her, a quizzical smile on his face.

For a moment she thought she was still dreaming. She stared up at him sleepily, her eyes moving lovingly over the planes of his face—the high cheekbones, the strong arrogant nose, the firm chin, the lips . . . He was smiling now, his eyes brilliant blue as he watched her slowly swim up through the mists of sleep. She struggled upright against the pillow.

'John?' she murmured.

Then, half-blinded by tears, she flung herself from the bed and running barefoot across the carpet she hurled herself into his arms. 'John! Oh, John!'

He swung her off her feet, covering her face with kisses. 'My darling,' he murmured. 'I was so frightened they had taken you too. Then when I saw your face at the window and I realised they had not recognised you . . .' His lips found hers at last, hungry and demanding, putting a stop to all speech and she returned his kisses, half-fainting with joy and relief and ecstasy.

It was a long time before he drew away from her, laughing. He held her at arm's length, his eyes still devouring her. 'My grandmother would be horrified if she knew where I was at this moment,' he said severely.

Stella blushed. Then she laughed too. 'I don't believe she would at all. She is a quite remarkable lady.'

John nodded. 'But, remarkable or not, she is determined to see us married before the day is out.' He drew her against him again, holding her hands against his chest. 'Is that what you want, too, Stella?'

Stella looked up at him through her long lashes, unable to breathe for a moment. Her heart was dancing and she was drowning in his gaze, as slowly she managed to nod.

She did not ask about his capture or his rescue then. Not till many months later could she bring herself to talk about the events of the past few weeks. Now the only thing which mattered was that he was there and that he loved her.

It was a long time before he withdrew his lips from hers and reluctantly let her go. 'I must go down, sweetheart, and you must dress. There is much to do today.' He looked solemn suddenly. 'You do realise, my darling, that we cannot stay in England more than a few hours longer? One of the cross-channel packets sails on the tide. We shall be aboard her.' He caught her hands again and held her close. 'I hope our exile won't be for very long, sweetheart. Grandmama has already talked to my uncle the earl into approaching Her Majesty on our behalf. She is sure we shall be given a royal pardon.' He laughed boyishly. 'We may yet return to walk the streets of Hay and Brecon together. And, until that happens we shall regard our sojourn abroad as a honeymoon. Do you agree?' He kissed her hands. 'Now, hurry and dress, sweetheart and come downstairs, Or I shall forget myself,' and he was gone, leaving her in a glow of breathless happiness.

She did not ring for Summers. Her fingers flew as she dressed, unbraided her hair and twisted it up into a chignon, then, pulling the fringed sash tightly around her waist, she ran to the door and made her way, her heart singing, down to the parlour.

John was there ahead of her. He held out his hands to her with a smile. 'Grandmama had told me she has ordered dresses and shoes and pelisses by the score for you. She won't have it either that we are fleeing the country, sweetheart. She sees our exodus as a Grand Tour of Europe. What is it, my darling?'

A shadow had passed over Stella's face as she looked out of the window to the dank shrubbery outside. She shivered. 'How do you know they won't come looking for you here?' she whispered.

'They might.' He drew her against him tenderly. 'But, my sweetheart, you and I will hide while my grandmother denies all knowledge of our existence.' He laughed softly, his lips on her hair. 'And it would take a brave man to call her a liar to her face. And even if they did persist, and searched the house, there are one or two priestholes here that have saved the necks of my ancestors in the past. They shall do the same for us. And by tonight we'll be gone, Stella. And we'll be safe.'

Reassured, she raised her lips to his, just as the doorbell pealed through the house. John stiffened. Then he smiled, his fingers on his lips. 'Bellwood will deal with it,' he breathed. 'If there's danger, he'll warn me.'

They stayed where they were, staring at the parlour door, as footsteps approached along the passage. There was a timid knock.

'Come in,' John called after a fraction of a second's hesitation. The door opened and one of the parlour-maids peered in.

'Mr Vivian, sir; there's a gentleman here, says he's a friend of yours—' she began. She broke off with a squeal as she was pushed aside and a burly figure appeared behind her in the doorway.

'Who is it? Where's Bellwood?' John thundered and he thrust Stella behind him as Owen Morgan walked into the room.

Owen bowed. 'Your butler was otherwise occupied, so this young person let me in.' He inclined his head gravely towards the maid, who had gone chalk white when she looked at John's grim face. 'Don't blame her, Vivian.' Owen ushered her from the room and closed the door on her. 'I can be very persuasive.' He looked for the first time at Stella, and after a moment's hesitation, he smiled.

'I am so glad to see you looking so well, Stella, in spite of everything.'

'What do you want?' Stella's mouth had gone dry with fear as she stared at the familiar figure before her. 'Have you come to take me back?' Her legs were trembling so much she could hardly stand.

'That is my duty, Stella,' Owen said gravely. 'I should take you both under arrest. I am, I believe, still sworn as a special constable.'

John let out an exclamation and took a furious step towards him, his fists raised, but unexpectedly Owen laughed. 'No, no,' he said, apologetically, backing away, his hands raised in mock surrender. 'I said I should arrest you. I did not say I was going to. On the contrary.' He threw himself down in a chair and looked from one to the other and back. 'I can't pretend to approve of your activities any more now than I did before. But the Royal Commission of enquiry does throw a slightly different light on things. It means that you had some sort of case. Besides, I am not so unforgiving that I would want to see you punished, Stella. No, I shall say nothing about seeing you both here.'

John relaxed. 'What are you doing here then, Morgan?' he asked suddenly. 'I don't believe you are one of my grandmother's cronies?'

Owen laughed. 'No. But my mother is. I came on an errand for her.' He sobered suddenly. 'Vivian, seeing that we all find ourselves here, I must ask you to allow me to talk to Stella alone. There is something I very much wish to say to her in private.'

John took Stella's arm protectively. 'Stella is about to become my wife, sir. You can have nothing to say to her which cannot be said to me as well.' His hand found Stella's and he squeezed it reassuringly.

'Very well.' Owen cleared his throat uncomfortably. 'Stella, I wanted to explain. You may remember my mother paid you a visit in September. She was much intrigued by the idea that Eliza was,' he hesitated, glaring at John, 'or thought she was, interested in Vivian here.'

John grimaced, but Owen went on without giving him the

chance to interrupt. 'She wrote to Lady Ambleston to enquire as to your prospects, I believe, Vivian. And was perplexed by the reply which gave Mama to understand that you were in love with Stella and not Eliza at all. She brought the letter to me and suddenly I began to understand everything.' He paused.

'And it was then that you decided to denounce me to Stella's father, I suppose,' John said dryly.

Owen nodded sheepishly. 'And it was then I realised I had lost Stella,' he said slowly.

'You never said anything!' Stella interrupted at last.

'No,' Owen looked at her. 'But I knew at that moment our engagement was at an end.'

'And you have now decided to console yourself by marrying Eliza instead,' John put in cynically.

Owen coloured. 'We were thrown together by circumstances later. And I have always had the highest regard for Eliza,' he said defensively. 'You both know that . . .'

'And I'm sure you more than make up for her disappointment in not winning me,' John grinned unfeelingly. 'So . . . Do I gather that you wish to tell us that you and I are soon to be brothers-in-law?'

Owen nodded slowly. 'Eliza and I are to be married in the spring.'

'Oh, Owen. I am so glad.' Impulsively Stella ran to him and kissed his cheek. 'You'll be so happy with Eliza, I know you will.'

Owen took her hand shyly and raised it to his lips. 'I wish you every happiness, too, Stella. I . . .' He hesitated for a moment with a glance at John. 'I have something here which I want you to keep. Call it a wedding-present.' He produced a small box and pressed it into her hand. She knew without opening it what it was. 'My brooch?' she breathed, looking up at him with tears in her eyes.

He nodded. 'I had it mended and cleaned. I'd like you to keep it, Stella.'

She opened the box and stared down at the bright jewel in its nest of lambswool. 'I shall treasure it, Owen,' she whispered. 'Thank you.'

The door behind them opened and the countess hurried in, closely followed by Bellwood and one of the footmen.

Both men carried pistols.

'Mr Vivian, I'm sorry.' Bellwood stammered, levelling his weapon at Owen with a shaking hand. 'The girl only just told me—'

'It's all right, put up your guns.' John waved them aside. 'Mr Morgan is not going to give us away.'

'Mr Morgan?' The countess stared at Owen, who was still standing beside Stella, his mouth agape as he saw the gun pointing at his head. 'Not Alicia Morgan's son?'

'The very same, Grandmama.' John laughed. 'He is to marry Stella's sister.' He frowned at his grandmother suddenly. 'I understand that Lady Morgan wrote to you enquiring as to my prospects as a prospective son-in-law on Mrs Vaughan's behalf. May I ask what you said?'

Lady Ambleston opened her mouth to comment. Then she laughed. 'Certainly not, my boy. That is information which I would divulge to no one but the mother of your bride.'

She took Stella's hands. 'My dear. I know you must be sad about leaving your parents like this. Will you allow me to try and make things all right with them? I am sure I can talk your father round. Mr Morgan will help me, will you not, sir?' She smiled artfully at Owen. 'And,' she clapped her hands in excitement suddenly, 'I have just had the most delightful idea. You shall stay for the wedding and give Stella away.'

Stella glanced at John apprehensively, not at all sure that he would agree with her that there was no one better, but he was smiling as he ordered Bellwood to fetch some refreshment.

Owen looked at each of them in turn, then at last he, too, smiled. He took Stella's hand and raised it to his lips. 'I should regard it as a great honour,' he said.

Bellwood returned with a silver tray and a cut glass decanter. Setting them on the table, he poured the wine and handed it round, then bowed and withdrew. John stepped forward. He looked at Owen and smiled mischievously, raising his glass.

'May I propose a toast. To the lady who brought us all together first.'

Owen looked puzzled. 'Maria Williams?'

John laughed. 'No. To Rebecca.'

'Rebecca,' the countess echoed, smiling at Stella and, after a moment's hesitation, Owen raised his glass as well.

Stella sipped her wine and gazed up at John's face. But he was no longer looking at her. His eyes had strayed to the window, and she saw him stiffen as he stared out through the clustered laurels towards the long drive.

'My God, Morgan!' he said explosively, 'You've tricked me! Why, you . .'

'What? What do you mean, tricked you?' Owen whirled to face him, his face white with anger.

'You had the house surrounded all the time!'

Stella gasped. She turned in dismay towards the countess. 'But Owen wouldn't . . .'

'No,' Owen confirmed, his voice calm once more. 'No, I wouldn't. Don't be a fool, man. If I had meant to arrest you do you think I would have walked in openly as I did?' He strode to the windows and peered out. 'What do you mean, surrounded? I see no one there.'

But even as he spoke they all saw the flash of colour as a scarlet uniform showed itself for a moment in the bushes and vanished.

Stella caught John's arm in a panic. 'Hide. You must hide!' she breathed. 'Quickly. Oh, quickly. Owen won't betray you—'

She broke off as Bellwood, too shaken even to knock, threw open the door. 'Your ladyship! Mr Vivian! There are soldiers at the door.'

Lady Ambleston straightened her shoulders calmly. 'Tell them I shall attend to them at once,' she said. 'And, Bellwood, you may show the officers into the library. The men are to wait outside. Serve the gentlemen brandy, if you please, and then go to the chapel and see that all is ready.'

Bellwood mastered himself with an effort and bowed. Then he withdrew. The countess looked round. Then she smiled, catching Stella's hand.

'Sweet child. There is no time now to do more than kiss you. Go with John to the chapel. The priest will be there. He shall marry you without delay. Then you must both be ready to leave the house at once.'

Stella stared at her, her eyes round. 'But Lady Ambleston—'

'No time, my dear. No time. Take her, John. My blessings on you both!' And the countess had gone.

Stella looked from Owen to John and back, then at the window, where the shrubbery seemed once more deserted.

John took her hand. 'Ready, sweetheart?'

She nodded. Her heart was pounding as, gently, he led her to the door and put his head against the polished oak panels, listening.

Owen put his hand on John's shoulder. 'Let me go first,' he whispered and, cautiously, eased open the door.

The dark passage was deserted.

'Turn left and up the staircase at the end,' John breathed in his ear, his hand tight around Stella's. Owen nodded and began to tiptoe in front of them through the long passage. Twice they stopped and held their breath, but on each occasion they moved on again. Stella had caught up her skirt, afraid the slight rustle of her petticoats might be heard.

In front of her Owen tensed as he reached the end of the passage, and she saw him flatten himself against the wall and peer round. For a moment he did not move, then he turned to throw her a quick smile. He put his finger to his lips, and with a small beckoning gesture for her to follow, he slipped out of sight. She crept to the corner and leaned forward to see round it. The main hall, dimly lit by the tall half-curtained windows looking out over the front gardens, stretched out before her to the huge ornate front door. To her left a narrow secondary staircase wound up steeply to the floor above. Owen, following John's whispered directions, had already disappeared up it, two steps at a time.

Taking a deep breath, she ran across the broad expanse of hall and from the corner of her eye she glimpsed a door opening in the distance. She gained the stairs and ran up them, her heart slamming against her ribs with fear. Behind her, John still waited in the passage. Owen was crouching on the landing. He caught her hand and dragged her into an alcove.

'This is madness,' he whispered fiercely. 'Does it really

matter so much that you marry the man now? You've got to get away from here, Stella!'

Stella's eyes were troubled, but there was no time to reply. Owen was already peering back down the stairs.

There was no sign of John, but from below they heard the sound of strident voices in the front hall, followed by a barked command.

Stella's hand flew to her mouth to stifle a gasp of fear, and she looked mutely at Owen. He was listening intently, his brow concentrated into a frown.

'You do understand, your ladyship,' a harsh voice was saying. 'I am forced to do this. I realise he is unlikely to have come here, but my orders are to search this house . . .' The words became indistinct as the speaker turned away, and they heard the rattle of locks as the front door was opened.

Below them, quiet as a shadow, John slipped across the polished wood floor and up the stairs.

He joined them in the alcove, motioning them to be quiet as he reached for Stella's hand. Then he was pulling her against him, his mouth lost in the silkiness of her hair. 'Follow me, quickly,' he breathed, and he had released her again.

He ran lightfooted along the passage, pulling her with him, and behind them came Owen, puffing slightly from the unaccustomed exertions. The long passage was hung with tapestries and on one side a line of full-length windows looked out over the back of the house. Two soldiers were standing on the rainswept terrace, bayonets fixed to their weapons.

Stella felt the fear bitter in her throat as she caught a glimpse of them, but John had not stopped. He hurried her through yet another doorway and up another staircase and then allowed her to stop at last before a carved wooden door. He smiled at her, his blue eyes intense.

'Do you still want to marry me, Stella?'

She stared at him in wonder. 'I love you, John.'

'Then you will marry me. Now.'

She was conscious of Owen behind her, his hands resting lightly on her shoulders, but all she could see were the eyes of the man she loved. Stepping towards him, she put her hands in his and kissed him.

He turned and opened the door, ushering her inside.

The small chapel was richly furnished, the painted ceiling and walls reflecting deep crimsons and blues in the light of the candles which burned everywhere. There, before the altar with its cross of carved gold, knelt the chaplain. He turned as they entered, and rose to his feet with a smile.

Stella moved as if in a dream as Owen took her hand and led her towards the altar. Behind them there were other figures, kneeling at the back of the chapel. She recognised Lloyd, and the maid, Summers, and two other servants from downstairs, hastily summoned by Bellwood to act as witnesses.

In a daze she found herself looking at John, who stood beside her so tall and handsome, and then up at the golden cross glinting in the candlelight before them.

John took her hand and they stood before the priest as, hurriedly, he began to weave the age-old words around them which would bind them for ever as husband and wife.

In the distance, Stella dimly heard shouting and the sound of running feet, but she did not look round. Her eyes were on John's hands as he took hers.

Silently Owen moved back and stood squarely before the door of the chapel, his broad shoulders leaning against the carved wood panels, watching with a wistful smile as John drew off the heavy gold signet-ring he wore and placed it on Stella's finger.

Then it was over. The priest was smiling his congratulations, but she saw his eyes skim warily over their heads towards the door.

John kissed her once, a long hard kiss which contained a world of passion and anguish and longing, and then he had caught her by the hand and, taking up a candle from the credence table by the altar, he was dragging her towards a small door covered with hangings behind the priest's chair.

The passage behind it smelt musty with disuse and was cold after the candlelit warmth and fragrance of the chapel.

Stella stumbled and almost fell, but John steadied her, his arm round her shoulders. No one had followed them. Owen and Lloyd and the servants had remained in the chapel with the priest as the sound of the search grew closer, and the hangings had fallen back into place over the hidden door. It was as if they had never been there.

The passage began to slope steeply downwards, the uneven stone flags which paved it broken now and then by a step.

Stella's heart hammered with fear, though she could no longer hear anything of the search behind them. The silence was intense, save for the sound of their own footsteps.

Then suddenly she could smell the sweet damp scent of wet earth. John slowed his pace warningly, as the candle-flame in his hand flared and streamed before an unseen draught. By the light of the flame she saw him smile reassuringly, then he was moving on.

The passage ended abruptly in a dank cavern hung with ferns. Beyond, a stone façade, flanked by lichened statues running with moisture, marked the bleak site of some old-time folly built by an Earl of Ambleston a hundred years before.

John grinned at her. 'Nearly safe, my love. Hang on just a little longer.' His arm was steady round her shoulders. 'If Grandmama's plan has worked, there will be a closed carriage waiting somewhere near—'

He pushed her down gently on to a marble seat, soft with damp moss. 'Wait here, sweetheart. While I check if it is safe to move.'

Stella clutched at his hand.

'Don't leave me—'

'Only for a second.' For a moment his finger touched her lips and she saw him smile. Then he was gone.

She shivered violently. Until that moment she had been kept warm by his vibrant presence, by his arm around her shoulder, by fear and the speed of events. Now she was alone, and, she realised, dressed only in the yellow dress which John had produced for her a lifetime before in the inn at Wales, and a thin shawl which was growing every second wetter in the cold damp atmosphere of the cavern.

She hugged herself numbly, staring at the gleaming cold figure of the statue before her, and the curtain of sleet sliding down through the ferns around the entrance. Then suddenly she caught sight of the heavy gold ring on her finger. Was it true, then? Was she really married? She touched the cold metal to her lips and prayed that John was safe.

He was gone for an agonisingly long time. But when he returned, he was smiling. She watched as he walked towards her, his hands outstretched.

'It's all right,' he called. 'They've gone. Grandmama chased them away after the briefest of searches. Come,' he folded her in his arms. 'Bellwood has been dispatched to the cellars for champagne, and the grooms are loading the coach with fripperies for my wife to take to France on her honeymoon!'

He kissed her gently. 'Well, what are you waiting for?'

She glanced up shyly. 'It's really going to be all right?' she asked at last.

'Yes, my darling.' He smiled down at her once more. 'It's really going to be all right.'

EPILOGUE

THEY STOOD together in the stern of the ship, staring back at the shore. The waving hands were out of sight now: the countess, Owen, and Lloyd Pugh who, with tears in his eyes, had driven with them to the quayside. Nothing remained to be seen but the receding shore-lines of England to the south and to the north of them almost out of sight the coast of Wales.

Above them lay the darkening sky shredded white with scudding cloud, and the black smoke from the funnel which fanned in torn rags round the bleached canvas of the packet's sails. Beneath their feet the engines throbbed, and the small ship churned through the choppy water towards the open sea.

Tears of loneliness filled Stella's eyes suddenly as she stared back towards that northern shore and all it hid: her home, her parents, George, Eliza and her happy sunny childhood. In front lay the Channel and eventually a foreign land, where she knew no one but the tall dark silent man at her side.

Then, as if he knew what she was thinking, he smiled at her, his arm once more round her waist, pinning down her billowing cloak. And his eyes on hers were warm and smiling, full of love and reassurance as he pulled her close to him and there, in front of the other passengers and the crew, he kissed her once again till the world spun on its axis and the sky and the smoke and the streaks of crimson light from the setting sun mingled with the spray and the shrieks of the gulls. And she knew that her home was in his arms, and the past and the future no longer mattered, and that she would follow him if he demanded it even to the ends of the earth.

**Fill in and send this coupon back today
and we will send you**

2 Introductory
Historical Romances
FREE

At the same time we will reserve a subscription to
Mills & Boon Masquerade Historical Romances for
you. Every two months you will receive Four new,
superb titles delivered direct to your door. You
don't pay extra for delivery. Postage and packing is
always completely free. There is no obligation or
commitment – you only receive books for as long as
you want to.

**Just fill in and post the coupon today to MILLS & BOON
READER SERVICE, FREEPOST, P.O. BOX 236, CROYDON,
SURREY CR9 9EL.**

**Please Note:- READERS IN SOUTH AFRICA write to
Mills & Boon, Postbag X3010,
Randburg 2125, S. Africa.**

- -

FREE BOOKS CERTIFICATE

**To: Mills & Boon Reader Service, FREEPOST, P.O. Box 236,
Croydon, Surrey CR9 9EL.**

Please send me, free and without obligation, two Masquerade Historical Romances, and
reserve a Reader Service Subscription for me. If I decide to subscribe I shall receive,
following my free parcel of books, four new Masquerade Historical Romances every two
months for £5.00, post and packing free. If I decide not to subscribe, I shall write to you
within 10 days. The free books are mine to keep in any case. I understand that I may cancel
my subscription at any time simply by writing to you. I am over 18 years of age.

Please write in BLOCK CAPITALS.

Signature _____

Name _____

Address _____

_____ Post code _____

SEND NO MONEY — TAKE NO RISKS.

Please don't forget to include your Postcode.

Remember, postcodes speed delivery. Offer applies in UK only and is not valid
to present subscribers. Mills & Boon reserve the right to exercise discretion in
granting membership. If price changes are necessary you will be notified.

4M   Offer expires July 31st 1984.

EP